ALWAYS AGNES

MICKEY DUBROW

Library of Congress Control Number: 2023934691

Cover Design by: Alexios Saskalidis

www.facebook.com/187designz

For information please contact:

Brother Mockingbird, LLC

www.brothermockingbird.org

ISBN: 978-1-960226-02-0 Paperback

ISBN: 978-1-960226-04-4 EBook

Dedicated to all the time travelers. Now is always the best time to tell someone you love them.

PROLOGUE

Sunday, October 26, 2008

Claudia Cook started her car and turned the heater on full blast, glancing in the rear-view mirror at the closed garage door before switching on the radio.

"Good morning!" shouted the deejay. "Our classic rock weekend continues with another thirty minutes of uninterrupted music from your favorite classic rock artists. Let's kick this Sunday off with thirty minutes of R.E.M."

The opening chords of "Talk About the Passion" played through the car's speakers. Claudia loved too many R.E.M. songs to have a favorite, but she was rather fond of this one. She agreed with Michael Stipe that not everyone could carry the weight of the world. She could barely carry herself. Claudia shut her eyes and let the music sooth her.

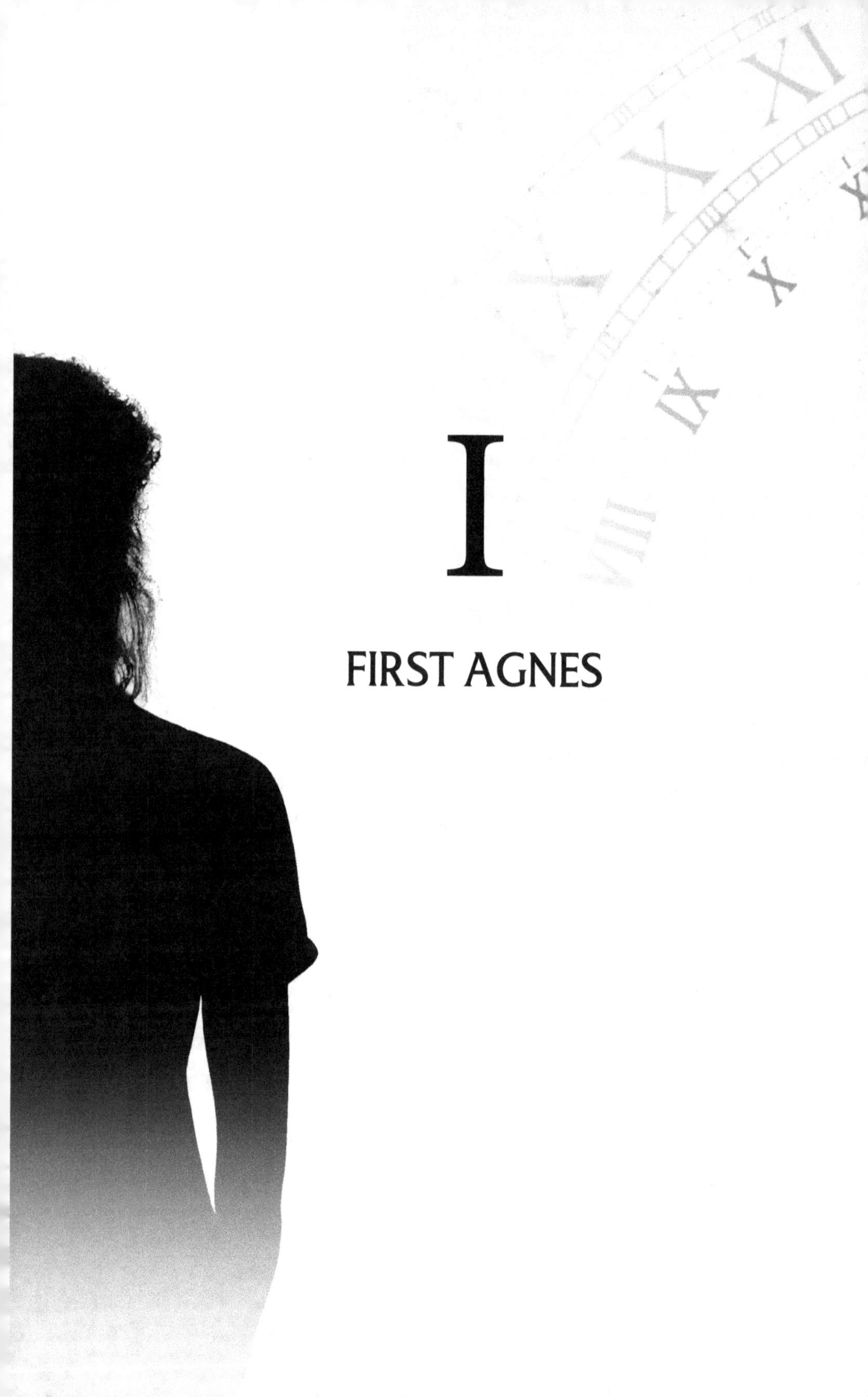

I

FIRST AGNES

CHAPTER

I

Friday, June 8, 2007

Agnes checked the time.

If she hurried, she could conduct one more experiment before she had to go. A plume of smoke rose as she soldered the wires connecting a metal box to a digital clock. Agnes wrinkled her nose. She didn't care for the smell of burning metal. When she was done, she placed the box and its attached timer on a table. Scooting over to her camcorder, she squinted into the viewfinder.

"You need to work this time," she scolded the box.

Agnes started the camcorder and took a stopwatch out of her lab coat pocket. She spoke into her voice recorder.

"Transport solid object attempt number forty-eight in three…two…one."

Turning on the machine, she started the stopwatch. The box and clock shimmered as if they were a mirage and then flattened into metal pancakes.

"Okay, don't work. See if I care."

Agnes stopped the stopwatch and turned off the camcorder. Eleven seconds. That was all the time needed for the experiment to fail. She wrote the details of the failed attempt in her journal and then put her recording devices, tools, spare parts, lab coat, and journal into her locker. She wrapped the squashed items in a copy of *Technique*, the Georgia Tech student newspaper, before stuffing them into her backpack.

Agnes checked the time.

The meeting with her laboratory director Howard Levin was scheduled to begin in nine minutes. Barring any obstacles, she was confident it wouldn't take more than seven minutes to take the elevator from the laboratory on the second floor to Levin's office on the fifth floor. Agnes wasn't expecting any obstacles because it was 7:51 a.m. and the Centennial Research Building was usually a ghost town until nine fifteen.

As she rode the elevator, which always smelled like French fries, Agnes worried about the meeting. Levin hadn't told her what he wanted to talk about.

Did he find out about my project? Agnes thought. *Hope not. It's too soon. Too soon.*

The goal of Levin's research lab was to apply Einstein's relativity theories to advance the study of time travel. The experiments conducted in the lab hoped to prove objects could travel through the fourth dimension by observing a time traveling neutron. Levin believed the work they did today would assist scientists in the future build a functioning time machine.

Agnes wasn't content to let future scientists have all the fun. She was determined to build a time machine *now*. As if her self-appointed task wasn't daunting enough, Agnes believed she didn't need a super strong container to survive the crushing impact of traveling faster than light speed, but rather a device that would allow her to slip from one point in time to the next.

Certain that Professor Levin wouldn't allow her to deviate so radically from the stated purpose of his laboratory, Agnes kept her experiments a secret. She had tremendous respect for Levin, so it pained her to go behind his back. She had no doubt that when she finally revealed a functioning time machine, he would forgive her.

During the day, Agnes worked on experiments Levin assigned his lab assistants. At the end of the day, Agnes went to her dorm room and slept until mid-evening. Then, she came back to the lab. Other than the security guards, she had the place to herself, so she worked on her own experiments until daybreak.

She had no social obligations to get in the way of her personal project because she had no friends. Agnes did get lonely at times. She'd had a habit of talking to herself since she was seven. On the weekends when all the other students were at parties or on weekend trips, the only voice she heard was her own. But most times, she was too absorbed in her experiments to be lonely.

"If he does know," Agnes said, "I wonder how he found out. There are no security cameras inside the lab. Maybe Professor Levin has x-ray vision, and he saw the failed experiments I hid in my backpack." She scratched her forearm. "No. That's silly. X-ray vision is still unreliable and only available to the labs sponsored by the military."

Agnes talked to herself quite often. Her mother had worried about this habit until she read a magazine article that said it was normal and a sign of advance intelligence.

Agnes' footsteps echoed in the empty halls as she approached Professor Levin's office. His door was open, she could hear him chanting. Professor Levin stood behind his desk. A leather strap was wound around his left arm and fingers. Another leather strap attached to a small box was draped over the cap on his head. He wore a prayer shawl on his shoulders and cradled an open book in his hand.

Agnes grew up in a neighborhood that only had Baptist and Methodist churches but had gone through a phase where she became curious about non-Christian religions and read many books about other beliefs. She was aware that Professor Levin was an Orthodox Jew, and he was reciting his morning prayers. She was going to wait in the hall until he was done, but Professor Levin spotted her and without pausing his chanting, motioned for her to enter and take a seat. Agnes did as she was instructed. She took off her backpack and placed it beside her chair.

Levin sang in a deep baritone that rolled over the Hebrew words like a melancholy journey through hills and valleys. Agnes was mesmerized by the sound and the feeling it stirred inside her. When Levin finally closed his prayer book and put it on his desk, Agnes resisted the urge to applaud.

"That's all?" she asked. "No more?"

"For now," Levin said.

"I've never seen you do that before."

"I normally do my morning prayers before I leave the house, but I was running late."

"It was lovely."

"Yes, prayer is lovely."

Levin unwrapped the leather strap from his arm. Agnes could see it was attached to a leather box identical to the one he had on his head.

"The shawl is a called a tallit and the beanie cap is a kippah?" Agnes asked.

"That's right."

"I can't remember what the black boxes with leather straps are called."

"They're called tefillin. They're part of the morning ritual."

"How do you use them? What's inside the boxes?"

Levin folded the prayer shawl and the tefillin and stuffed them into a velvet bag. He kept the kippah on his head. He always wore a kippah. As he put the bag and prayer book into his desk drawer, he smiled at Agnes.

"You're a true scientist," he said. "Always asking questions."

"Questions like what is the purpose of our meeting?"

Levin looked at her with surprise.

"I assumed you knew. Your mother called. She thinks I'm working you too hard. As she put it, you may be a genius, but you're still a sixteen-year-old girl who should be out doing the kinds of things normal sixteen-year-old girls do instead of being worked to death in a cold laboratory. You'll be happy to know I assured her that our labs have excellent heating and air conditioning."

Agnes' cheeks burned with embarrassment.

"I can't believe Mom called you without telling me."

"You did sign an agreement that gives Claudia permission to access your grades and to communicate directly with me."

"It would have been nice if she'd warned me."

Levin chuckled.

"I'm sure she meant well. And it was no bother at all."

Agnes suspected Professor Levin enjoyed her mother's calls. Men were naturally attracted to Claudia. Professor Levin was a happily married man, but his voice changed whenever he talked about her. Agnes would almost describe it as giddy.

The weird part was her mother made no effort to attract men. Claudia seemed oblivious she was a magnet that pulled them toward her. Agnes was relieved she hadn't inherited her mother's magnetism. The attention would have been bothersome and had caused Claudia more harm than good.

"Mom knows it was my choice to stay at Tech for Summer Semester," Agnes said.

"You're the only lab assistant in my group who didn't take this semester off," Levin said.

Agnes shrugged.

"I don't care what other lab assistants do."

"You can understand your mother's concern." Levin counted off on his fingers. "You're her only child. You're living away from home for the first time. You didn't come home for the summer or take a vacation from school."

Agnes stared at her tennis shoes. The left shoe had come untied. She resisted the urge to bend down and tie it.

"This is a vacation for me. If I weren't here, I would be beyond bored."

Levin stroked his thick beard. Agnes liked how his facial hair was a shade lighter than the dark brown curls on his head.

"Everybody needs to take a break once in a while," Levin said. "Even you. It helps recharge the batteries. I want you to take some time off. I don't want to see you in the lab for at least a couple of weeks. Okay?"

No longer able to hold back, Agnes reached down and tied her left shoe.

"Okay. Two weeks. And then I'm coming back."

She picked up her backpack and sulked out of Levin's office.

Agnes had been planning on moving her experiment to her dorm room at the end of the summer because the risk of discovery was greater during fall and spring semesters. Her mother's meddling just meant she had to make the move sooner.

Agnes checked the time.

Claudia would already be at Wendy's and too busy to talk unless it was an emergency. Agnes could call her late afternoon but by then she would have cooled down enough to admit she missed Claudia and a short vacation was a good idea.

"I'm a genius," Agnes said. "And yet Mom is always one step ahead of me."

Rushing to the lab for her tools, supplies, and journal, Agnes figured she had time to conduct one more experiment before she went home.

CHAPTER 2

Wednesday, July 4, 2007

Agnes buried her hand in the yellow sand. Beaches don't form naturally next to lakes, so Chattanooga built one. She pulled her hand out, shook off the sand, and shielded her eyes as she watched Claudia emerge from Chickamauga Lake.

"I think the reason they call this Chester Frost Park is because the water is freezing," Claudia said as she wrapped a towel around her shoulders.

"Actually, the park is named after Judge Chester Frost," Agnes said. "It was originally called Hamilton County Park."

Claudia laid her towel on the sand next to Agnes, took a tube of sunscreen from her bag, and squirted a glob into her hand.

"I was just making a joke," Claudia said as she vigorously rubbed the lotion on her arm. "Do my back."

Agnes reached out her hand while Claudia squeezed sunscreen into it. Agnes rubbed the lotion on Claudia's back including the R.E.M. logo tattooed on her left shoulder blade. The air smelled of suntan lotion, grilled meat, and lake water. Music blasting from portable radios competed with children shrieking and motorboats roaring across the water. Despite all the activity, Claudia and Agnes had plenty of space to spread out.

"I was afraid it would be more crowded," Agnes said. "Is this what happens when a holiday lands in the middle of the week?"

"It's early," Claudia said. "The beach will be packed tonight for the fireworks."

"We'll be home by then, right?"

Claudia sighed. "Yes, we'll be home by then."

She put on her sunglasses and floppy hat, then sprawled out on her towel. Agnes didn't understand why her mother enjoyed being exposed to the heat of the sun considering she spent her working hours next to hot stoves and sizzling oil. As for Agnes, if not for the health benefit of absorbing Vitamin D from the sun, she would have been perfectly happy to spend the day reading in her bedroom.

"Check out the cute boy," Claudia said.

Agnes had no difficulty figuring out which boy Claudia was referring to because he was the only boy on the beach who wasn't a toddler. Tall with a mop of blond hair, he wore cut-off jeans and tennis shoes with no socks. His hairless chest was smooth and muscular. He was checking out Claudia and Agnes while pretending he wasn't checking them out when he did a double take. He jogged over. Up close, he smelled of boyish sweat and Axe body spray.

"Hey, Ms. Cook," he said. "Remember me? I'm Josh Hawkins. You used to be part of our carpool when I was in grammar school."

Claudia pushed her sunglasses to the top of her forehead.

"Little Josh Hawkins? Look at you! You're not little anymore. You're all grown up. I can't believe you remember me after all these years."

"We always looked forward to the days you drove because your car always smelled like hamburgers."

"Sadly, it still does."

Josh gawked.

"Agnes? Is that you?"

Agnes felt overly exposed in her bikini. She had wanted to get a one-piece suit, but Claudia had talked her into the bikini. Agnes was tempted to use her towel to cover herself.

"Yes, it's me," she said.

"I haven't seen you since fifth grade. You skipped ahead. What grade are you in now?"

"Agnes is about to start her second year at Georgia Tech," Claudia said proudly.

Josh smacked his forehead.

"I'm such a dope. I read about you in the paper. You're like super smart. That's so cool."

Agnes couldn't help but smile. Josh was so big and friendly that Agnes felt like she was talking to a Labrador Retriever. She wouldn't have been surprised if he started licking her face. She wondered if all boys her age acted this way. That would be nice if it were true because Agnes liked dogs.

"Are you here by yourself?" Claudia asked.

"My family's over there," Josh said, pointing toward the campgrounds. "We spend a week here every summer. Dad loves the fishing here. The fireworks tonight are going to be awesome."

"We can't stay that late, so we'll miss them."

"That's too bad. They're something to see. Hey, it was nice seeing y'all again."

"Nice seeing you too, Josh."

"Good luck in school, Agnes."

Agnes was about to say she didn't need luck in school because she was completely capable of doing well on her own, but Josh had already walked away.

"That was nice of him to stop by," Claudia said. "Do you remember him?"

Agnes scratched her forearm.

"Yes. He sat in front of me and always smelled like onions."

"I never noticed," Claudia said. "Probably his onion smell blended in with my car's hamburger smell."

Claudia dug her ear buds out of her tote bag, inserted them into her ears, and called up a playlist on her phone. From the way her mother smiled, Agnes knew she was listening to her beloved R.E.M. Agnes tried to go back to reading *Einstein: His Life and Universe*, but the noise was too distracting. The loud music and loud children hadn't bothered her before but for some reason they did now. She didn't feel like getting in the water, never much of a swimmer even when the water was a comfortable temperature. She poked Claudia who took her ear buds out.

"I'm going for a walk," Agnes said.

"Okay," Claudia said. "I'll be here."

Wrapping her towel around her waist, Agnes made her way through the families lounging on the beach facing Lake Chickamauga to a trail that wound through the trees facing Dallas Bay. The opposite shore was covered with rocks instead of sand. She was glad she had thought to wear her sandals.

Except for two elderly men fishing, she had the rocky shore to herself. A few boats in the bay floated lazily with fishing lines trailing behind them, while the rest zoomed back and forth sending ripples across the bay and waves lapping the shore. Watching the speeding boats race past stagnant boats reminded Agnes of Einstein's theory that time is a river with faster and slower boats.

"Professor Levin was right," Agnes said. "I needed to take a break. I see now that getting out of my daily routine has given me a fresh perspective. I was bogged down and missed new avenues of exploration that were staring me in the face."

"Who's Professor Levin?"

Fear shot through Agnes as she looked for the source of the voice and spotted Josh Hawkins leaning against an oak tree. He was in the tree's shadow which was why she hadn't noticed him at first. As he stepped out into the sun, she saw he was pinching the stub of a hand-rolled cigarette between his forefinger and thumb. Having been in college for many years, Agnes was familiar with the cigarette's sweet smell.

"You're smoking marijuana," Agnes said.

Josh held out the joint toward her.

"Want some?" he said. "There's probably enough for one toke. If I'd known you were coming, I would have waited to light up."

Agnes wrinkled her nose.

"No, thank you. I have zero interest in clouding my mind with drugs."

Josh shrugged. He sucked on the stub then flicked it into the lake. It sizzled as it hit the water. Agnes would have been angry that he littered but paper was biodegradable, and marijuana was a plant causing little to no environmental damage.

"So," Josh said. "Who is Professor Levin?"

"Why do you want to know?" Agnes said.

"You brought him up."

"I wasn't talking to you. I didn't even know you were here."

"Do you always talk to yourself?"

"I'm not crazy."

Josh studied her with bloodshot eyes and grinned.

"I don't think it's crazy to talk to yourself. But since I'm here, you could talk to me."

Again, Agnes felt like she was talking to a Labrador Retriever.

"Professor Levin is my laboratory director at school," she said.

"He must be a great teacher if he told you to take a break from school," Josh said.

"He is a great teacher."

"It's too bad you're not going to be here for the fireworks tonight. Maybe you could talk your mom into staying. Me and some buddies scored a six pack of beer."

As they were talking, Agnes realized Josh was staring at her body. Though she wished she had gotten a one-piece bathing suit instead of the bikini, she was oddly flattered by his attention. She was accustomed to people seeing her as a brain with legs. Since she was always years younger than the other girls in her class, boys ignored her. As a result, she didn't give much thought to her appearance. She kept her unruly brown hair tied in a ponytail and never bothered to wear make-up. She didn't understand how Josh could have possibly found her attractive. Then again, his interest could have been triggered by teenage boy hormones and the fact he was high.

"Thank you for the invitation," Agnes said, "but my mother and I must leave before the fireworks."

Josh waded into the bay until his tennis shoes were submerged. He squatted, plunged his hands into the water, and scooped up a handful of rocks. He picked through them, keeping only the flat, smooth rocks and tossing the rest back.

"Want to skip stones?" he asked.

Agnes was about to say no and walk away, but this was such an unusual situation for her she became intrigued. Having never spent time with people her age, she felt no connection with them. But Josh was friendly and easy-going. His company was pleasant, and she had come to the park to relax.

"Yes, I would like that very much," Agnes said.

Josh handed Agnes half the stones. They took turns skipping stones across the water. They made a game of who could get the most skips before the rock sank. Agnes beat Josh easily with a minimum of eight skips on every stone. The surprised look on his face made her laugh.

"You didn't tell me you were an expert," Josh said.

"Skipping stones incorporates elements of physics, mainly hydrodynamics, momentum, and gravity," Agnes said, running her finger around a stone in her palm. "The spin stabilizes the stone and keeps it from falling into the water. Minimum speed must be obtained, or the stone will sink immediately. Flat round stones work best because the surface area creates a bounce on impact. But none of that matters unless you achieve the magic angle. That's how you get the largest number of skips."

Agnes looked up from the stone. Josh was staring not at her body but at her face. It was if he was more interested in who she was rather than what she looked like. This excited and embarrassed her at the same time. She caught herself wondering what it would feel like to kiss him.

"I should be getting back to my mother," Agnes said.

"Do you have to?" Josh asked. "What you said was so cool. I don't know any girls who are as smart as you."

Agnes blushed. "I guess we can hang out a little longer, but then I really do have to go."

A few white clouds floated in the blue sky. They gathered more stones. Agnes examined them carefully and smiled. She had found the perfect stone, flat and round. An electric current of excitement that was even better than Josh's attention spread through her. The answer she had been seeking was in her hand.

"Skipping stones," she said. "Time is a river. Downstream is the future and upstream is the past. When I skip a stone, I don't worry about which way the river is flowing. I merely have to find the right combination of hydrodynamics, momentum, and gravity to enter the time stream. Once I establish that, then it's just a matter of utilizing the force of the river to skip from one point in time to the next."

Agnes squeezed the perfect stone in her hand. She didn't want to lose it, so she took another stone and tossed it toward the water. It bounced three times across the surface before it sank.

"You forgot to use the magic angle," Josh said.

"Yes. I mustn't forget the magic angle." Agnes looked at Josh's smooth chest. "Thank you for a lovely time, but I have to go now."

She headed back toward the beach. Josh rushed to join her.

"You're leaving?" he asked.

"I must make notes while this new theory is still fresh in my mind."

"If you're not too busy between now and when you go back to school, maybe we could go out. I have a driver's permit. Dad lets me borrow the car."

Agnes' gaze stayed glued to the walking path.

"I don't go on dates."

"It doesn't have to be a date. We could be two people going to a movie and maybe getting something to eat."

"That sounds like a date."

"Come on. It'll be fun."

Agnes stopped, and Josh kept going. He caught himself and came back to her. She put her hand on his warm chest. His skin felt pleasant.

"I'm sorry, but I'm not interested in having sex at this time in my life. Maybe after I complete my experiment and only with proper protection. By the time I'm ready, you'll probably have a girlfriend. So really, what purpose would it serve for us to go on a date?"

Josh opened his mouth, but no words came out. Agnes continued on her way. She didn't look back.

CHAPTER
3

Tuesday, October 16, 2007

Claudia's feet were killing her. Her best employee Denise called in sick and as day shift manager Claudia had to cover for her. The lunch crowd had been heavier than normal. Construction crews kept pouring in, and they all wanted their food in a hurry. Their work boots tracked mud on the tile floor. After the crews, the stay-at-home mothers arrived with their crying babies. Ordering took forever because the mothers were too distracted by their offspring to check the menu before they came to the counter. Their children tossed most of their meal on the floor. And then there were the bathroom pukers, but Claudia didn't have to clean up after them. That was what trainees were for.

Now the restaurant was empty, and Claudia hoped it stayed that way for the next hour when her shift ended at five. Also, she hoped the night manager wasn't late again. Claudia was in her cramped office with one shoe off, massaging her foot, when she heard what sounded like a herd of children stampeding through the store. Anthony stuck his head in Claudia's office.

"Customer wants to talk to you," he said.

"Is there a problem?"

Anthony looked toward the counter and then at Claudia. He bounced on his heels like he had to pee.

"Lady and her kids came in. I asked for their order and the lady said she would like to speak to the manager. I swear I didn't do nothing wrong."

Claudia reluctantly put her shoe back on and trudged to the front counter. She laughed when she saw the mother.

"Megan! What are you doing here?"

"My boys are starving, and I don't feel like cooking," Megan said. "Can you help me out?"

Megan's three sons Ethan, Bobby, and Steven Jr. were seven, five, and three. They had round, freckled faces and their father's red hair. Steven Jr. clung to his mother's leg while Ethan and Bobby tried to climb the condiment table.

Claudia had Anthony get the boys' cheeseburgers and fries. She brewed a fresh pot of coffee and poured a cup for Megan and herself. They took over a table in the far corner of the store.

"I hope I'm not keeping you from anything," Megan said as she sipped her coffee.

"I have to go over my crew's timesheets, but it can wait," Claudia said. "What brings you down off the mountain?"

The "mountain" was Signal Mountain, one of Chattanooga's most affluent neighborhoods. Megan and Claudia had grown up in Red Bank. Most of its population was lower middle-class families. Claudia still lived in Red Bank.

"I took the boys to the mall to pick out Halloween costumes," Megan said.

Claudia looked at the three boys. "So, what did you guys decide on?"

"Spider-Man," said Ethan.

"A ninja," Bobby said.

Steven Jr. had to think about it before answering. "Power Ranger!"

Claudia and Megan had been best friends since first grade. Despite the years and their opposite economic status, they were still best friends. They called each other four or five times a week.

Claudia tried not to be jealous of Megan's good fortune but watching her with her three rambunctious boys after a shopping trip to spend money on something non-essential, Claudia couldn't help but feel a knot of envy in her stomach. She tried to swallow it down with coffee, but it was lodged too tightly.

"You'll have to send me pictures of them in costume," Claudia said.

"You should come over," Megan said. "They'll be done trick or treating by eight. You can see them dressed up before they crash from a sugar high. We'll drink wine and watch horror movies."

The knot in Claudia's stomach soured into something more painful.

"I can't. I have to work the next day."

Megan tilted her head, which she did to let Claudia know she was being serious.

"When was the last time you celebrated Halloween?"

"Why do you ask questions you already know the answer to?"

"You have to stop making the connection between what happened and the holiday. It could just as easily have been a birthday party or a Christmas party."

"Then I would avoid birthdays and Christmas."

Steven Jr. paused from trying to stuff a fry up his nose to ask, "What about Christmas?"

"Nothing, honey," Megan said as she pulled his hand away from his face. "We're talking about Halloween right now."

Megan tilted her head at Claudia again and Claudia tilted her head right back at her.

"I don't regret going to that party," Claudia said. "Not for a second. But I can't help feeling sad this time of year when I think about how my life would have been different if I hadn't gone."

Ethan burped, making his brothers giggle. This led to a burping competition between the three of them.

"You boys are disgusting," Megan said as she smiled at her sons. She turned back to Claudia. "I'm glad it wasn't a Christmas party. I don't know what I would do if we couldn't visit each other on Christmas."

"What about Christmas?" Steven Jr. asked.

Megan used a napkin to protect her fingers as she removed a fry from Steven Jr.'s nose.

"We're not talking about Christmas. We're talking about Halloween."

CHAPTER

4

Saturday, October 27, 1990

The bunny and the witch posed for the camera.

"You two are adorable!" Megan's mother said as she snapped the photo.

The two sixteen-year-old girls giggled. Claudia, the bunny, and Megan, the witch, had spent all week trying to decide on a costume for the Halloween party and ended up cobbling together whatever they could find in Megan's closet that afternoon. Claudia's bunny ears were liberated from an Easter outfit, and her tail was a mass of cotton balls pinned to the butt of her black leotard. Black eyeliner completed her transformation with a smudge on her nose and lines on her cheeks for whiskers. Megan had sworn there was no way she'd go as a witch since that was what she'd been for the last three years, but desperation made her reconsider. Besides, the witch's hat and cape still fit.

"Remember," Megan's mother said, "be home by ten thirty."

"But Mom," Megan whined. "It's Halloween."

"Okay, midnight. Don't try to push me any further or you'll end up walking to the party."

Megan's mother was letting Megan drive the family car to the party rather than chauffeur them. The girls waited until they were out of the cul-de-sac before Claudia inserted R.E.M.'s album *Green* into the car's CD player and turned the volume up as far as it would go. The station wagon vibrated as the girls sang along with Michael Stipe.

They lived in a neighborhood of compact three-bedroom ranch houses, each with a single lonely tree in the middle of a large front yard of trimmed grass. Behind the houses was the remnant of the forest that had been cleared away so the suburb could flourish.

"Did any of the guys say what they were going as?" Claudia asked.

Barry, Derrick, and Neal were a year ahead of Megan and Claudia at Red Bank High School. The five of them formed the nucleus of their social circle.

"Hell no!" said Megan. "I'm sure they did like us and threw something together at the last minute."

Claudia gazed dreamily out of her window and recited the playful mantra the girls had devised after a lengthy discussion about the boys' best attributes, "Barry's curly hair, Neal's blue eyes, and Derrick's amazing ass."

Megan turned onto Dayton Boulevard. A cherry red Trans Am with the firebird logo on the hood roared up behind the station wagon and flashed its lights. Before Megan could change lanes, the car sped around them.

"Redneck!" Megan shouted.

"God, I hate this town," Claudia said.

The girls sang along with eight songs on the CD before they arrived. Houses were bigger and more elegant in this hilly neighborhood. Luxury cars sat in the driveways instead of inside the houses' massive garages, because otherwise no one would see them.

The winding street was choked with cars. Megan had to park three blocks away from the party. They got out and joined the throng of costumed teenagers following the siren call of rock music coming from the big house at the top of the hill.

"When did it get so damn cold?" Claudia said. "I'm about to freeze my tail off."

"I'm sure it's plenty warm inside," Megan said.

"Oh, look. The redneck is here."

The red Trans Am that passed them earlier was parked in the driveway.

"I hope somebody steals his car," Megan said.

The girls were greeted at the front door by a young man dressed as Elvis. Despite his excellent Elvis wig, aviator sunglasses, and gold lame jumpsuit, he wasn't a convincing Elvis because he was too short and scrawny.

He struck a pose and pointed at them.

"Hello, pretty ladies," he drawled. "Welcome to the home of the king."

"Hey, Allan," Megan said. "You make a great Elvis."

"Thank you, thank you very much."

Megan was right. It was plenty warm inside. The house was a sauna heated by the dense crowd of witches, vampires, pirates, glam rockers, clowns, cats, slashers, bloodied victims, superheroes, and a few unique creatures never before seen by man.

"I can't believe Allan's parents let him throw this party," Claudia said.

"They didn't," Megan said. "They're in Bermuda."

"How do you know all this?"

"People talk and I listen. You should try it sometime."

"It looks like everybody in North Chattanooga heard about this party. We'd better find the free booze before they run out."

Megan pouted. "You know I can't drink. I'm the designated driver."

"Don't worry, I'll drink for you."

After a few false turns, they found the kitchen. Like the rest of the house, it was huge.

"If my mom had a kitchen with this much space," Megan said, "she would have thought she'd died and gone to heaven."

On a kitchen island were festive plastic bowls with the crumbled remains of potato chips and pretzels, containers of onion dip, and near empty two-liter soft drink bottles. The counter held an impressive assortment of hard liquor. In a corner, a beer keg sat in a metal tub of melting ice. A clown, a hobo, and the grim reaper guarded the keg, clutching a red plastic cup in one hand with their other hand in their pocket. Three Ninja Turtles sat at a breakfast table sharing a joint.

Still feeling the night chill, Claudia wanted something to warm her up, so she mixed herself a whiskey and soda. Megan made quick friends with the Ninja Turtles. They passed her the joint. She took a hit and passed it to Claudia, who gave her a puzzled look before inhaling.

"Just because I can't drink," Megan said, "doesn't mean I can't smoke. I'm a better driver stoned than I am sober."

Claudia laughed and coughed out the smoke in her lungs.

"If you say so," she said before passing the joint along.

Claudia and Megan left the kitchen with a pleasant buzz. The hallway was a gauntlet of costumed teenagers laughing and shouting over the stereo blasting the music of Concrete Blonde. The teens were no match against Johnette Napolitano singing about a boy name Joey.

From around a corner, a boy wearing a hockey mask and bloody coveralls leaped out at them. He held a machete above his head and appeared ready to plunge the blade into their soft skin. Megan squealed and Claudia stumbled back. The boy laughed as he lowered the machete and lifted his hockey mask.

"Derrick!" Claudia said, punching his shoulder. "You asshole. You made me spill my drink."

"You should have seen your faces," Derrick said. "Come on, we're in here."

He put his arm around Claudia's shoulder, and she leaned away from him because his breath was producing more alcohol than carbon dioxide. Derrick led them to a cozy study off the main hallway. The sweet smell of pipe smoke clung to built-in bookshelves. Bay windows faced the front lawn. Barry and Neal had claimed two leather chairs facing an overstuffed couch. In between the chairs and the couch was a coffee table covered with golf magazines.

As the girls settled onto the sofa, Barry pointed at Derrick.

"He's Jason, get it?" Barry said.

"Oh, we got it," Claudia said.

"I used real blood for the bloodstains," Derrick said.

"Eww!"

Barry was dressed as a vampire. He had a black cape and white make-up with streaks of red running down the sides of his mouth. Neal was dressed as a cowboy with a white cowboy hat, cowboy boots, and a cowboy holster with a cap gun.

Megan took out her camera and had the three boys pose with Claudia. Then Megan handed the camera to Claudia so she could pose with them. In each photo, Derrick held his machete ready to attack, Neal held his cap gun ready to shoot, and Barry pretended he was about to bite a neck.

"Hey, did you see my new car?" Barry said. "I parked it in the driveway so it wouldn't get scratched."

"Please tell me that red Trans Am isn't yours," Megan said.

"My dad gave it to me as an early graduation present."

"You almost ran us off the road!"

"I did? Where?"

"Dayton Boulevard."

Derrick and Neal laughed while Barry searched for a response.

"Sorry. I didn't know it was you."

"You can make it up to us by giving us a ride in it later," Claudia said.

Megan rolled her eyes, which brought more laughter from Derrick and Neal.

The five friends made the study their home base. Neal rolled joints on top of the golf magazines while Barry and Derrick took turns going to the kitchen for more beer and to refill Claudia's whisky and soda. Claudia and Megan entertained the boys by making fun of other people's costumes.

"It's a shame how Batman has let himself go," Megan said pointing to a boy in a Batman costume that stretched across his bulging belly. "I hear he's been binge eating ever since the Joker died."

An hour later, Claudia announced she had to pee. She stood up too quickly and the room spun.

"Oh shit. How did I get so drunk?"

"I'd better go with you," Megan said as she struggled against the couch's gravitational pull. "Otherwise, you'll never make it."

"You're too stoned to move."

Claudia looked down at the boys. The way they were gazing up at her made Claudia feel like the girl on that TV dating show who picks one of three eligible bachelors. She already knew who the winner was, the same boy she'd had a crush on since she first saw him in home room at the beginning of her freshman year.

"Barry, will you take me?"

Barry glanced at Derrick and Neal. He grinned.

"Sure. Let's go."

As they left the cocoon of the study, the sights and sounds of the party bombarded them. Barry put his arm around Claudia's shoulder and guided her through the crowd. Pressed against Barry's body, Claudia breathed in his boy smell, which made her think of a forest of pine trees on a fall night.

They were physical opposites. Barry was tall and loose-limbed with a mass of soft brown curls framing his long face. Claudia was petite with strawberry blonde hair and large brown eyes. Barry was so full of teenage insecurity that even his breathing seemed self-conscious. Claudia was a fresh-faced girl next door with a natural sensuality.

They found the bathroom, but there was a long line ahead of them. They found a second bathroom with an even longer line.

"Let's check upstairs," Barry said.

"Stairs? I don't know if I can do stairs."

"Don't worry. We'll make it."

Barry half carried Claudia up the stairs to the second floor. They passed people standing on the stairs and discovered they were the tail end of the line to the second floor bathroom.

"What do you have to do to pee around here?" Claudia asked. "Make a reservation?"

"Looks like you're going to have to water the bushes outside," Barry said.

"I can't. I'd have to take off the leotard, and I'm not going to strip naked where someone might see me."

They walked down the hallway to see if any of the doors led to a bathroom. A couple of bedroom doors were open to reveal guests lounging on beds and sitting on the floor underneath clouds of marijuana smoke. The end of the hallway turned into a half corner and ended at a closed door with a sign taped to it that read KEEP OUT.

"I bet this is Allan's parents' bedroom," Claudia said.

"You think?" Barry asked.

"I bet they have their own bathroom."

"We can't go in there. The sign says keep out."

"But it doesn't say keep out Claudia and Barry."

Claudia checked to make sure nobody was looking in their direction before opening the door. She pulled Barry inside with her and closed the door. The room was dark. She felt around on the wall, found the light switch, and flipped on the lights. Claudia's scalp tingled. The bedroom was bigger than her family living room. Even the king-sized bed couldn't compete with the scale of the room. The air smelled of perfume and pipe smoke.

Claudia tried to imagine what it would be like to live in this home. It would be fun, but she couldn't see Barry ever making the kind of money necessary to support a rich lifestyle. That was okay with her. A loving home was all the wealth she needed.

"You're right," Barry said. "Here's a bathroom."

Claudia almost peed when she heard relief was near. She was about to close the bathroom door when she grabbed Barry's cape.

"Someone might see the light under the bedroom door and realize we're in here," she said. "Turn off the overhead light."

"But then I'll be standing here in the dark," Barry said.

"You're a vampire. You're supposed to be to see in the dark."

She closed the door before Barry could say anything else. Once inside, she lowered the toilet seat, wiped it down with toilet paper, and then wiggled out of her leotard and rolled it down to her ankles. Then finally, she emptied her bladder.

Barry turned out the bedroom light. There was a full moon and plenty of windows, so he wasn't totally in the dark. He slipped his key ring onto his finger and twirled his car keys. He liked twirling the keys because it was a reminder he had a sweet ride waiting for him outside.

The ring spun off his finger and landed silently on the carpeted floor. In a panic, Barry fell to his knees and felt around for the keys. Ten possible scenarios flashed through his mind, each one more horrible than the one before, of what his father would do to him if he didn't find the keys. His fingers touched the cold metal cluster of keys and relief washed over him. He stood and waited for his heart to slow down.

"Barry?"

The bathroom door was cracked and all he could see of Claudia was her face peeking out.

"Hey, Claudia. You done?"

"You know I like you, don't you?"

Barry knew this was an important question, but the pot and the beer were clouding his mind. He tried to concentrate.

"I kind of thought you did."

"Do you like me?"

"Sure."

"I mean really like me the same way I really like you?"

The room felt warmer. Barry liked Claudia, but not enough to be her boyfriend. Then again, he liked her enough to have sex with her. He was fairly sure this conversation was leading toward sex.

"Yeah, I like you the same way."

Claudia came out of the bathroom. She hadn't put her leotard back on. Barry had often imagined what Claudia would look like naked but actually seeing her was so much better. Claudia walked over to Barry and raised her chin for a kiss. Instead of kissing her, Barry grabbed her breast and squeezed too tightly. Claudia winced and pulled his hand away. She led him to the king-sized bed and waited nervously while he fumbled with his clothes.

They made awkward, messy love. Though they didn't know this about each other, this was only the second time for both of them. Barry came as soon as he entered Claudia but kept going for another minute hoping she wouldn't notice. The bed sheets smelled of candied perfume and adolescent sex.

Afterwards, Claudia hurried to the bathroom to retrieve her leotard. When she looked at herself in the mirror, she saw streaks of white make-up on her face and breasts. She felt guilty dirtying a plush towel with make-up and semen but didn't have a choice. Once she was done cleaning up, she stuffed the towel in the clothes hamper and prayed Allan's mother didn't notice when she did the laundry.

Claudia peeked out of the bedroom door to make sure no one was around. She and Barry stepped out and closed the door behind them. They were about to turn the corner in the hallway when Claudia felt her head. "I have to go back," she said, grabbing Barry's arm. "I forgot my bunny ears."

"We can't go back. Somebody will see us."

"If Allan finds my bunny ears in his parents' bedroom, he's going to know I was in there. Wait here."

Claudia hurried back to the bedroom. Her bunny ears were on the bathroom counter. She jammed them on her head and looked in the mirror to make sure they were straight.

She rejoined Barry in the hallway. Only a few streaks of white vampire make-up remained on his face. As they turned the corner, they ran into Allan.

"What are you guys doing here?" he demanded.

Barry opened his mouth, but no words came out. Claudia did the talking for them.

"We were looking to see if there was another bathroom."

"There isn't."

"Yeah, we figured that out."

"You didn't go into my parents' bedroom, did you?"

Barry was still trying to speak, but only faint sounds came out.

"Which room is your parents' bedroom?" Claudia asked.

"The one with the sign that says Keep Out."

"We didn't go in there because the sign told us not to."

"That's right," Barry blurted out. "The sign told us not to."

Allan narrowed his eyes at Barry and Claudia.

"The lines to the bathrooms are starting to thin out," he said. "Just hold it a little longer."

"I will. Hey, great party."

Allan struck an Elvis pose.

"Why thank you, thank you very much."

Back in the study, Claudia was no longer drunk. Instead, she was light-headed. She watched Barry for signs that their relationship was different now, but he acted like he always did.

"Does anybody know what time it is?" Megan asked.

"It's ten thirty," Derrick said, pointing at a clock on the wall.

Neal checked his wristwatch. "That clock's wrong. It's eleven thirty."

"Oh shit, we have to go," Megan said.

"Do we have to?" Claudia asked.

Megan gave her a look that made it clear she was in no mood for an argument. Claudia hooked her arm around Barry's.

"Maybe you could give me a ride home," Claudia said. "In your new car."

"My dad told me not to let anyone else ride in the car," Barry said.

Derrick snorted.

"You have to go with me," Megan said. "You're staying at my house tonight."

Claudia looked at Barry with her best puppy dog eyes.

"Will you walk me to the car?" she asked.

Barry looked sheepishly at the guys and then shrugged.

"Sure. Let's do it."

Stepping outside reminded Claudia it was a cold night. Barry avoided

Claudia's attempts at conversation. At Megan's car, he gave Claudia a lingering kiss while his hand roamed her butt. Barry jerked his hand away when Megan took a photo of their embrace.

"See you at school," Barry said before hurrying back to the party.

Megan waited until they were driving on Dayton Boulevard to state the obvious.

"You screwed him, didn't you?"

Claudia turned the heater on as high as it would go.

"I did," she admitted. "Do you disapprove?"

"He's cute as hell. Given the right circumstances, I'd do him."

"Too late. I got him first."

"Please tell me you used a condom."

Claudia felt a new chill go through her. She'd been so drunk and nervous she forgot to ask Barry if he even had one.

Megan patted Claudia's knee.

"Don't worry. I'm sure it'll be okay."

CHAPTER 5

Friday, December 7, 1990

Claudia sat on the hallway floor across from the gym and waited for basketball practice to end. She wore her R.E.M. Green World Tour T-shirt because it was her favorite, and she felt she could tackle anything when she wore it. Five weeks had passed since the Halloween party. During that time, Barry had made it crystal clear he had no intention of being Claudia's boyfriend. He avoided talking to her and generally treated her like a complete stranger.

She dozed off and was awakened by the gym doors slamming open. Sweaty boys poured out, joking, and pushing each other. Claudia climbed to her feet and slipped on her backpack. Barry spotted her as soon as he came out. He looked startled and Claudia feared he'd run away, but he regained his composure and sauntered over to her as if he was the coolest kid in school.

"Hey, what's up, Claudia?"

"I saw you give Shannon Tendler a ride. I thought your dad said you weren't allowed to let anyone in your car."

"Shannon's allowed because she goes to our synagogue. Is that why you're here? Are you jealous?"

Claudia chewed on her lower lip.

"We need to talk."

"That doesn't sound good."

"It depends on your definition of good. I'm pregnant."

Claudia crossed her arms as Barry studied his tennis shoes.

"Do you know who the father is?"

"Yeah, I know."

"Is it me?"

"Yeah."

"Are you sure?"

Claudia stomped on Barry's toes. He yelped and hopped in place. His teammates laughed and pointed at him. He grabbed Claudia's elbow and limped as he led her outside the building. They sat on a brick wall next to the walkway. Barry took off his sneaker and rubbed his toes.

"I have all the symptoms," Claudia said. "Missed my period, morning sickness, bloating. Just to be sure, I peed on a stick, and it came out positive."

"Sometimes those tests give false positives. You should see a doctor."

"Damn it, Barry. I know I'm pregnant."

Barry stared at the night sky. A half-moon peeked through the clouds.

"I have some money left over from my summer job. That should cover half if you can cover the other half."

"Half of what?"

Barry looked around nervously.

"The abortion," he said in a stage whisper.

Claudia punched him in the arm as hard as she could. Barry moaned and rubbed his arm.

"I am not getting an abortion."

"Then what do you expect me to do? My dad's going to kill me when he finds out. I'm going to college next year. I can't deal with this right now."

"And I can?"

Barry examined the inside of his shoe.

"What do you want me to do? Just tell me."

Claudia hugged her stomach and fought back the nausea creeping up her throat. Once her stomach settled, she could see her future ahead of her, and Barry wasn't in it. She slid off the wall.

"Forget it," she said.

As she walked away, she wondered how she was going to tell her parents. Holding the sneaker in his hand, Barry skipped after her.

"Where are you going? I said I would help."

Claudia spun around, and Barry stopped skipping. Though he towered over her, her fury scared him.

"I don't want your help," she said.

"Just tell me what you want me to do. Do you want to ride in my car?"

"I hope somebody steals your car! No. I hope somebody crashes into it and destroys your stupid car."

When Claudia reached the parking lot, she looked over her shoulder. Barry stood on the sidewalk with one sneaker on and one sneaker off.

CHAPTER
6

Monday, August 4, 2008

Agnes felt a tingling at the base of her neck. She was certain that today, her birthday, she would have a major breakthrough. Her reasoning was wholly unscientific. She turned seventeen today. Her mother was seventeen when she had Agnes, making today the perfect day for Agnes to give birth to a functional time travel device.

Despite her optimism that today's experiment would be a success, she didn't consider any of the past year's experiments to be failures. Each one brought her closer to finding the "magic angle" that would allow objects to skip across the river of time.

Her stopwatch was missing.

"I can't conduct the experiment without a stopwatch," Agnes said. "Of all things to go missing. Ethel! Did you take it?"

Ethel Owl, Agnes' childhood stuffed animal, stared at Agnes from the bookshelf, offering no comment. After a brief search, Agnes found the stopwatch on her bedside table next to a half-eaten cup of yogurt.

Agnes lived on the third floor of the Stein House, the women-only residence hall. Her dorm room contained two narrow bedrooms with a shared bathroom. As a gifted student years younger than her fellow students, the administration decided it would be better if Agnes had her own room, while instructing all Stein House faculty and students to act as big sisters and keep an eye on her. Agnes used her extra bedroom as her lab. She found using her dorm room as her lab had both advantages and disadvantages. On the plus side, she could work on her experiments whenever she wasn't scheduled to be in Professor Levin's laboratory. If she got an idea in the middle of the night, she could roll out of bed and five steps later, she would be in her lab.

The best time was during summer semester. Hardly anyone was in the building, and nobody complained about sulfur and burnt plastic smells coming from her room.

On the negative side, several experiments grinded to a halt because she didn't have the parts to continue. Most of the raw materials were pilfered from other labs. Agnes was a careful thief, taking a few wires from one lab and a stack of metal plates from another. She got the circuit boards from her own lab. She could have requested the supplies she needed from the university, but she would have needed Professor Levin's approval. Since her experiment was still top secret, that wasn't an option.

Agnes double-checked the wires connecting the digital clock to the metal box, not wanting a repeat of what happened on July fourth. She had convinced Claudia to let stay at school during the holiday. While Atlanta celebrated America's birth with hot dogs and fireworks, Agnes was in her dorm room lab. Unlike her earlier boxes, it didn't shimmer or explode or become a metal pancake. What it did was both remarkable and mundane. The box disappeared. One second it was on the desk and the next second it wasn't.

Overjoyed, Agnes threw her arms out and spun around while outside her dorm window fireworks exploded into bouquets of sparking color. She had done it.

Watching the fireworks, Agnes thought how one year earlier she had skipped stones with the boy she knew from grammar school. Josh something. That was the day she had her epiphany about how to build her machine. Tonight, she had succeeded in casting her machine into the time stream.

"Oh shoot!" Agnes said.

Staring at the empty space where the box had been, she had to laugh at her own foolishness. Agnes had forgotten to attach a timer. The box had nothing to tell it when to return. It was skipping through time without a destination and would keep skipping downstream for eternity.

"The purpose of experiments is to learn from our mistakes," Agnes said.

After going over her checklist one last time, Agnes was ready to begin the experiment. She set the clock, started the camcorder, and spoke into her voice recorder.

"Transport solid object attempt number three hundred twenty-five. Goal is for object to travel sixty seconds forward in time. Begin in three… two…one."

Agnes flipped the switch, activating both the box and the clock simultaneously. Immediately, they disappeared. She started the stopwatch.

Her phone rang. She grudgingly answered.

"Who is this? What do you want?"

"Happy Birthday to you, Happy Birthday to you, Happy Birthday my darling Agnes, Happy Birthday to you."

"Thanks, Mom. Can I call you later? I'm in the middle of something."

Agnes studied the stopwatch. Fourteen seconds had passed. Forty-six seconds to go.

"Are you celebrating your birthday with your friends?"

"Nobody I know is in town right now. I'm doing an experiment that requires my complete attention."

Twenty-five seconds passed. Thirty-five seconds to go.

"I'm going to call Professor Levin. He's pushing you too hard again. He didn't even let you come home this weekend to celebrate your birthday."

"We've been over this a hundred times, Mom. It was my decision to stay."

Thirty-nine seconds passed. Twenty-one seconds to go.

"I know, but I still want to see you. I miss you."

"I miss you too, Mom, but this is really important to me. Summer semester is almost over. I'll come home during the break."

Fifty seconds passed. Ten seconds to go.

"At least tell me you did something special for your birthday."

At exactly one minute, the time machine reappeared.

"Yes, Mom. I did."

CHAPTER 7

Saturday, August 10, 2002

"Sorry I couldn't be here last weekend," Barry said. "Did she have a big birthday party with all her friends?"

"My parents took us out to dinner, then we came back here for cake and ice cream," Claudia said.

"That's it? Doesn't Agnes have any friends?"

"She has friends, but none her own age. How are things in Nashville?"

Barry took a sip of iced tea to buy time. He didn't want to admit that his job sucked, he hated Nashville, and the only reason he moved in with his girlfriend was to save money on rent.

"Things are great. Nashville is the bomb."

Agnes joined her parents in the living room. She wore plaid shorts and a beige T-shirt. A pink headband kept her mass of frizzy brown hair out of her face. She had her purse slung over her shoulder to show she was ready to go.

"There's the birthday girl," Barry said. "Your mom tells me you got the gift I mailed you."

"Yes, I did. Thank you very much."

Barry had gotten Agnes a Bratz, a girl doll with an oversized head that wore too much make-up and dressed like a slut. Agnes had no plans to take the thing out of its box.

"We should get going," Barry said, looking at his watch.

"Go on out to the car, Agnes," Claudia said. "I need to talk to your father."

Barry winced. This couldn't be good. He and Claudia watched Agnes trot across the front lawn to Barry's car.

"Your check is late," Claudia said. "Again."

"I had to choose between sending you a check or getting Agnes a birthday present," Barry said. "I'm that fucking broke."

"Dolls aren't that expensive. Do I have to call Family Services again?"

"You'll get your damn check. Now if you don't mind, I'd like to spend some quality time with my daughter."

When Barry got in the car, Agnes was in the passenger seat with her seatbelt on. She waved at Claudia as they drove away.

Agnes was an exotic animal to Barry. He had meant to be more involved in her life, but never seemed to find the time. Other than occasional holiday visits, he rarely came around. Even finding out Agnes was a bona fide genius didn't get him back to Red Bank as often as he should. But now that he was older and more mature, Barry was determined to get closer to his daughter.

He had planned to begin the bonding process by exposing Agnes to rock groups other than Claudia's lame favorite REM, but his plan was derailed by Agnes' endless questions.

"Where do you work?"

"Radio Shack."

"What do you do at Radio Shack?"

"I'm assistant manager."

"Did you know Mom's an assistant manager at Wendy's?"

"Yes, I know."

"Do you like country music?"

"It's okay."

"A large number of country music stars live in Nashville. Do you know any of them?"

"No, sorry."

"When are you going to take your car in for a new clutch?"

"My car doesn't need a new clutch."

"Do you hear how your transmission grinds whenever you shift gears? That means your clutch either needs an adjustment or it's worn out. From the way it's grinding, I'd say you definitely need a new clutch."

Barry gripped the steering wheel tightly. He was sensitive about his red Trans Am. The car had impressed a lot of girls when he was in college, but it was getting old and cranky. Most of the hood's firebird decal had peeled off and half of his paycheck already went to keeping it functional enough to stay on the road. There was no way he could afford a new clutch.

The Bijou Cinema 7 sat under a parking garage a few blocks from the Tennessee Aquarium. Barry found a spot on the third floor of the garage, and they took the elevator down. A young woman with big breasts, big hips, and big blonde hair stood at the theater entrance. Agnes thought she looked like a country music star. The big blonde smiled and waved at them. Agnes looked at Barry and he blushed.

"That's my girlfriend," he said. "I thought it would be better if Claudia didn't know she was going to hang out with us."

The girlfriend leaned over. Agnes could see down her shirt.

"You must be Agnes."

"Yes, I am. Who are you?"

"Agnes, this is Stacy," Barry said. "Stacy, Agnes."

Stacy held out her hand and Agnes politely shook it.

"Your daddy has told me so much about you," Stacy said.

"He hasn't told me anything about you."

Stacy glared at Barry. He pointed at the marquee.

"Let's decide which movie we want to see."

They craned their necks to study the titles on the marquee.

"We girls want to see *Divine Secrets of the Ya Ya Sisterhood*, don't we, Agnes?" said Stacy. "I love me some Sandra Bullock."

"Seen it," Agnes said. "Mom liked it. It was okay."

"How about *Lilo & Stitch*? It's a Disney movie," Barry said. "Would you like that, Agnes?"

"That's a kid's movie. I'd rather see *The Time Machine*."

"That's an old movie. You can watch it on TV."

"This is a remake. It just came out."

Stacy and Barry searched the movie posters along the side of the theater until they found the poster for *The Time Machine*.

"What do you know?" Barry said. "They did make a new one. The guy from *Memento* is in it."

"Hated that movie," Stacy said. "I couldn't follow it."

"I liked it," Agnes said. "Having the movie move backwards chronologically was fascinating."

Barry paid for the tickets. Stacy bought popcorn and sodas. The smell of liquid butter filled the lobby. Anticipating the chill from the air conditioning, Agnes slipped on the hoodie she had tied around her waist. Barry sat between Agnes and Stacy. Ten minutes into the film, Stacy lost interest and went to watch the Sandra Bullock movie, taking the popcorn with her. Agnes sat still and kept her eyes on the screen. When Barry asked her if she wanted more popcorn, she didn't answer. Her full attention was on the movie. It was like she was in a trance. The idea that a kid, even a genius kid, could pay attention to anything for more than ten minutes amazed Barry.

The movie ended before the Ya Ya Sisterhood divulged all their secrets. Barry and Agnes sat in the lobby and waited for Stacy.

"How'd you like the movie?" Barry asked.

"It was different from the book."

"You read the book?"

"When I was eight. It's okay that the movie wasn't the same. I like that the time traveler went back in time to try and save his fiancée."

Stacy's movie finally let out. Leaving the theater, they were blasted by the hot afternoon sun as they walked to Lupi's Pizza Pies. The intoxicating smell of freshly cooked pizza greeted them. The walls were covered with posters for bands playing at local rock n' roll bars.

Barry ordered three slices, Stacy ordered a salad, and Agnes ordered one plain cheese slice. Barry got a pitcher of beer to share with Stacy and a soda for Agnes. While waiting for the food, Stacy gushed about the Sandra Bullock movie. She tried to explain the plot but kept backing up to add details and though she'd just seen the movie, she couldn't remember which character did what. Agnes didn't bother reminding Stacy she'd already seen the movie.

The waiter brought their food and talking ceased while everyone dug in. Barry couldn't get over how proper Agnes acted. She sat up straight in her seat and didn't fuss. She acted more like a mature woman than a child. He wondered how much of her behavior was due to her advanced intellect and how much was due to how Claudia raised her. Barry secretly wished Agnes had inherited her big brain from him, though he couldn't think of anyone in his family who was super smart. On the other hand, Claudia didn't have any Einsteins in her family either.

"We need another pitcher," Stacy said as she emptied the last dregs into her glass.

"I don't know," Barry said. "I don't want to get plastered."

"Come on. I've seen you drink a lot more beer than this before you got drunk."

Barry glanced at Agnes.

"I don't think it's a good idea."

"Don't worry. I'll pay for it."

Barry relented and ordered another pitcher. Stacy finished her salad and took Barry's third slice.

"Tell me, Agnes," Stacy said as she bit into the pizza. "Does your mom have a boyfriend?"

"You don't have to answer that," Barry said.

"Mom doesn't have time for a boyfriend," Agnes said. "She works all the time."

"I work a lot, too," Stacy said. "But come on. She has to find time to go on dates. Everybody goes on dates."

Agnes swung her legs.

"You asked if she had a boyfriend. Not if she went on dates."

"What's the difference?" Stacy asked.

"A steady boyfriend is more of a time commitment than a casual date."

Stacy glanced at Barry.

"Good point. Does your mom go on dates?"

Agnes nodded. "Yes, she goes on dates."

"But nobody special?"

"No."

"Too bad."

"What's your point, Stacy?" Barry asked.

Stacy leaned into Barry pressing her ample breasts against his arm and spoke in a low voice, but not low enough that Agnes couldn't hear her.

"Claudia needs to find a boyfriend and get married, so that *my* boyfriend won't have to keep paying child support."

Barry covered his eyes with his hand. Agnes pulled napkins out of the dispenser on the table and wiped pizza grease off her hands.

"Family Services could have taken child support payments directly from Barry's paycheck," Agnes said. "They could have based those payments on gross income instead of net income. At Mom's request, Family Services made sure Barry only pays what he can afford."

"Barry said you were eleven," Stacy said. "You sure know a lot for a sixth grader."

"I'm not in sixth grade."

"I told Stacy you were super smart," Barry said. "You skipped a grade, right?"

Agnes straightened her shoulders and beamed.

"I start college in two weeks."

"College?" Stacy said. "You're lying. Eleven-year-olds don't go to college."

"Well, I'm going."

Stacy nudged Barry.

"Are you paying for her to go to college?"

"I have a full scholarship to UTC," Agnes said. "I wanted to go to Georgia Tech, but Mom insisted I get my bachelor's degree here in Chattanooga. She says I'm too young to live away from home."

Stacy emptied her beer glass and dabbed her upper lip with a napkin.

"You sure she's your kid? I love you Barry, but you're not the sharpest knife in the drawer."

"I'm smart," Barry protested. "I'm an assistant manager."

"Of a Radio Shack."

The waiter arrived with the second pitcher of beer. For the rest of the dinner, Barry and Stacy argued. Agnes watched them and wondered what it would be like to have a real father. Afterwards, Barry drove back to Claudia's house with Agnes in the back seat. Stacy rode shotgun and talked the entire trip. Whenever Barry tried to include Agnes in the conversation, Stacy talked over him.

At the house, Barry got out of the car to give Agnes a goodbye hug, but she scurried past him without saying goodbye. Barry watched his daughter until she disappeared inside her house. His shoulders slumped, and he got into the car. He reminded Stacy not to tell his parents they took Agnes to the movies.

The sound of the door slamming brought Claudia out of her bedroom where she'd been folding laundry. She found Agnes standing at the living room window, watching Barry drive away.

"How was the movie?" Claudia asked. "Did you have a good time?"

Agnes rushed over to Claudia and wrapped her arms around her mother's waist.

"What did you ever see in that man?" Agnes asked.

Claudia ran her fingers through her daughter's unruly hair. There were some questions she couldn't answer.

CHAPTER

8

Saturday, September 6, 2008

After successfully sending inanimate objects (an ink pen, a cupcake with vanilla frosting, her stuffed animal Ethel Owl) into the future and back to the present, Agnes felt confident she was ready to transport a living test subject. There had been a heavy rainstorm the night before and the skies were full of dark gray clouds. An occasional ray of sunlight broke through and lit up patches of earth. In the lounge, girls and their male visitors watched the Georgia Tech Yellow Jackets play the Boston College Eagles on TV.

"This is quite an honor, Mr. Rat," Agnes said, as she attached a rat-sized harness to the brown and white fancy rat she bought at a pet supply store. "You are the world's first time traveler."

Mr. Rat's busy nose sniffed the harness and the wires attached to it that led to the metal box. In movies, time machines were much more elaborate than a metal box, but this box was Agnes' time machine and it really worked. Agnes checked the camcorder to make sure both the machine and

Mr. Rat were in the frame, then began recording.

"Transport living test subject attempt number one," Agnes said into the voice recorder. "Goal is for healthy rodent to travel five minutes forward in time. Begin in three…two…one."

Agnes flipped the switch. The time machine along with the furry time traveler disappeared. Agnes started the stopwatch then made notes in her notebook.

As the first minute passed, Agnes regretted setting the clock for five minutes. She wasn't worried about the length of Mr. Rat's journey. Waiting in real time was annoying. She had nothing to do for the next four minutes. She thought about calling Claudia, but there was no such thing as a four minute phone call with her mother. Agnes had no choice but to be patient and wait.

Finally, five minutes passed. The time machine and Mr. Rat reappeared. Mr. Rat lay on his side, his eyes closed, and his body very still. A careful examination confirmed Agnes' worst fear. Mr. Rat was dead. There was no sign of injury.

For the rest of the afternoon, Agnes grieved the loss of Mr. Rat. Intellectually, she had known his death was a possibility, but still she was crushed. That evening, while most of the campus celebrated the Yellow Jackets' narrow victory over the Eagles, Agnes left the dorm with a shoebox containing Mr. Rat's corpse, a rusted garden trowel she'd found in the janitor's closet, and a flashlight.

Agnes walked a block a parking garage with tennis courts on top and inched her way down into the ravine than ran alongside the structure. The rain had soaked the ground, making it easier for her to dig a small grave under a mimosa tree. An itchy feeling between her shoulder blades warned her that she was being watched. She looked around. No one was there. The only sound she heard was the whistle of the wind. Agnes blamed her guilty conscience for the false alarm and continued digging.

Agnes never let a failed experiment get her down because she didn't consider them failures. By definition, an experiment was a test performed to learn about something not yet known. Mr. Rat's death was different.

Other than the occasional bug or spider, she had never killed a living, breathing creature before.

After the burial, Agnes covered the grave with leaves. She felt she should say something, but she choked up and hurried back to her room with tears in her eyes.

CHAPTER
9

Monday, August 7, 2000

Agnes sat up straight in her chair. This was a day of firsts. Her first day at a new school and the first time since first grade she was excited about being in school. First grade had been miserable. Agnes finished her assignments way before any of the other students and then was forced to sit around bored out of her mind.

The crushing boredom continued until third grade when Claudia finally convinced Red Bank Elementary to test Agnes' intelligence. When the school saw the results of the tests, they acted like they knew all along Agnes was gifted. The school recommended Agnes skip not one, but three grades which was why at age nine, Agnes was starting seventh grade at Red Bank Middle School.

Aware that twelve-year-old seventh graders would be bigger than her, Agnes had grabbed a seat in the first row. As the other students came into classroom, pushing past Agnes to find an empty desk, they looked like a stampede of giants. A boy sat behind her, scraping the desk on the floor, grunting as he settled in. Not only was he bigger than Agnes, he was the biggest kid in the class. Big enough to be in high school. His size and age intimidated her more than she thought it would. She felt like a mouse with a bear about to scoop her up in one bite. Screwing up her courage, she turned in her seat and faced him.

"Hello. I'm Agnes."

The boy pushed aside the dirty blond hair that hung over his eyes. Acne spread across his cheeks and chin.

"I know who you are," he said. "You're the egghead freak they let into our class."

Agnes quickly turned around and stared straight ahead. She knew some of the kids might resent her because she was younger than them, but she didn't think anyone would lash out at her like the boy did. She wanted to change seats but was too afraid to move.

The boy leaned forward. Agnes could feel his nasty breath on her neck.

"You'd better be as smart as they say you are," he said. "Because I'm going to be copying your test answers from now on."

"But that's cheating," Agnes said.

"Did I say you could talk back to me?"

Agnes shivered with fear. She didn't talk back again.

* * *

Four months later, Agnes brought home her first seventh grade report card. Claudia read the card and then read it again.

"Agnes," Claudia said. "I don't believe what I'm seeing. You're failing all your classes."

Agnes hung her head. She knew she should say something, but she was too scared. The boy said he'd hurt her and Claudia if she told anybody. Agnes didn't know if he'd really do anything, but she didn't want to find out.

"I'm sorry," Agnes said. "I'll do better. I promise."

Claudia placed the card on the dining room table. Agnes ignored the peanut butter and jelly on crackers and glass of milk in front of her. Her stomach was churning too much to eat.

"Maybe we moved you too fast," Claudia said. "Three grades were a lot. Maybe we should have just had you skip one grade. I could see about getting you moved back to elementary school."

"No!" Agnes said, fearing failure more than bullying. "Please don't do that. I can do this."

"Are you sure?"

Agnes couldn't keep her anxiety inside any longer. She burst into tears.

"There's a boy in my class. He sits behind me and says terrible things to me. He cheats off my papers and then blames me if he gets a bad grade. He bumps into me in the hallway. One time he tripped me as I was coming into class, and I dropped my books and scrapped my elbow. I can't concentrate on what the teacher is saying because I'm too scared."

Claudia rushed around the table and put her arms around Agnes.

"Does this boy have a name?" Claudia asked.

* * *

The following week, Claudia sat on one side of Principal Milligan's desk. Scott and Kristy Dobbs sat on the other. Principal Milligan laced his fingers and knitted his brow.

"We take bullying very seriously here at Red Bank Middle School," Milligan said.

"We do, too," Scott said. "But I can assure you our Trey did not bully this woman's daughter."

"He's a good boy," Kristy added.

"Are you suggesting my daughter is a liar?" Claudia asked.

Principal Milligan held up his hands.

"Now, Ms. Cook," he said. "I'm certain that's not what Scott meant."

"Sorry," Claudia said. "What did you mean, Mr. Dobbs?"

Scott glared at Claudia.

"Your daughter..." he said.

"She has a name," Claudia said.

"Sorry. Agnes is very young, younger than the other kids in her class. I've been told she has a high IQ. A girl that young and if she's as intelligent as you claim, a girl like her would have an active imagination and a desire for attention."

Rage burned through Claudia. It took all her will power not to bite the man's head off.

"The bruises on Agnes' back weren't caused by her active imagination," Claudia said. "They're from when Trey slammed Agnes into her locker."

"Trey denies ever touching her," Scott said.

"Did anyone see Trey do it?" Kristy said.

Claudia, Scott, and Kristy looked at Principal Milligan.

"A student said he saw Trey bump into Agnes," Milligan said, "but that it was an accident."

"Well, there you go," Kristy said, waving her hand. "It was an accident."

"It's an accident that happens every day," Claudia said.

Scott leaned forward in his chair and placed his fists on his thighs.

"I don't appreciate you making these unfounded accusations against our son," he said. "He was raised in a Christian home with two parents. He would never harm a girl. We raised him better than that."

Claudia ground her teeth. She really hated these people.

"And even if Trey did happen to tease Agnes once or twice," Kristy said. "I'm not saying he did, but if he did, he probably did it because he likes her."

"Boys will be boys," Scott said.

"She should appreciate his attention. He's a fine boy."

Claudia groaned.

"Principal Milligan, what are you going to do to ensure my daughter's safety?"

Milligan held out his hands in a helpless gesture.

"We take bullying very seriously here at Red Bank Middle School, but until a student or a teacher comes forward to corroborate Agnes' accusation, it's one student's word against another's."

"Then what the hell am I supposed to tell Agnes?" Claudia asked.

"Really," Kristy said. "There's no need for such language."

Scott and Kristy stared at Claudia as if she were some kind of heathen.

"If someone bullies her," Milligan said. "She should report it immediately to her teacher."

"Or to a parent, which is exactly what she did," Claudia said.

Milligan straightened his desk calendar.

"Mr. and Mrs. Dobbs. Thank you for coming in. I'd like to speak to Ms. Cook alone."

The Dobbs left but not before looking down their noses at Claudia.

"Is it possible," Milligan said, "that Agnes made this whole thing up?"

"My daughter is not a liar," Claudia said.

Milligan held up his hands in a defensive gesture.

"Hear me out. Agnes skipped three grades. That's a long way to go, both academically and emotionally. I am aware of her lackluster grades. Evidence suggests she's in over her head, but rather than admit it and disappoint you, she made up this story about Trey bullying her as an excuse for not being able to keep up."

Claudia took a moment to push her anger aside and compose her thoughts. She had to be clear and concise. For Agnes' sake.

"Agnes doesn't lie. If she were failing because she couldn't keep up, she wouldn't make up a story about a bully. She would admit it and face the consequences."

Milligan gave Claudia a condescending smile.

"We're talking about a nine-year-old. They make up stories."

"A normal nine-year-old does," Claudia said. "But we're talking about Agnes."

"I will give her until the end of the next semester. If her grades don't approve by then, I won't allow her to remain in this school."

"What are you going to do about the bully?"

"If someone bullies her, she should report it immediately to her teacher," Milligan repeated.

Claudia's heart sank. She had failed to protect her daughter. She felt like the worse mother in the world.

* * *

Agnes devised a solution to the problem of Trey the bully during Christmas break. She told no one of her plan, especially not Claudia. She would have tried to stop Agnes.

She executed her plan the first day after Christmas break. She got to school before other students arrived, telling Claudia she had to be at school an hour early to meet with the science teacher about an extra credit assignment to help boost her grades.

Even though the halls were empty, Agnes cringed every time the school's warped floor creaked as she made her way to Trey Dobbs' locker. She got to his locker just as a teacher came walking down the hall from the opposite direction. Agnes pretended to search for something in her backpack, her heart pounding in her ears, until the teacher went past. She took a deep breath to calm her nerves, then slowly turned the dial of Trey's combination lock while applying pressure to the shackle. Using this technique, she found the three numbers of his lock, writing them down on a piece of paper. She spun the dial to the three numbers and the lock opened with a satisfying click. Stuffing the piece of paper with the numbers into her mouth, she chewed it up, and swallowed.

Agnes opened Trey's locker and reared back in disgust. The interior smelled like old sweaty gym socks and spoiled food. Ignoring the stench, Agnes removed brand new, never opened schoolbooks from the top shelf and placed them at the bottom of the locker. She took a U-shaped slingshot and a homemade stink bomb from her backpack.

Installing a booby trap on the top shelf of Trey's locker put her at ease. Agnes was in her element. When it became painfully obvious the school wasn't going to protect her from Trey, she made a list of possible solutions. Agnes settled on hitting him in the face with a stink bomb water balloon. Throwing a water balloon at him wouldn't work. She might miss. Or if she did hit him, he might try to kill her. Better to set a trap and let him walk into it while she was a safe distance away.

Since the school lockers didn't have much depth, Agnes designed a slingshot that would fling an object at maximum velocity in a limited space. Trey wouldn't know what hit him until it was too late.

The stink bomb was the simple part of the plan. She created ammonium sulfide, which smelled like rotten eggs, by mixing matchstick heads, ammonia, and water inside a balloon then let it sit for four days. Agnes added an extra ingredient that would react with the oil in Trey's skin and cause the odor to stick to him for days, no matter how many times he bathed.

Trey wasn't the type to simply open his locker. He always slung it open, the door clanging on the locker next to his, the metallic sound echoing in the hallway. Agnes flinched whenever she heard that noise. It was the same noise she heard whenever Trey pushed her into a locker. She attached a wire from the slingshot to one of the angled slats in the locker door. Trey would trigger the booby trap himself when he flung open his locker.

Her work done, Agnes closed the door and relocked the combination lock. She checked the time. Students would arrive soon. Agnes slung her backpack onto her back and hurried away.

She loitered outside her first period classroom. Students entered the building sounding like a herd of animals migrating to their classrooms. After the first wave of students passed, Agnes entered the classroom and took her usual seat in the front row.

Staring at the blackboard, her legs bounced as she waited for Trey to arrive. The last wave of students entered the classroom and took their seats. Still, there was no sign of Trey. Agnes worried that maybe he was sick and wasn't coming to school today. The trap would wait, but Agnes wasn't sure she could.

The bell rang as late students rushed into the room. The teacher put the day's assignment on the blackboard. Agnes wrote it down in her notebook and tried to ignore the rapid beating of her heart. The seat behind her, Trey's seat, was empty.

Five minutes into the class, the door slammed open. The teacher turned to see who had disrupted her class.

"Trey Dobbs," she said. "How nice of you to decide to join us."

Trey's hair was soaking wet. His wet shirt was plastered to his skin. His open mouth showed gritted teeth. He pointed at Agnes.

"Wait until I get my hands on you," Trey said.

Agnes sunk in her seat.

"Trey!" the teacher said. "What is wrong with you this morning?"

"Agnes," he said. "She did it."

"Did what?"

"This!" Trey pointed at his head.

"Agnes has been here all morning." Trey started to argue but she shushed him. "Now take your seat. You've disrupted class long enough."

Trey glared at Agnes as he lumbered to his seat. He barely had time to sit before the girl behind him jumped to her feet.

"Oh, my God!" she said, holding her nose. "You stink! You smell like stale farts."

Students laughed and then groaned when Trey's odor reached them. The teacher tried to regain control of the classroom, but then his foul odor reached her.

"What on earth have you been doing?" she said covering her nose. "Don't bother to explain. Just leave the room. Go see the nurse. And somebody open a window."

"Yeah," the girl said. "Get out of here, Fart Boy."

The students laughed and chanted "Fart Boy! Fart Boy! Fart Boy!"

Trey's cheeks glowed apple red.

"Stop it! Stop it!"

"Fart Boy! Fart Boy! Fart Boy!"

"I mean it. Stop it!"

"Fart Boy! Fart Boy! Fart Boy!"

"Go to the nurse now!" the teacher said.

Trey stumbled to his feet and hurried out of the room. Agnes felt a swell of pride. He would try to get revenge on her, but she wasn't worried. If he did, she'd just build another booby trap.

* * *

The next day, Claudia sat on one side of Principal Milligan's desk. Scott and Kristy Dobbs sat on the other. The principal and the Dobbs glared at Claudia. Claudia looked at her nails.

"Will someone please explain why I'm here? Some of us have jobs."

"You know what your daughter did," Scott said.

Claudia glared at him.

"She has a name."

"Agnes hit our son with a stink bomb. He could have been seriously injured."

"How do you know it was her?"

"It had to have been Agnes?"

"Did anyone see her do it?"

Claudia, Scott, and Kristy looked at Principal Milligan. He shook his head.

"Nobody saw her," Milligan said. "But I think we can safely say it was Agnes."

"Really?" Claudia said. "Do you have any evidence?"

Milligan sighed.

"Red Bank Middle School has many bright students. None of them are as gifted as Agnes. She's the only one who could have rigged the booby trap inside Trey's locker."

"Not too long ago, you implied Agnes wasn't smart enough to be in seventh grade," Claudia said.

"I was wrong. She is plenty smart. Maybe too smart for her own good."

"Admit it," Scott said. "Agnes attacked Trey."

Claudia looked at Scott with as much innocence as she could muster.

"Y'all swore Trey never laid a finger on her. Agnes never does anything unless she has a good reason. She's stubborn that way. According to y'all, she had no reason to do what you're accusing her of."

Kristy sneered at Claudia.

"I never swear. I leave that to godless heathens like you and your demon spawn."

Milligan rose to his feet.

"Please, Mrs. Dobbs. Refrain from name calling."

"Even if Agnes did set this trap," Claudia said. "And I'm not saying she did. How do you know she didn't do it because she likes Trey? Girls will be girls. He should appreciate her attention."

"You're not helping, Ms. Cook," Milligan said.

Claudia directed her righteous indignation toward him.

"Why should I? You refused to believe my daughter, but someone hits their precious boy with a water balloon, and you immediately blame Agnes. How do you know Trey isn't bullying other students and one of them decided they'd had enough?"

Principal Milligan sat back in his chair. He looked like his lunch didn't go down like it was supposed to. Kristy broke into tears.

"Everyone keeps calling him Fart Boy," Kristy said. "He's too embarrassed to go back to school."

Scott put his arm around his wife's shoulder, she leaned against him. For a moment, Claudia envied Kristy for having a partner by her side. Then she realized she'd rather die alone than have a partner as big a jerk as Scott.

"The name calling is bad enough," Scott said. "But we've scrubbed Trey raw. He still stinks to high heaven. What the hell did Agnes put in that balloon?"

"Please," Claudia said. "There's no need for such language."

Scott and Kristy glowered at Claudia. Claudia shot daggers back at them. Principal Milligan placed his hands on his desk.

"I've made my decision," he said. "Agnes will be suspended for a week."

"Suspended?" Claudia said.

"For just a week?" Kristy said.

"That's my decision," Milligan said. "Ms. Cook. I'll have the front desk fetch Agnes."

Scott and Kristy grumbled but accepted the punishment. They left without saying goodbye. Once they were gone, Milligan gave Claudia a weak smile.

"I'm sorry, Ms. Cook. I'll make sure Agnes' teachers send her homework to your house, so she doesn't get behind."

"Even if they didn't send her anything," Claudia said, "it wouldn't take Agnes long to catch up. Might even give her a bit of a challenge."

Principal Milligan chuckled.

"As a gesture of good will, could you get Agnes to tell us how to make Trey stop stinking?"

Claudia crossed her arms.

"That would be an admission of guilt."

They said their goodbyes. Claudia waited at the front desk for Agnes. She arrived wearing her winter coat and carrying her backpack. Her frizzy hair looked like a cloud around her head. For some reason, she was always losing her elastic hair ties. They were cheap, and Claudia bought them by the dozen, but every penny counted. She fished one out of her purse and handed it to Agnes.

"Hey, Mom," Agnes said as she tied her hair back.

"Hey, pumpkin," Claudia said.

"Am I in trouble?"

"You've been suspended for a week."

Agnes looked down at her shoes.

"I knew I was suspended when my teacher told me I was going home. But I didn't know for how long. A whole week."

Claudia put her arm around Agnes' shoulder.

"Come on. Let's get out of here."

As they left the overheated school, they were blasted by a cold winter wind. They didn't speak until they were in the car and had pulled out of the school parking lot.

"They know I did it, don't they?" Agnes asked.

"Principal Milligan can't prove it," Claudia said. "But decided to suspend you anyway."

"Should I confess?"

"Hell, no. Don't give them the satisfaction."

"What will I do for a week?"

"You'll come to work with me. I can't leave you at home by yourself."

Agnes stared out the window at passing cars.

"I'm sorry," Claudia said.

"Why?" Agnes said. "I'm the one who did something bad."

Claudia reached over and squeezed Agnes' hand.

"I'm sorry I wasn't able to protect you," Claudia said. "I'm sorry you had to do it."

"I would have told you what I was going to do," Agnes said. "But I was afraid you'd stop me."

"You're damn right I would have. You're lucky Trey didn't catch you."

Claudia drove past the turn to their neighborhood. Agnes watched the street go by but didn't say anything.

"At least something good came from this experience," Agnes said. "I've decided I want to be a scientist."

"Is that so?" Claudia said.

"Science solved my problem. I used chemistry to create the stink bomb and physics for the slingshot."

"Did you solve your problem? Trey will probably try to get you once you're both back at school."

"I admit it wasn't the best solution. But now he knows I'm not helpless. I can hurt him."

Claudia pulled into a Waffle House parking lot.

"What are we doing here?" Agnes asked.

"I'm getting a slice of chocolate pie and a cup of coffee," Claudia said. "You can get whatever you like, but I know how much you love pecan waffles."

Agnes narrowed her eyes at Claudia.

"You're getting me waffles?"

"The school thinks you should be punished. I think you deserve a reward. The slingshot was impressive, but the stink bomb water balloon?" Claudia snorted. "That was pure genius."

Agnes' face lit up. When she smiled like this, Claudia was reminded Agnes was still a young child. Then Claudia noticed Agnes' hair was loose, and the hair tie she'd just given her not ten minutes earlier was missing. How did she manage to lose them so quickly? Maybe there was a scientific solution to that mystery. Claudia opened her purse and handed Agnes another hair tie.

CHAPTER
10

Sunday, September 7, 2008

The rain clouds had left town leaving a clear blue sky. Curled up on her bed with her computer, listlessly surfing the Internet, Agnes could hear students outside her room laughing and talking in the hallway. Nothing kept her interest, not even old standbys like the latest quantum physics articles on the international science sites.

Agnes considered going to Professor Levin's lab. She was way behind on her assigned experiments, having allowed her personal project to get in the way of her lab duties. She didn't want to risk losing her scholarship but observing neutrons inside swirling light beams seemed so crushingly boring after what she'd accomplished in her dorm room. Besides, she was too depressed to leave her room.

Agnes scrolled through her saved bookmarks for anything that might distract her and came across web pages she'd saved about tefillin. Watching Professor Levin pray with tefillin had fascinated her. She researched the ritual and watched instructional videos on YouTube, but it wasn't enough.

She wanted an actual demonstration. After weeks of badgering, Professor Levin finally agreed to show her.

The demonstration took place in his office. Agnes understood Levin wouldn't have done this for any other lab assistant. He gave her special treatment because of her young age and gifted status. They often ate lunch together. Levin never ate meals with any of his other lab assistants. If the assistants were jealous Levin was more personable toward her, they didn't show it. Instead, they treated her like their celebrity mascot which in some ways was worse.

In his office, Professor Levin removed the leather boxes from his velvet bag and laid them on his desk. He took a box and unrolled the straps attached to it.

"The first box goes on the weak arm," he said. "I'm right-handed, so I put in on my left, like this."

He slid the box up to his bicep.

"That's the *shel yad*?" Agnes said.

"Correct. You wind the strap, which is called the *retzu'ot*, around the arm seven times and three times around the middle finger like this." He wrapped the leather strap around his arm. The skin between the straps puffed out slightly. "The other tefillin goes on your head like this with the straps hanging down. I'm skipping some steps and the prayers so that we can concentrate on how to put it on."

He positioned the box above his forehead on the middle of his head so that it was directly above the point between his eyes. The straps from the box came together in a knot at the base of his skull and the straps dangled on either side of his head.

"That's the *shel rosh*," Agnes said. "The purpose of the ritual is to bind mind, heart, and deed?"

Professor Levin chuckled. "I bet your mother never had to worry if you'd done your homework."

Agnes pushed her hair out of her eyes and smiled shyly.

"How did you know?"

"It's a bit obvious, Agnes," Levin said. "Yes. the purpose of the ritual is to bind mind, heart, and deed. The scrolls inside are the *parshiyot*. They're handwritten torah passages that describe the mitzvah of tefillin."

After he removed the tefillin, Levin allowed Agnes to hold the shel rosh. She rubbed her fingers over the Hebrew letter embossed on the side. She wanted to put the tefillin on herself, but her research said only Jewish men were allowed.

Of all the things Professor Levin had taught Agnes at Georgia Tech, putting on tefillin was her favorite. Agnes relished the memory as she wrapped her hair around her finger. She re-watched one of the instructional YouTube videos she'd bookmarked. The rabbi in the video said something Professor Levin had also said during the demonstration in his office.

"The purpose of the ritual is to bind mind, heart, and deed."

That was the answer she was looking for. Agnes bolted out of bed and hurried into the bedroom she used as her lab, taking her computer with her. She sat at her desk, opened her notebook to a clean paper, and began to furiously make notes.

She understood why Mr. Rat died. An inanimate object has no inner energy source, but a living organism has an intricate system both interior and exterior that gives it life. Agnes needed to lock the unified energy source to the time machine. When she sent Mr. Rat skipping over time, she hadn't bound him mind, heart, and deed to the time machine. That was why his life had been snuffed out.

She went to the pet store's web page for their hours of operation. Agnes checked the time. She should be able to catch a bus to the store before they closed. She hoped they weren't out of fancy rats, but if they were, a hamster or a gerbil would suffice.

When she arrived at the pet store, there were two fancy rats left, a male and a female. The female was bigger and appeared more robust. The cashier remembered Agnes from when she bought Mr. Rat and asked if the new rat was a girlfriend for her boy rat. Agnes was going to explain a relationship wasn't possible because Mr. Rat was dead, but she held her tongue. She was afraid the cashier might refuse to sell her the rat if he knew she had killed the last one.

"Depends on how they get along," Agnes said as she stared at her shoes.

On the bus ride back to campus, Agnes peered at the rodent through the holes in the cardboard carrier.

"Ready for an adventure, Ms. Rat?" Agnes asked. Ms. Rat twitched her whiskers.

Back on campus, Agnes went to the dining hall and picked up two large bran muffins. She hadn't eaten all day and was ravenous. The second muffin was for Ms. Rat. Agnes wanted her to have a wonderful last meal in case the experiment failed.

Ms. Rat gorged on the bran muffin while Agnes broke open the metal box and transferred the circuits into two smaller boxes. She created miniature tefillin by connecting wire straps to the boxes. That was the easy part. The hard part was getting the tiny tefillin onto Ms. Rat. She kept wiggling out of it. Having cold metal boxes next to her chest and head was disturbing, Ms. Rat wanted nothing to do with them.

Agnes wrapped the wire straps in soft fabric and gently wound one strap around Ms. Rat's arm and tied the other strap round her pointed head. Agnes had no idea which arm was Ms. Rat's weak arm. Rodents probably didn't favor one arm over the other, so Agnes chose her left arm. This time, Ms. Rat sniffed the straps but didn't try to remove them.

With the clock set for five minutes and her equipment ready to begin, Agnes pressed record on her voice recorder.

"Transport living test subject attempt number two. Goal is for healthy rodent to travel five minutes forward in time. Begin in three…two…one."

She was so caught up starting the experiment she didn't notice Ms. Rat gnawing on the strap wound around her arm.

"Stop that!" Agnes said.

Agnes meant to reach for the rat but flipped the switch instead. Ms. Rat was still gnawing away when she disappeared.

Agnes paced the room for the next five minutes, imagining every possible outcome to Ms. Rat's destruction of the strap, all of which involved the rodent returning with at least one body part missing or her body turned inside out.

At the end of the five minutes, Ms. Rat reappeared. Agnes put her hand on her heart and gasped with relief. Ms. Rat was completely whole and alive. The strap was intact, and she no longer gnawed on it. She stood still and stared straight ahead. If a rat could look amazed, then that was how Ms. Rat looked.

"You made it," Agnes said. "Oh my God, it worked. It really worked. Ms. Rat, you are the first successful time traveler. Congratulations!"

Ms. Rat wiggled her nose and swiveled her head from side to side. She sat on her hind legs while slowly flexing her front paws. She bit Agnes when Agnes tried to remove the time machine. Agnes went out and got Ms. Rat another bran muffin. She figured the rodent earned it.

CHAPTER

11

Thursday, May 12, 2005

Claudia, Megan, and Neal watched Agnes stare open-mouthed at the large, rectangle pizza the waitress brought to their booth.

"It's not circular," Agnes said. "What kind of pizza is this?"

Claudia put her hands on her cheeks in mock surprise.

"I can't believe I know something you don't know. Agnes, that's deep-dish pizza."

Agnes didn't wait for the others. She pulled off a square, using her finger to sever strands of melted cheese clinging to it. After taking a bite, Agnes closed her eyes and smiled.

"I like deep dish."

Claudia, Megan, and Neal pulled off squares for themselves. The pizza restaurant sat at the end of a strip mall. It was brightly lit and had the plastic veneer of a chain restaurant. Though it wasn't packed, the waitresses busily buzzed from table to table like bees pollinating flowers. Neal looked around the restaurant and then addressed their table.

"There are plenty of family and friends here tonight at this fine establishment, but I think it's safe to say we are the only ones celebrating a certain someone getting a full scholarship to Georgia Tech to earn her doctorate in physics."

Agnes blushed as she ate her pizza. She didn't know that much about Neal. He had beautiful blue eyes and dressed well. He was a part of Claudia's close group of high school friends. From the way Claudia talked about him, Agnes got the impression he was a nice man and so far, her impression had proved correct. Plus, he didn't eat with his mouth open. Agnes hated when people ate with their mouth open.

"This calls for a toast," Megan said. She held up her soda cup. Claudia and Neal did the same. "To Agnes, who shall soon be Dr. Agnes, master of physics!"

"To Dr. Agnes," Neal said.

Everyone sipped their soda.

"We're also celebrating Neal coming to town," Claudia said. "I'm so happy you could join us tonight."

"I'm glad you invited me. I really missed you guys."

Agnes looked across the table at Neal.

"Where do you work?" she asked.

"Rite Aid," Neal said.

"What do you do at Rite Aid?"

"I'm a pharmacist."

"How many years of college did it take for you to learn to be a pharmacist?"

Claudia tried to halt Agnes' interrogation, but Neal waved her off.

"Four years undergraduate then four years at a pharmacy college," Neal said.

"Do you like jazz music?"

"I do. I like all kinds of music. You and Claudia should come to New Orleans for JazzFest. You can stay at my place."

"Does R.E.M. play at JazzFest?"

"I don't know. They have different musicians every year."

"Mom only likes R.E.M."

"That's not true," Claudia said. "I like lots of different music. R.E.M. just happens to be my favorite band, has been since high school. I used to have huge crush on Michael Stipe."

"What made you decide to finally come crawling back to Chattanooga?" Megan asked.

Neal choked on his pizza. He coughed and drank soda to clear his throat.

"I thought you knew," he said.

"If I knew then I wouldn't have asked," Megan said.

"Barry's getting married."

Agnes felt a hot flash of anger.

"Mom. Did you know?"

Claudia crossed her arms.

"I haven't talked to Barry in over two years."

"You might as well give us all the details," Megan said.

Neal looked around as if worried someone might eavesdrop on them.

"Derrick's the best man. The wedding is going to be at Barry's synagogue. His father is paying for everything, but he's keeping it very low key because of the circumstances."

"Ooh, I love that word *circumstances*," Megan said. "It implies something is amiss."

"The bride is pregnant and starting to show. I don't know if you've ever met her. Her name is Stacy."

"I met her," Agnes said. Everyone looked at Agnes. "I told you about her, Mom. She was with Barry that time he took me to see a movie."

"That was like five years ago," Claudia said. "It was the only time Barry took you to do something. And the idiot brought a date."

Everyone turned back to Neal. He shrugged.

"That's it. The wedding is this Sunday. I came to town early so I could catch up with old friends like you guys."

Claudia wiped her hands with a napkin.

"I wonder how Stacy got Barry to marry her. It had to be something more than getting pregnant."

"If he's been with her for five years, then it must be true love," Neal said.

Megan punched Neal's arm then nodded at Claudia. He blushed.

"Hey, forget that loser," Megan said. "We're here to celebrate Agnes' scholarship."

"You're right," Claudia said. "Tonight is about Agnes."

She took a bite of her pizza and chewed slowly. Suddenly, she stood and rushed to the bathroom. Megan followed her.

"I suppose I should go as well," Agnes said.

"Okay," Neal said, "but don't be surprised if there's no pizza when you get back."

Agnes glanced at the pizza. He had to be joking. Few humans could consume that much pizza. In the bathroom, Agnes found Megan with her arm around Claudia while Claudia wiped her eyes.

"I don't get it," Claudia said. "Barry's scared to death of his father. He never talks to his parents about Agnes. They pretend Agnes doesn't exist, and Barry lets them do it. It's like he's ashamed of us."

"I think Barry is more scared of Stacy than his dad," Megan said. "She's making him marry her and he's too afraid to say no. You could have made him marry you."

"I'm glad you didn't," Agnes said.

Claudia grabbed Agnes' hand and squeezed it.

"Megan's right," Claudia said. "We should forget that loser."

"We should get back to the table," Megan said. "We left poor Neal all alone."

Despite the group's best efforts, they couldn't finish the pizza. They had the waitress box up the leftovers. Neal insisted on paying the check.

"My gift to Agnes," he said.

As they stepped outside into the warm night, Agnes looked down the strip mall stores past the chiropractor and the sandwich shop to a place she'd always wondered about.

"Mom," Agnes said, tugging on Claudia's sleeve. "Can we go in there, please?"

Agnes pointed at a billiards club.

"You want to play pool?" Claudia said. "But you've never played before."

"Pool is based on math and physics, things I understand very well, so I should be able to play. Come on, Mom. Please."

"I could go for a game of pool," Neal said.

"Me too," Megan said.

Claudia threw her hands up in surrender.

"Let's go play pool."

The billiards club was a cavernous room with a bar in the middle, a line of dartboards on one wall, and a battalion of pool tables. Classic rock music played on the loudspeakers at a low volume so as not to drown out the sound of sports on the wide screen TVs mounted from the ceiling. Each screen had a different sporting event. Despite the smoke eaters on the ceiling, a haze of cigarette smoke floated throughout the place. Agnes knew the smell would stick to her but didn't care. She was finally inside this place that fascinated her.

Most of the pool players were middle-aged men in ball caps and southern rock T-shirts that barely covered their beer bellies.

"Anybody want a drink before we get started?" Neal said.

"I could use an adult beverage," Megan said.

"Nothing for you, Agnes," Claudia said. "You may be a college graduate, but you're still underage."

They converged on the bar. While Claudia, Neal, and Megan studied the sign listing various drink specials, Agnes admired the row of shiny chrome beer taps with its array of fancy handles molded to reflect the brands of beer available.

"Oh my God," Claudia said. "They have one-dollar beers for people who work in the service industry."

"You have to prove it," Megan said.

Claudia fished her nametag out of her purse. She showed it to the bartender and ordered a light beer. She stuck her tongue out at the others.

"Don't you wish you worked in a fast-food restaurant? Don't answer that."

Claudia, Megan, and Neal got beers and Agnes got a soda. They found an empty pool table in a corner.

"Okay, how are we going to do this?" Megan said. "Are we playing doubles or taking turns?"

"Actually, I just want to watch," Claudia said as she hoisted herself onto a tall stool next to a small round table.

"Then we'll take turns playing Agnes," Neal said. "You want to go first, Megan?"

"No, you go first."

Neal put quarters into the pay slot and the balls rolled out into the well. He racked the balls while Agnes chose a cue stick. She liked the smooth feel of the lacquered wood. She ran her fingertip over the tip. It left a trace of gritty aqua green powder she rubbed between her forefinger and thumb. While Neal chose a stick, Agnes walked around the table, running her hand on the green felt surface. She studied the diamonds embedded in the wood rails. They were evenly spaced. Using them as guides, she imagined lines of mathematical models on the table. She calculated the various ways to use the angles. This was going to be easier than she thought.

"You want to break?" Neal said.

"What's that?" Agnes asked.

"That's how you start the game. A player shoots the cue ball at the balls to break them apart."

"Yes, I would like to break."

Agnes took the cue ball and placed it carefully at the head of the table. She held the stick the way she'd seen people hold it on the Internet. She pushed the stick, but instead of a smooth forward motion, her hand wiggled and the ball jumped off the table. Neal hurried after the rolling ball and snatched it off the floor. He placed it back on the table.

"May I try again?" Agnes asked.

"Of course," Neal said. "We're just having fun. But before you do, you should add chalk. Gives you less chance to miscue."

Neal showed her how to apply the chalk to the blue tip of her pool cue and the proper way to use the cue stick. Agnes did a few practice strokes, feeling it slide through her fingers. When she shot the white cue ball the next time, it rolled forcefully into the triangle of balls. With a loud, satisfying clack, the balls moved in all directions. A striped ball teetered on the edge of a corner pocket before falling in.

"Okay, you're stripes and I'm solids," Neal said. "Take your next shot."

After a careful study of the angles and the positions of the balls on the table, Agnes selected a striped ball and the hole she wanted it to drop into. She took her second shot. The cue ball smacked the ball sending it rocketing to the foot rail. It bounced off the rail and rolled into a side pocket. Agnes grinned. She liked pool.

Agnes stalked the table, leaning down to study positions of the balls and their proximity to pockets, noting the obstacles in their paths. With each shot, she gained confidence and soon the table was cleaned of stripped balls.

"May I knock the solid balls in as well?" Agnes asked.

Neal laughed.

"Go for it, Agnes."

She methodically cleared the table. Neal racked the balls and watched her clear the table again. Megan and Claudia sipped their beers and chatted. Agnes knew they were talking about her. She could hear their conversation. The music was too loud for them to whisper. They probably wouldn't have lowered their voices anyway. Agnes was used to people talking about her as if she wasn't there, because people often treated her advanced intelligence as a disability. She was "special" in their minds much the same way a mentally handicapped person was special.

Claudia talked about Agnes as if she wasn't there because that's what mothers do. They talked openly about their children no matter how much it embarrassed the child.

"Poor Neal," Claudia said. "He had no idea what he was getting into."

"He does really well with Agnes," Megan said. "You should have slept with him instead of Barry."

"He was awfully cute back in high school."

"He's seriously cute now. Why don't you hook up with him now? He always liked you. Hell, all the guys liked you. Used to make me so damn jealous."

"He has a life in New Orleans. I can't worry about what might have been."

Agnes wondered if Neal heard Claudia and Megan talking about him. If he had, he acted like he hadn't. His full concentration seemed to be on watching Agnes shoot pool.

One of the middle-aged men sauntered over to the table to watch Agnes play. He wore a Lynyrd Skynyrd T-shirt, a Harley Davidson ball cap, and had a chain connecting his wallet to his belt. He stood so he wouldn't get in Agnes' way. After she emptied the table, Neal paid for another game and racked the balls.

"Hey little lady," the man said. "You play pretty good. How long you been shooting pool?"

Agnes looked at her watch.

"Thirty-five minutes."

He took off his ball cap and scratched the few thin hairs left on his scalp. He turned to Neal.

"Can I play the next game?"

"I gave up," Neal said. "At this point, I'm just watching her."

Agnes leaned against the table

"I'll play a game with you."

"Name's Kyle," the man said. "What's yours, little lady?"

"Agnes."

They shook hands. Kyle put a quarter on the table. His friends came over and took positions around the table. Kyle flipped a coin to see who would break and he won. He sank three shots before missing the fourth.

Agnes didn't miss any of her shots and won the game.

"Gawd da…!" Kyle caught himself before uttering the full curse word.

He nodded at Claudia. "Sorry, ma'am."

Kyle's friends teased him.

"That little girl just mopped the floor with you"

"Did you get a sudden case of arthritis?"

"Arthritis? Or a sudden case of senility."

Kyle's face flushed a deep red.

"She was just lucky. I'll get her next game."

Another member of the group strutted to the table. He wore a black leather vest over a Charlie Daniels T-shirt and a Budweiser ballcap. He placed a quarter on the edge of the table.

"You had your chance, Kyle. Time for a real pro. Hey, Agnes. I'm Robby."

"Hi, Robby," Agnes said. "Should we flip a coin to see who breaks?"

"Naw. You go ahead."

"You sure?"

Robby chuckled. "Yeah. I ain't worried."

Neal put his pool stick back on the wall racks and went to get another round of beers. By the time he got back, Agnes had won the game.

"Thought you was so smart, didn't you, Robby?" Kyle said.

Robby glared at Agnes.

"She's not a little girl. She's a midget pool shark in disguise."

The next member of Robby and Kyle's group came forward to take on Agnes.

Neal rejoined Claudia and Megan with three beers and sat on a barstool next to Claudia. Agnes had mastered the game well enough she could eavesdrop on them while playing.

"Agnes is amazing," Neal said. "You must be very proud of her."

"I am," Claudia said.

Agnes suppressed a smile. She was used to compliments from Claudia and Megan but hearing one from a handsome man somehow made a difference.

"I don't have children, so I don't really understand," Neal said.

"Understand what?" Megan asked.

He looked at Claudia.

"How can you let her go to college in another city when she's only fifteen? It's obvious she's not an ordinary fifteen-year-old. But aren't you worried?"

Agnes flubbed her shot. The cue ball sailed past its intended target and fell into a pocket.

"Finally!" Kyle said. "Turns out the little girl is human after all."

Her opponent sank four balls before missing the pocket. Agnes didn't notice. She was waiting for Claudia's response to Neal's question.

"I have to," Claudia said. "I mean look at her. You think she's amazing now, imagine how amazing she's going to be four years from now. She won't make the same mistakes I made. She won't get stuck in Red Bank like I did. But even if she wasn't gifted. Even if she was just a normal girl, I would let her go if it meant she got a chance to do something with her life. I want her to have the opportunities I didn't have. I don't want her to end up like me."

Neal put his hand on Claudia's.

"You didn't turn out so bad."

Her opponent tapped Agnes on the shoulder. He wore a Widespread Panic T-shirt and no ballcap.

"It's your turn, little lady."

"Sorry," Agnes said.

She quickly cleared the table. Kyle stepped forward for a rematch. Agnes defeated Kyle and then won a rematch with Robby. After defeating the man with Widespread Panic T-shirt, Claudia waved her arms in the air.

"That's enough. Play time is over. Time for Agnes to go home."

"She can't leave," Kyle said. "We was just about to make a comeback."

The men laughed. Kyle shook Agnes' hand again.

"Good game," he said.

"I hope I didn't hurt your feelings," Agnes said.

"Maybe a little bit, but I'll get over it. You're something special. Don't let nobody tell you different."

In the parking lot, Megan hugged everyone before driving off in her minivan. Claudia offered her hand to Neal, but he held out his arms instead. They hugged.

"Let's stay in touch," he said.

He congratulated her again on her scholarship. Claudia and Agnes waved from the sidewalk as he drove away.

"I like him," Agnes said. "It's unfortunate he doesn't live in Chattanooga."

"Yeah," Claudia agreed. "Unfortunate."

"I heard what you told him."

"I know you did."

"He's right. You didn't turn out so bad."

Claudia put her hands on her hips.

"Since when did you grow a sense of humor?"

"Did I say something funny?"

CHAPTER
12

Saturday, September 13, 2008

Agnes ran her fingers over the finished time machine sitting on her desk. The two shiny metal cubes were 1 ¼ by 1 ¼ by 1 ¼ inches and contained microprocessors she stole from the communications lab. The cubes were attached to half-inch wide by three and a half foot long strips of silver Mylar, which covered the red and blue wires inside. A digital clock the size of a chocolate bar with Velcro strips was attached to the end of one set of straps. The contraption resembled silver tefillin, which was why Agnes named it the Time Tefillin. She was eager to put the Time Tefillin on, yet deathly afraid of it.

"What do you think, Ms. Rat?" Agnes asked. "Should I experiment on a larger animal first or go ahead and test it on me?"

Ms. Rat was asleep in her cage and not available for comment. Agnes had sent her on five trips of varying time limits. She exhibited no side effects.

Agnes didn't need anyone's input. Her desire to test the Time Tefillin on herself outweighed her fear. She fastened one cube on her head and the other on her left bicep, wrapping the strap attached to around her arm and fingers. She set the digital clock for five minutes into the future, then used the Velcro strips to secure the clock to her wrist.

She was dressed in jeans, tennis shoes, and a T-shirt. Perhaps not the best outfit for a time traveler's maiden journey, but she decided comfort was more important than formality.

In the middle of her dorm room, a camcorder on a tripod faced a hard plastic chair with metal legs. Outside her room, she heard two girls chatting as they walked down the hall. Their voices receded until there was silence. When it was quiet like this, Agnes' room felt like a planet she lived on alone. She started the camcorder then sat in the chair. She held the voice recorder in her hand.

"Transport living test subject attempt number seven. Goal is for primary scientist to travel five minutes forward in time."

Her throat tightened with fear. Agnes couldn't begin the countdown. Once she flipped the switch, there was no going back. This single action would either change her life or end it. She left the chair, stopped the camcorder, and stood by the window. She gazed at the well-tended lawn around her dorm. In the middle of the lawn was a maple tree with fiery red leaves.

"I don't know what Ms. Rat saw or she felt when she traveled through time," Agnes said. "It could be wonderful or terrifying. I may not survive the experiment. Perhaps I should have notified someone considering the potential danger. There are moments in science when the only way to learn is to take chances."

Agnes started the camcorder and retook her seat. She rested her finger on the switch to the Time Tefillin.

"If I don't survive, please let my mother know I love her very much." She started the countdown again. "Transport living test subject attempt number seven. Goal is for primary scientist to travel five minutes forward in time. Begin in three…two…one."

Agnes flipped the switch.

A surge of electric energy coursed through her body. For one panic-stricken moment, she couldn't breathe, as if an invisible giant hand squeezed the air out of her lungs. She thought of an earlier experiment when the time travel box was flattened. Was she about to become a pancake? A loud droning like a song played at low speed forced her to cover her ears. Then, she was breathing normally again, but she wasn't sure what she was breathing since there didn't seem to be oxygen. The droning was replaced with a complete absence of noise. The floor dissolved below her, and she floated in space. The objects in the room melted into blobs of color. She felt like she was inside a lava lamp.

The numbers on the clock sped by. The blobs of color evolved into shimmering orbs. The invisible hand grabbed her again and pulled her down as the droning returned and the floor reappeared. The orbs became her dorm room. She was back where she started. The journey lasted about ten seconds.

Agnes hopped out of chair as if it were electrified.

"I did it. I time traveled."

She stopped the camcorder. The video playback showed Agnes sitting in the chair one second and gone the next.

"I disappear just like that." Agnes snapped her fingers.

She watched the video again from the beginning. After she disappeared, the chair sat empty for five minutes, then Agnes reappeared. Furiously, she scribbled down everything she saw and felt during the few seconds she traveled in time.

She went into the bathroom and studied herself in the mirror. There didn't seem to be any damage. She stuck out her tongue. Shedding the Time Tefillin along with her clothes, she looked for signs she had changed, but she appeared normal.

"Normal?" Agnes asked her reflection. "Normal no longer exists."

CHAPTER
13

Saturday, October 4, 2008

Though Agnes time traveled a half dozen times, she had only gone downstream into the future, incrementally expanding the time skip from five minutes to five hours. Most theories on time travel claimed traveling to the future was possible but not the past. And a sturdy spaceship was necessary to survive the journey. Agnes proved she didn't need a spaceship. A trip upstream into the past was necessary before she could proclaim the Time Tefillin fully operational.

The sun shone brightly through her dorm window as Agnes put on the Time Tefillin. She was happy she had frizzy hair because it made it easier to hide the device on her head. For added concealment, she wore a baseball cap with the Georgia Tech yellow jacket logo. The sleeves of her yellow raincoat covered the strap on her left arm and the digital clock on her right wrist. She purchased the raincoat and cap from the campus bookstore the day before, making this the first time she had worn school colors for any place she'd attended.

Traveling to the past wasn't the only thing Agnes was doing for the first time. She was also going to her first college football game. Her dorm was across the street from Bobby Dodd Stadium, yet for the two years she'd lived here, she had never attended a Georgia Tech football game. She had never attended a sporting event of any kind.

Joining the crowd of students, parents, and alumni funneling through the stadium gates, a white-haired man tapped Agnes' shoulder. He wore a yellow sport coat and an identical Georgia Tech baseball cap.

"Like your hat," he said, tugging on the bill of his cap.

"Thank you, sir."

"Why the raincoat, young lady? It's not supposed to rain today and there's hardly a cloud in the sky. Perfect football weather."

"Yes, sir. There is no rain in the forecast today. However, it did rain on September sixth."

"September sixth? That was a month ago."

"Twenty-eight days, or six hundred seventy-two hours, to be precise."

The white-haired man moved away from her quickly.

Agnes found her seat number on the metal bench in the student section. Students sat behind the end zone. The marching band was seated in the section in front of her. Agnes liked their smart uniforms and shiny brass instruments.

Agnes had her camcorder in one pocket of the raincoat and a notebook with pen in the other. Her time destination was already set on the clock. She only needed to flip the switch to begin her journey. But first, she needed Georgia Tech to score a touchdown.

According to Agnes' research on football and audience behavior during games, when the home team scored the students jumped to their feet and cheered. Their full attention was on the field. No one would notice a single student's sudden disappearance.

Agnes wasn't as worried about disappearing as she was about showing up out of nowhere and having to explain how she got there. She wanted to be somewhere on September sixth where there was the least chance of others being around. That included her own dorm room since her past self would be in there, preparing Mr. Rat for his tragic journey.

On September sixth, the Georgia Tech football team played against Boston College in Chestnut Hill, Massachusetts, which meant no one would be at Bobby Dodd Stadium.

As Agnes waited for today's game to begin, she wished she had brought something to read. The stadium slowly filled with people. A light breeze carried the smell of hot dogs and spilled beer. The stadium was packed by the time the football players ran out onto the field.

Nobody scored during the first quarter. The sun was blazing hot. Agnes felt like napping.

In the second quarter, a Georgia Tech player kicked the ball through the goal post but that didn't generate the level of distraction Agnes required. During the third quarter a Georgia Tech player finally entered the end zone. Everyone around her jumped to their feet. The cheering was deafening.

Agnes flipped the switch.

She felt the familiar squeeze followed by weightlessness. The roar of the crowd slowed down to an echoing hum. Thousands of yellow blobs floated over larger green and blue blobs. Agnes floated with them in silence. The yellow blobs dissolved away and were replaced with white blobs. The blue blobs were replaced with dark gray blobs. She floated for what seemed like five minutes and then the blobs began to shimmer. A deep drone rang in her ears as gravity pulled her down.

Agnes was alone in an empty stadium. And it was raining. She jumped to her feet and cheered.

The heavy rains tapered off into a light drizzle. Agnes placed her camcorder on a stadium bench and climbed down three rows, so she could look directly into the lens.

"Transport living test subject attempt number fourteen in progress. Primary scientist traveled backward in time six hundred seventy-two hours to Saturday, September 6, 2008. On this day, I made my first attempt to transport a living test subject. The test subject, Mr. Rat, did not survive. The goal for this experiment is to observe my past self as I bury Mr. Rat.

The presence of my present and past self in the same space and time will prove I built an operational time machine."

Agnes checked the time. Her past self was in her dorm room right now sending Mr. Rat to his death. She wouldn't bury him until the sun went down. That was five hours away, plenty of time to get a cup of tea and make notes on the progress of the experiment.

She turned off the camcorder and put it into the pocket of her raincoat. The stadium's main entrance was locked, barring her from leaving the way she came in. It took her fifteen minutes to find an exit.

Outside on the wet sidewalk, the air smelled the same as it always did. Her feet touched the ground the same. But it wasn't the same. Agnes was in the past. She wanted to shout to the passing cars she had come from the future. Instead, she giggled, sharing a private joke with herself.

Agnes froze.

Professor Levin saw her the same moment she saw him. It was too late to change direction, too late to hide. They were headed toward each other on the sidewalk. She jammed her hand into her coat pocket so he wouldn't see the silver straps of the Time Tefillin wrapped around her fingers.

"Agnes," Professor Levin said, "I'm glad I ran into you. Can you spare a minute?"

"Of course, Professor," she said, kicking herself. She was too panicked to come up with an excuse saying the first thing that popped into her head.

"Where were you headed?" he asked.

"I was on my way to Brittain Hall for a cup of hot tea."

"A cup of tea sounds lovely."

At the entrance of Brittain Hall, Agnes paused to admire the dining hall's Doric pillars.

"Archimedes," she said, pointing at the face carved into one of the pillars.

"The father of mathematical physics," Levin said. "Is he your hero?"

"I know you're teasing me, but he is in fact one of my heroes."

Brittain Dining Hall was the students' least favorite dining hall, but Agnes loved its cathedral ceiling and stain glass windows. She didn't care that the food was mediocre, and the serving area always smelled like rotting vegetables. Agnes and Levin got cups of hot tea and entered the dining hall. A few students watched the football game on a wide screen television. Levin chose a table on the opposite side of the room.

"I have things to do in the lab before Monday. I'm taking a break," Levin said.

Agnes' leg bounced. She could barely contain herself. Scared to death she would say something that would alert him she had traveled to the past, she also wished she could tell Professor Levin time travel was not only possible she was living proof. Now was not the right time. She needed more evidence like the kind she hoped to get tonight.

"You're doing great work in the lab," Levin said as he dipped his tea bag. "The other lab assistants think highly of you. The reports on your experiments are detailed and complete."

"Thank you, Professor Levin."

"But I've been around you long enough to know you could be doing better. Something is distracting you. The others may not notice it, but I do."

Agnes took a sip of her tea. It was too hot and burned her tongue. She broke out into a nervous sweat. Her raincoat felt sticky and heavy.

"You're right, Professor," Agnes said. "I haven't been doing my best. I will put my complete concentration on my lab work."

"I only brought it up because I'm concerned about you, Agnes. Is there something going on I should know about? Is everything okay with your mother?"

Agnes' cheeks burned from anger and embarrassment. She was angry Levin was thinking about Claudia. She was embarrassed she was jealous of Claudia. She shouldn't be feeling either emotion. Professor Levin was happily married to a very nice woman.

"Mom's fine," Agnes said. "I've just had a lot on my mind lately."

The straps of the Time Tefillin began to itch. Agnes resisted the urge to scratch her arm.

Levin held up his hands in surrender. "I didn't mean to pry, but my door is always open if you ever want to talk."

"Thank you, Professor Levin."

Levin blew on his tea before taking a sip. He added honey. They drank their tea and talked about the latest developments in the lab. Agnes' stomach churned from the effort to avoid mentioning things that had happened in the lab since September sixth.

The students watching the game groaned in unison. Levin peered at the TV.

"Tech is losing sixteen to ten," he said, though it was obvious from his tone of voice he didn't care if they won or lost.

"It's okay," Agnes said. "They'll win in the fourth quarter."

Levin chuckled. "What makes you so sure?"

"I just have a feeling they'll win."

Levin leaned back in his chair and crossed his legs.

"The other physics professors and I have an ongoing argument about time travel, and I'd like to get your take on it. Let's say you're in a time machine and you look out the window. What do you see? We're split between streaks of light because you're traveling so fast or black emptiness because you're passing through a black hole."

"Neither. You see slowly floating blobs of color like a lava lamp."

"Lava lamp?" Levin said, laughing. "Aren't you a little young for lava lamps?"

"They're still around. They just aren't as popular as they used to be."

They finished their tea.

"I better get back to the lab," Levin said. They were headed for the exit when the students watching the game cheered. Levin looked at the screen. "Hey, Tech scored a touchdown. They're winning. Looks like your feeling is right, Agnes."

Agnes suddenly remembered a conversation she had with Professor Levin in mid-September. One of the lab assistants was really into football and worried way too much about the games. Levin suggested the lab assistant talk to Agnes because she was good at predicting the outcome of the games. At the time, Agnes thought Levin was teasing her about being a know-it-all, but now she realized it was because he believed she had predicted the winner of today's game.

The air outside was misty and cool. Levin headed toward the Centennial Research Building while Agnes pretended to head toward her dorm room. She checked the time. Past Agnes wouldn't bury Mr. Rat until three hours from now. Rather than risk running into anyone else she knew, Agnes hurried to the parking garage with tennis courts on the top floor.

The courts were empty. Agnes sat on a concrete wall outside the fence surrounding them. She was above the street that ran next to the parking garage. She had a good view of the sidewalk that led to her dorm. With time to kill, she took out her notebook and wrote down the progress of the experiment including her chance meeting with Professor Levin.

As the hours crawled by, the temperature dropped with the sun. Sitting on the rain-soaked concrete, water seeped through Agnes' jeans, leaving her butt wet and clammy. She got up and stomped her feet for warmth. Worse than the chill in the air, she really needed to pee.

A trickle of people passed by on the sidewalk, pools of light from the streetlamps illuminated their way. Agnes' heart skipped a beat when she spotted herself. Her first thought was she never realized she had such a dorky walk. Her second observation was she was rather cute. She'd never given much thought to her appearance, but this was more than a photograph, a video, or the mirror. It was Agnes in real life.

She pressed record on the camcorder and held it at arm's length with the lens pointed at her face.

"Transport living test subject attempt number fourteen in progress. Second report. Primary Scientist successfully traveled twenty-eight days into the past and has been here for five hours and twelve minutes. Primary Scientist's present goal is to observe and record her past self as she buries deceased test subject number one in the ravine below my position. For details on Mr. Rat's demise, please refer to my notes from that day. Primary Scientist of September sixth is unaware I have traveled back to observe my past self and if the experiment goes as planned, she will remain unaware. Since this is her present, I will refer to myself as Future Primary Scientist and her as Present Primary Scientist."

Future Agnes turned the camcorder around and zoomed in on Present Agnes. At first, shadows hid her Present Agnes' face, but then she walked under a streetlamp and was clearly recognizable. Future Agnes stayed on her until she reached the ravine.

When Present Agnes reached the ravine, she looked around to see if she was being watched. Future Agnes quickly squatted behind the wall. She inched her way back up and peered down. Present Agnes slid down into the ravine. The light from her flashlight bounced around as she looked for a good place to dig. Future Agnes recorded the burial. Afterward, Present Agnes climbed out of the ravine and headed back to the dorm. Once Future Agnes was certain she was gone, she turned the camcorder back on herself.

"This concludes this phase of transport living test subject attempt number fourteen."

She turned off the camcorder. Midnight was three hours away. Present Agnes would be asleep. That was when Future Agnes planned to sneak into her dorm room then travel back to October 4.

Her stomach grumbled. After her initial time skips, Agnes felt like she'd been punched in the stomach and had been unable to eat until the pain subsided. Many trips later, the opposite was true. The longer the time skip, the hungrier she felt.

She decided to go to the Varsity, an Atlanta institution established in 1928. The fast-food restaurant had drive-in service and a maze of dining areas. Agnes loved their disgustingly greasy onion rings. However, the first thing Agnes did upon entering the Varsity was hurry into the bathroom to pee.

The restaurant had a long counter with numerous cashiers shouting, "What'll ya have? What'll ya have?" Normally, there was a horde of people jostling for a chance to order, but tonight the crowd was sparse. Agnes stepped forward to a waiting cashier and ordered a plain hot dog on a bun, an order of onion rings, and a large soda. She carried her food tray to an empty booth in a glassed-in room. The clouds had cleared, and she could see the moon.

Dipping a greasy onion ring in a pool of catsup, Agnes wondered what would happen if she went to her dorm room, knocked on the door, and Future and Present Agnes met face to face. She could tell Present Agnes not to worry, Mr. Rat didn't die in vain. She would solve the problem the very next day. But that would be wrong. Contact with Present Agnes would contaminate the experiment.

Once she finished eating, Agnes pushed aside her tray and took out her notebook. She checked the time. She had been in the past for six hours and fifty-four minutes. Six minutes later as she was writing wrote down her observations, she felt a surge of electricity. The Time Tefillin had been activated.

But she hadn't touched the switch.

Agnes checked the time. She had been in the past for exactly seven hours. The familiar squeeze and weightlessness came over her as the room melted into a sea of red and yellow blobs resembling catsup and mustard. She floated for what seemed like five minutes before the time skip ended. She was still seated in the Varsity booth, but everything else had changed. It was a sunny afternoon, the restaurant was crowded, and there was a very confused boy seated across from her.

"How did you do that?" he asked.

Agnes noticed a tray of half-eaten food in front of her. A girl wearing too much make-up and too tight pants came to the table and glared at Agnes.

"Who the hell is this?" she asked the boy.

"I have no idea. She appeared like magic."

"Magic? I leave to go the bathroom and you start up with another girl."

"I swear she came out of nowhere."

"Excuse me," Agnes said. "I didn't mean to bother you."

Clutching her notebook, Agnes stumbled out of the booth. As she hurried away, she could hear the angry girlfriend yelling at her confused boyfriend. Once outside the Varsity, she checked the time and date. She had returned to Saturday, October 4 at the exact time she had left.

In her dorm room, she played back the video of Future Agnes observing Present Agnes burying Mr. Rat. Though technically, she was Present Agnes watching Past Agnes. Whatever. The video clearly showed two of her occupying the same time and place. A giddy thrill rippled through Agnes. Here was definite proof she had traveled to the past. However, the unplanned return trip concerned her.

Seven hours. That was the limit for how long she could travel to another time. She made a cup of tea and wondered why it was seven hours and not six or eight, or why there was a time limit at all. As she lifted her teabag out of her cup, she noticed the ripples it created.

"I get it," Agnes said. "Time ripples."

A time traveler skipped across time like a stone skipped across a river. A skipping stone created ripples lasting a little while before the river settled. The time ripples she created lasted seven hours before the river of time settled. Agnes would have to plan her time skips more carefully. She didn't want to suddenly appear in a stranger's booth again.

"Seven hours?" Agnes said. "Who cares? I proved the Time Tefillin works."

As soon as she put together a proper presentation, she would show her invention to Professor Levin and together they would share it with the scientific community. Time travel would no longer be a secret. A shiver of pleasure raced down her spine. She was about to change the world.

CHAPTER
14

Friday, October 24, 2008

Claudia kicked off her shoes as she sifted through the mail. Bills, bills, and more bills. Then she came to a large caramel envelope. From the high-quality paper and the thickness, she could tell it was a wedding invitation. The return address was in New Orleans.

Her heart raced as she tore open the envelope and read the invitation. She placed it on the coffee table, went into the kitchen, and took half a bottle of white wine out of the refrigerator. Pouring her a glass, she wondered if she had more wine because half a bottle wasn't going to be enough.

She carried her wine glass into the living room and put R.E.M.'s *Automatic for the People* in the CD player. She sat on the couch and re-read the invitation. When the song "Everybody Hurts" began to play, she turned the volume down and dialed Agnes' number.

The phone rang and rang before going to voicemail.

"Agnes, it's Mom. Call me when you get a chance. Love you."

Claudia listened to music and drank wine until she finished the bottle.

There wasn't a second bottle. She tried calling Agnes but got her voicemail again. She didn't leave a message this time.

As soon as she hung up, her phone rang.

"Agnes?"

"Nope, it's Megan. Did you get the invitation?"

"Came today."

"I can't believe it. Neal's getting married."

"Well, he is of legal age. I don't know who the lucky girl is, but then I haven't talked to him in over a year."

As they talked, Claudia remembered she had a bottle of rum she received as a Christmas gift. She stashed it away because she wasn't much of a rum drinker. Until tonight.

"Are you going?" Megan asked.

"Even if I could get the time off, I can't afford it. What about you?"

"I haven't talked to Steven yet, but we'll probably go."

Claudia located the bottle of rum on the top shelf of the cabinet. Reaching for it, she could only touch the base of the bottle with her fingers. If only she were a little taller.

"You should go. I'm sure the boys would love New Orleans."

Using the tips of her fingers, she inched the bottle toward the edge of the shelf. Part of her knew she should get a chair to stand on, but another part of her really needed a drink.

"How did Agnes react when you told her?"

Claudia paused. The bottle was sticking out over the edge and her fingers kept it from dropping.

"She's not answering her phone, but I know what she'll say. Nothing. She doesn't really know Neal."

"Are you worried she's not answering her phone?"

"She's probably in the middle of a project. You know how she is. Gets so deep in her head I can't talk to her until she's done. If I don't hear from her soon, I'll call her dorm peer leader and have her make sure Agnes is okay."

"I'd come over, but I have to get dinner ready."

"You don't need to come over. I'm fine."

"You don't sound fine."

Claudia inched the bottle a little closer. It slipped away from her, fell to the floor, and shattered. The dark amber fluid gushed out covering the kitchen floor.

"Damn it!" Claudia shouted.

"Are you okay?" Megan asked. "That sounded like a gunshot."

Claudia stepped through the sticky mess and slumped into a dining room chair.

"It's okay. I just dropped a whole bottle of rum and now it's all over the kitchen."

"I'm sorry, Claudia. You're having a really bad day."

"I'm having a bad life." Claudia began to cry, which escalated quickly into heavy sobs. "Everybody I know is married or getting married. Everybody has somebody but me. I'm stuck here in Red Bank going nowhere. I feel like such a loser. I don't get it. How did this happen to me?"

Megan let Claudia cry for a minute then said softly, "You have Agnes."

"She's growing up fast. Soon she'll be gone and then I'll really be alone."

"That does it. I'll have Steven take the boys out for pizza. We're going to go out and get knee walking drunk."

Claudia looked at the lake of rum in her kitchen.

"Thanks Megan, but I can't. I have the early shift this weekend. Besides, I have to clean the kitchen. Some idiot spilled a bottle of rum all over it."

CHAPTER
15

Monday, October 27, 2008

Agnes studied her reflection in the mirror. The dark blue dress was the fifth outfit she'd tried on this morning. She wasn't in the habit of fussing over her appearance. Days would go by without giving any thought as to what clothes she wore or how her hair looked. She prided herself on being neat and clean, but fashion was a mystery she had no interest in solving.

Today was different because she was about to make science history, and for such a momentous occasion she wanted to look her best. She doubted Professor Levin would notice she took the time to tame her hair into an attractive braid. The secret was hair gel. Lots of hair gel. Levin might miss the hair, but certainly he would notice Agnes was wearing make-up, something she only wore on super special occasions.

She opened her backpack for the tenth time, making sure her computer and the Time Tefillin were inside. Satisfied they were inside just as they had been the first nine times she checked; Agnes zipped up her backpack.

According to her watch, she didn't need to leave her dorm room for another thirty minutes, but she was way too antsy to wait any longer. She put on her coat and slung her backpack over her shoulder.

Agnes was about to put her phone into her coat pocket when she noticed it was off. She forgot she turned it off so she wouldn't be disturbed while putting together her presentation. The phone must have been off for days.

Agnes turned the phone on. She had one voice message and four missed calls, all from Claudia. Agnes listened to her voicemail.

"Agnes, it's Mom. Call me when you get a chance. Love you."

Agnes dialed Claudia's number. After three rings, it went to voicemail.

"Hey Mom, it's me. Looks like we're playing phone tag. You're probably doing the early shift and have your phone off. Sorry I missed your call. I should have warned you I was on a deadline and couldn't be disturbed. I'm really excited about the presentation I'm giving this morning. I can't wait to tell you about it."

Just as she finished sending the message, there was a knock at her door. Agnes couldn't imagine who it would be. Other than the peer leader on her floor and an occasional invitation to share something one of the students baked in the shared kitchen, hardly anyone knocked on her door. She opened it to find Terri, the building director, and Megan Wallace. Agnes wasn't surprised to see Terri. She stopped by twice a month to check on her. But Megan. That was a surprise.

Agnes felt a sharp pain in her stomach. She could think of only one reason why Megan drove to Atlanta to see her without Claudia. Plus, Megan's eyes were red.

"I'm glad we caught you before you went to class," Terri said. "Ms. Wallace needs to speak to you."

"What happened to Mom?" Agnes asked.

Megan and Terri glanced at each other.

"You two should speak privately," Terri said. "And not out here in the hall. I'll be in my office if either of you need anything."

"Thank you, Terri," Megan said.

Megan entered Agnes' room and looked around. This was the room

Agnes slept in. There were no posters on the wall and other than Ethel Owl and a photo of Agnes and Claudia, no attempt was made to personalize the room. Normally, it was very neat, but the Time Tefillin experiment had completely consumed Agnes, and the room was a mess. Dirty clothes littered the floor, and the trash can was full. Megan nodded at Ethel Owl. She had given Agnes the stuffed animal as a birthday gift when Agnes turned six.

Megan held out her arms. "Come here," she said.

Tears filled Agnes' eyes as they hugged.

"Is she hurt or is she dead?" Agnes asked.

"I'm so sorry, Agnes. Claudia's dead."

Megan held Agnes as she sobbed.

"She tried to call me," Agnes said. "But I turned my phone off. I should have kept it on. I should have been a better daughter."

"Don't say that," Megan said. "Don't you dare think it. Claudia was very proud of you."

They sat on Agnes' unmade bed. Megan held Agnes' hand.

"How did it happen?" Agnes asked, wiping away tears with the heel of her hand.

Megan took a tissue from her purse and handed it to Agnes. She got another tissue to wipe away her own tears.

"Claudia didn't show up for work yesterday and she didn't answer her phone," Megan said. "One of her employees went by the house to check on her. Claudia was found in her car in the garage with the car running and the garage door closed. She died from carbon monoxide poisoning."

Agnes wanted to believe this was some terrible joke. But she knew it wasn't.

"Did she do it on purpose?"

"I don't believe she did," Megan said.

"But she might have."

"Let's not go there, Agnes. We need to get you home. I'll help you pack."

Agnes slipped off her backpack with the Time Tefillin inside. She let it slip to the floor and pushed it under the bed with her foot. She got her suitcase out of the closet while Megan went through her dresser.

"I'll call your professor to let him know what's going on?" Megan asked.

"Thank you," Agnes said. "I can't think about school right now."

* * *

Megan pulled into the driveway and turned off the motor. The garage door was closed, but she and Agnes knew Claudia's car was inside even if they couldn't see it.

"Want me to come inside and keep you company?" Megan asked.

Megan had always been like a second mother to Agnes. For a week, Megan neglected her own family and stayed in the house with Agnes, helping her with funeral arrangements and financial decisions. But sooner or later, Agnes was going to have to be in the house alone. She might as well start now.

"No thank you," Agnes said.

"Let me know if you change your mind," Megan said.

"Thank you for everything."

Agnes waited until Megan drove away before going inside. The house smelled of coffee and Claudia. It felt so empty. In her mother's honor, Agnes put R.E.M.'s *Out of Time* on the CD player and played the song "Shiny Happy People." Claudia taught Agnes to dance to the song. At least, she tried to teach Agnes to dance.

Agnes wandered through the house and in each room, she could see Claudia. There was Claudia in the kitchen making grilled cheese sandwiches. There was Claudia in Agnes' bedroom, taking care of her when she was sick. There was Claudia at the dining room table, pouring over bills and worrying about how she was going to pay them. There was Claudia in the living room, dancing with Agnes.

When the song ended, Agnes turned off the CD player. She sat on the couch and listened to a saved voicemail on her phone.

"Agnes, it's Mom. Call me when you get a chance. Love you."

Megan still refused to believe Claudia committed suicide, but admitted that Claudia had been depressed the last time she talked to her. If only Agnes hadn't turned off her phone maybe Claudia would have told her what was bothering her. Maybe Agnes could have talked her out of killing herself. Maybe Claudia would still be alive. Maybe, maybe, maybe. Agnes played the message again.

"Agnes, it's Mom. Call me when you get a chance. Love you."

When Agnes discussed her feelings of guilt with Megan, Megan insisted it wouldn't have made any difference. Claudia had obviously made up her mind. Agnes shouldn't blame herself.

"Agnes, it's Mom. Call me when you get a chance. Love you."

"Agnes, it's Mom. Call me when you get a chance. Love you."

"Love you."

CHAPTER
16

Saturday, November 1, 2008

Agnes tugged at the hem of her black dress. She didn't own a black dress. This one belonged to Claudia. Agnes realized it was her dress now. She didn't want it. She wanted her mother.

The reverend gave a lovely sermon at Claudia's memorial service. He talked about what a wonderful mother she'd been and how much she would be missed. Agnes noticed two words that he didn't use in his sermon: suicide and heaven.

The service was held at Red Bank United Methodist Church. The Cooks' had been attending the church for generations, though Claudia and Agnes had been a *chreasters*, church goers who only came on Christmas and Easter. Agnes was agnostic. She preferred the rigors of science over the demands of faith. With Claudia gone, she didn't have much reason to attend church, not even as a chreaster.

Agnes couldn't afford a coffin and burial site, so she had Claudia cremated. The cardboard box containing her ashes and bits of bone sat by the fireplace in the living room. Agnes planned to scatter her ashes from the Walnut Street Bridge onto the Tennessee River. Claudia and Agnes had loved watching the river from the bridge.

Agnes began to cry. Again. She didn't know she was capable of being so sad, but Claudia had been more than her mother. She'd been her best friend. There were times when Claudia was Agnes' only friend.

If only Agnes hadn't turned off her phone, she would have answered Claudia's call and talked her out of killing herself. But would Claudia have told Agnes what she was about to do? Agnes knew how hard Claudia struggled to get by as a single mother without a college education. But other than complaining about bills and her job, Claudia never showed the warning signs of depression. Maybe she hid them from Agnes because she didn't want to worry her. Typical Claudia behavior. Answering the phone probably wouldn't have saved her.

But that didn't stop Agnes from thinking about other "if onlys." If only Claudia hadn't gotten pregnant at sixteen. She would have gone to college and gotten a degree. Agnes had no idea what Claudia would have majored in and the fact she knew so little of her mother's interest made her want to cry harder.

Whatever subject Claudia chose Agnes was certain Claudia would have done well at it. Her mother never backed down from a tough challenge. She would have gotten her degree and had a career. She would have found a better man than Barry. That would have been the easy part. Claudia would have married a good man, and Agnes would have had siblings. A sister would have been nice.

If only, if only, if only.

Agnes looked around the sanctuary. Wendy's employees sat in pews to her left. Claudia's friends and former classmates sat in pews to her right. Along with hymns sung by a member of the Sunday choir, Megan arranged for two young musicians to sing "I'll Take the Rain," one of Claudia's favorite R.E.M. songs.

After the service, everyone filed over to the Fellowship Hall for refreshments. Denise came over to Agnes and hugged her tightly. She had worked with Claudia longer than any Wendy's employee.

"I'm so glad you could make it," Agnes said.

"I don't know what we're going to do without her," Denise said. "The place is going to be so quiet. Claudia won't be back in her office playing her music."

"Especially her R.E.M."

Denise rolled her eyes. "Don't I know it? She would sing along and sometimes she'd even get up and dance."

"Were you the one who found her?"

Denise swallowed hard and nodded. Agnes hugged Denise. She had never been a hugger but today was different.

"I'm sorry, Denise," Agnes said.

Mourners lined up to give their condolences. Neal brought his fiancé, a pleasant woman named Susan. She had honey blonde hair and an easy laugh. She reminded Agnes of Claudia. A tall man with curly brown hair approached Agnes. It took her a moment to recognize her father.

"How are you holding up?" Barry asked.

He tried to hug her, but she stepped away from him. Just because she was hugging people today didn't mean she was going to hug *him*.

"My mother died," Agnes said. "How do you think I'm doing?"

"She was my friend. I'm hurting too," Barry said.

Agnes looked around the room. "Where's Stacy? And what about the baby? Do I have a half-brother or a half-sister?"

Barry dug his hands into his pockets. "A brother. His name's Nathan. I don't know if you heard, but Stacy and I got a divorce. I'm paying so much in child support I had to come back to Red Bank and move in with my parents."

"Do your parents know you're here?"

Barry winced.

"Let's not do this today, Agnes."

Megan came over and grabbed Barry's arm.

"Barry," she said. "Why don't you and Agnes join us? It's been years since the old gang has been together."

Groups of people were seated at round tables, eating, and chatting. Megan steered Agnes and Barry to a table near the back wall. Neal and Susan sat side by side. Steven sat next to an ugly man Agnes didn't know. Megan and Agnes took seats between Neal and Steven while Barry sat next to the ugly man. He had bad skin and greasy hair with a receding hairline. He wore a wrinkled suit, scuffed dress shoes, and stank of alcohol. Everyone was drinking, but this guy was sweating booze.

Megan noticed Agnes staring at him.

"Agnes, I don't think you've ever met Derrick."

"No, I haven't."

"Claudia and I lost touch after high school," Derrick said.

Agnes had seen photos from Claudia's high school days that included Derrick. The Derrick in those pictures was a cute boy with a blonde mullet and a cocky smile. Agnes found it hard to match him with the disheveled wreck sitting across from her.

In an attempt to be gallant, Steven fetched Agnes a paper plate filled with food she didn't want. To be polite, Agnes snacked on carrot sticks and celery. As she ate, she listened to Megan, Neal, Barry, and Derrick share stories about Claudia.

"And then Claudia walked up to you and said, 'You're rude, crude, and socially unacceptable,'" Megan said.

The old friends laughed.

"What can I say?" Derrick said. "When she's right, she's right."

"The way you talk about Mom," Agnes said. "She sounds like she was a funny, happy person."

"She was," Neal said.

"Neal has told me so much about her," Susan said. "I'm sorry I didn't get a chance to meet her."

"She was hot," Barry said. Everybody stared at him. "Well, she was."

"The Claudia I grew up with was always worried and tired," Agnes said.

Everyone glanced at each other except for Derrick who sat forward.

"That's because she got knocked up when she was sixteen," Derrick

said.

Though Agnes had been thinking the same thing, she hated how he said it. Derrick's tone of voice seemed to suggest Claudia had been a trollop. And that Agnes had been a burden.

"Why do you always have to be such a dick Derrick?" Megan said.

Derrick rolled his eyes.

"Oh, come on. Let's not dance around the obvious. If Barry and Claudia hadn't done the dirty deed at the Halloween party, then Claudia wouldn't have gotten pregnant, she wouldn't have dropped out of high school, she would have gone to college, and probably marry a rich guy like Megan did."

"What the hell is that supposed to mean?" Steven asked.

Derrick patted Steven's back. "Calm down, big fella. I meant it as a compliment."

Maybe Agnes was searching for any kind of relief from her grief, but what Derrick said made sense even if she still thought he was a jerk. If Claudia hadn't had sexual intercourse with Barry, then her life would have been much better.

"You make it sound like Agnes ruined Claudia's life and that's just not true," Neal said. "Agnes, your mother adored you."

"Then why did she leave me?" Agnes asked.

Everyone looked down at the floor as if the answer was hidden under the table.

"How's school, Agnes?" Susan said, changing the subject. "Neal tells me you're getting your doctorate in physics."

Agnes answered Susan's question but was still thinking about what Derrick said.

"I have two more years."

"Wow. So soon. What classes do you have left to take?"

"I don't take classes. I work in a laboratory."

"That sounds cool. What do you do in the lab?"

"We're doing experiments on the possibility of time travel."

"You know what you should do?" Derrick said, putting his elbow in his plate of food and pointing at Agnes. "You should build a time machine, go back to 1990, and stop Barry from hooking up with Claudia. Then Claudia would still be alive."

Agnes gasped. It was if he had read her mind. Barry stood and loomed over Derrick. He did his best to look fierce, but Derrick just grinned right back at him.

"If she did that, then Agnes wouldn't exist," Barry said.

"Sure, she would. She'd just be younger with a better father."

Barry punched Derrick in the face with a loud meaty smack. Derrick fell to the floor, his chair clattering as it went down with him. Agnes had never seen anyone get hit before. Other mourners looked over to see what was going on. Derrick struggled to his feet. His lip was bleeding. He smirked at Barry as he wiped away the blood. Steven and Neal quickly escorted the two men out of the building.

"I thought Barry and Derrick were best friends," Susan said.

"They are," Megan said. "They're like an old married couple. Occasionally, they have a lovers' spat."

"I shouldn't say this, but I don't care for Derrick."

"He's a mean drunk. Always has been." Megan put her hand on Agnes' arm. "I'm sorry he was so terrible. You have enough to deal with today without that kind of behavior."

"It's okay," Agnes said. "He gave me an idea. A very good idea."

CHAPTER
17

Thursday, November 27, 2008

Agnes brought a green bean casserole to Megan's house for Thanksgiving. It was the only dish she had confidence making with any degree of success.

"The fried onions are slightly burnt," she confessed, "but it should still be edible."

"Burnt onions add extra flavor," Megan said.

Megan led the way to the kitchen where she put the casserole in the oven to keep it warm. The kitchen smelled of cooked turkey and fresh bread. Steven and the three boys were in the den watching the Tennessee Titans beat the crap out of the Detroit Lions. Agnes thought about how much Claudia loved Megan's house and all the things she would have done if she'd had this much room.

"Thank you for letting me invite Barry," Megan said. "He was desperate to get out of the house. Would you like something to drink?"

"Just water," Agnes said. "I was going to contact Barry anyway. Seeing him tonight works well for me."

     Mickey Dubrow

Megan got Agnes a glass of water.

"That's good to hear," Megan said. "More than just getting away from his parents, he really wanted to see you. I think it took Claudia dying for Barry to realize how much he missed out by not being part of your life. He's not a bad guy. You should give him a chance."

Barry arrived an hour later with a six-pack of beer. He thrust an envelope into Agnes' hands.

"What's this?" Agnes asked.

"An early Christmas gift," Barry said.

Inside the envelope was a check for one hundred dollars made out to Agnes. She folded the check and put it in her back pocket. Every little bit helped.

Dinner was a noisy affair with most of the volume provided by Steven and Megan's three sons. Agnes knew their names but could never remember which name went with which boy. They were in perpetual motion, punching and wrestling one moment and stuffing turkey into their mouths the next.

Barry sat across from Agnes and blushed whenever their eyes met as if they were on a date instead of a father and daughter trying to make a connection after many years apart. Agnes barely ate and turned down dessert. She hoped it wasn't obvious she was waiting for meal to end.

The meal didn't officially end, rather Steven and the boys took their third helpings to the den to watch the Cowboys play the Seahawks. Barry helped Megan and Agnes clear the table. While the women washed the dishes and put the leftovers away, Barry drifted to the den.

Once they were done, Megan suggested they join the "men folk."

"Actually, I would like to speak with you alone," Agnes said.

"Sure," Megan said. "What about?"

"Wait here."

Agnes went to the hall closet and got a notebook and pen from her coat pocket. She motioned for Megan to join her at the dining room table. The smell of turkey and cooked vegetables hung in the air. Agnes removed a stack of old photos from a pocket in the back of the notebook and fanned them out on the table. Agnes could see the surprise on Megan's face. The photos were from the night of the Halloween party.

"I need you tell me everything you can remember about Saturday, October 27, 1990," Agnes said. "Any detail, no matter how minor."

"Are you planning some kind of legal action against Barry?" Megan asked.

Agnes straightened her spine.

"Why would I want to do that?"

"Claudia told me he stopped paying child support."

"Mom thought it was a waste of time trying to get him to pay. I agreed with her." Agnes thought of the check in her back pocket. "I'm curious if Stacy is having the same problem."

"I don't understand why you want to know about that night. Besides, shouldn't you talk to Barry about this?"

"I'm going to interview him after we're done."

Megan slumped in her chair.

"Can you at least explain why you're doing this?"

"I never thought about when I was conceived until that man, Derrick, brought it up at Mom's funeral. I went through Mom's stuff for anything that pertained to that evening, but I need more information."

"That doesn't really answer my question."

"I know."

Megan stared at Agnes, then picked up a photo of her and Claudia. She was dressed as a witch and Claudia was dressed as a bunny. They looked so young and innocent.

"You and Claudia are a lot more alike than you might realize," Megan said.

"My advanced intellect is probably a fluke of nature," Agnes said. "But there is no question in my mind I inherited my fierce determination from my mother."

Megan sighed.

"You can say that again. Okay, I'll tell you what I can remember, but first I'm going to need more wine."

Three glasses of white wine later, Megan finished telling Agnes everything she remembered about Saturday, October 27, 1990. From Megan and Claudia's frantic creation of Halloween costumes to Barry almost running them off the road in his new Trans Am on the way to a big Halloween party. From Megan and Claudia getting high with Neal, Derrick, and Barry to Claudia and Barry leaving the group to find a bathroom. From Megan and Claudia leaving the party to Claudia providing a detailed description of having sex with Barry during the drive back to Megan's house. As she talked, Agnes scribbled steadily in her notebook and didn't ask questions until Megan was done.

Most of Agnes' questions had to do with time. What time did Megan and Claudia leave the house? What time did they arrive at the party? What time did Barry and Claudia leave to find a bathroom? What time did they return?

"I have no idea," Megan said. "I wasn't wearing a watch."

"Did you have a curfew?"

"I'm sure I did, but I don't remember what it was. I can't imagine my mother letting me stay out past midnight. I'm sorry, but it was a long time ago."

Agnes wrote midnight down in her notebook and underlined it.

"Thank you, Megan. This was very informative. I'd like to speak to Barry now."

They went to the den. Megan sat on the couch next to Steven. He put his arm around her shoulder. One of her boys jumped into her lap.

"You okay?" Steven said. "You look tired."

"I'll tell you later," Megan said.

"Barry," Agnes said. "Would you please join me in the dining room?"

Barry looked at Megan. She avoided his gaze.

"Sure," Barry said.

Once they were seated at the dining table, Barry looked nervously at Agnes' notebook.

"Tell me everything you can remember about Saturday, October 27, 1990," Agnes said. "Any detail, no matter how minor."

"Why? What happened on that day?" Barry asked.

"That was the night you had sex with Claudia. It's the night I was conceived."

Barry leapt out of his chair and hurried to the den. He motioned for Megan to join him in the hallway. Agnes spied on them from the kitchen. "She wants to me to tell her about having sex with Claudia," Barry said.

"She asked me the same thing," Megan said.

"Why the hell does she want to know that?"

"I don't know. Ask her."

"What kind of person asks that kind of question?"

"You've been around her enough to know what kind of person she is. You know she doesn't think and act like normal people. Maybe this is her way of dealing with the loss of her mother. If you want to be closer to Agnes, then you have to meet her on her terms."

Agnes rushed back to the dining room and sat in her seat. Barry sulked in, plopped down in his chair, and crossed his arms. For years Agnes tried to understand why Claudia was attracted to Barry. He was generically handsome, but even when Claudia and Barry were teenagers it had to have been painfully obvious to Claudia his intelligence was substandard. Agnes no longer hated Barry, but she found his immaturity tiresome.

"What do you want to know?" Barry said.

"Megan didn't remember where the Halloween party was held."

"Allan's house. I don't remember his last name. I can show you the house."

"Good. Take me there tomorrow. What do you remember about that night?"

Barry sighed dramatically.

"I drove my new car to the party. We smoked a lot of pot. I had sex with Claudia. The end."

"Megan said that you and Claudia left to find a bathroom. How did that lead to intercourse?"

Barry clenched his fists.

"It was her idea. I didn't take advantage of her. She'd been drinking, but no more than me."

"I'm not suggesting it wasn't consensual."

Barry unclenched his hands and placed his palms on the table.

"Hey, it's not like I hadn't thought about having sex with Claudia. She was hot. But I wasn't planning anything."

"Just tell me what happened."

"Fine. If you think you can handle it."

"I can handle it."

Barry repeatedly glanced in the direction of the den as he talked.

"Claudia announced to everybody that she had to pee. Megan was going to go with her, but she asked me to go with her instead. I should have known she was up to something because girls usually go together. That's what you do, right?"

Agnes paused from taking notes.

"I don't, but you're right, most women do. Please go on."

"There were mile long lines to every bathroom in the house," Barry said. "Claudia didn't want to pee outside. She said it because she was wearing a leotard. We were on the second floor and there was a sign on a door that said KEEP OUT. We figured it was Allan's parents' bedroom. And it was. It had a bathroom."

Barry stopped talking. Agnes waited. He picked at the edge of the tablecloth.

"Then what happened?" Agnes asked.

"This is not how normal fathers and daughters act together," Barry said.

"How do normal fathers and daughters act together?" Agnes asked. "I've never had a father long enough to know."

Barry sat up straight in his chair.

"Claudia went into the bathroom to pee. When she came out, she was naked."

"I assume the lights were on," Agnes said.

"No. I remember Claudia telling me to turn off the lights so nobody would know we were in there."

"Then how do you know she was naked?"

"The blinds were open. I guess it was a combination of moonlight and streetlights. I could see she wasn't wearing anything."

Agnes made a note about the lighting conditions in the room.

"Continue."

"We had sex on Allan's parents' bed. Then we went back to the party. Not long after that, Claudia and Megan went home. I stayed with Neal and Derrick for at least another hour. Then the three of us left the party and met up at Krystal's for burgers and fries. After I ate, I drove home. The end."

Agnes looked up from her notebook.

"One more question and then you can go watch the game. Do you have any idea what time you were in the bedroom?"

"9:30."

"How do you know the exact time?"

"There was a clock next to the bed. That night with Claudia was the third time I'd ever had sex. I'm sure you remember every detail about the first guy you slept with."

"I'm a virgin."

Barry blushed, realizing he'd been talking about sex with his daughter and wasn't prepared to discuss the subject with her. He pointed at her notebook.

"What are you planning on doing with that stuff you wrote down?"

"If I told you, you wouldn't believe me," Agnes said.

"Try me."

"I'm going to travel back in time and stop you and Mom from having sex. If she hadn't gotten pregnant and had me when she was sixteen, then her life wouldn't have been ruined. She wouldn't have killed herself. She might have me later or she might never have me, but it's a risk I'm willing to take. I'm the reason she's dead and I can't live with the guilt."

Barry stood, his chair scraping the floor as he pushed it back.

"Fine, don't tell me, but you didn't have to make up a crazy story."

"Don't forget. Tomorrow, show me the house where the party took place."

"I won't forget."

Barry went into the den. Agnes gathered her photos and notebook. She put them in her coat, took her casserole pan out of the dish drainer, and said her goodbyes. She had a lot of work to do and the sooner she started, the better.

CHAPTER
18

Wednesday, December 24, 2008

Agnes squinted at the photo clipped to the side of the mirror, then continued teasing her hair to match the photo. Once she got it full enough, she feathered her bangs. She squinted at the photo again before putting on the bunny ears she'd found in the bottom drawer of Claudia's dresser. She scrutinized them in the mirror, turning her head from side to side.

The photo was of sixteen-year-old Claudia dressed as a bunny and was taken on October 27, 1990, before she left for the Halloween party. Agnes' decision to dress as her mother did that night was based on something Barry told her.

Barry claimed intercourse was Claudia's idea. Agnes believed him. Considering Barry's passive personality, it was more likely Claudia initiated the act. Agnes had to either make Claudia believe she didn't want to have sex, or make Barry believe Claudia wasn't interested. Either way, it had to be Claudia making the decision to abstain from intercourse.

Agnes considered entering the bedroom and announcing to Barry and

Claudia that she was their daughter, and they should stop what they were doing immediately. There were many flaws to that plan. The biggest was they probably wouldn't believe her. Her best option was to enter the dark bedroom, masquerade as Claudia, and tell Barry in no uncertain terms nothing sexual was going to happen between them.

Agnes wasn't sure how she was going to do this, and that unknown variable worried her. It was a crucial detail. The entire journey depended on her taking decisive action during a very narrow window of time. Agnes considered delaying her plan until she had solved the unknown variable to her satisfaction, but then she remembered another crucial detail. She was a genius. She'd figure it out.

The black leotard was the most uncomfortable thing Agnes had ever worn. The fabric kept riding up her butt. The stone washed jeans fit perfectly. She remembered Claudia taking them out of a dark corner of her closet. Agnes asked where they'd come from. Claudia said she'd had them since high school and hoped someday she would fit back into them. Agnes asked her why she would want to wear such ugly pants. Claudia put them back in the closet, sighing as she often did when Agnes asked a question. The bomber jacket, Skechers tennis shoes, and pink fanny pack came from a vintage clothing store.

Agnes had researched 1990. Few people had a personal computer or a mobile phone. The World Wide Web wouldn't be available to the public until the following year. Security cameras were around but not as abundant, plus the video quality was grainy. This pleased Agnes. There was less chance of her leaving any significant evidence of her presence.

The biggest hurdle was money. United States currency had changed in design and security features since 1990. Agnes had to spend more than she wanted to at a rare coin shop for a set of eight 1985 twenty-dollar bills and eight 1975 quarters.

Before putting on the bomber jacket, Agnes strapped the Time Tefillin to her head and arm. She felt giddy as she went through her pre-travel ritual. She hadn't realized how much she missed time traveling.

"I'm going out soon, Ms. Rat," Agnes said as she poured food pellets into the cage. "I'm going to time travel. You know what that's like."

The phone rang. Agnes debated on whether to ignore the call. The only person she thought might be calling her was Megan, but it was 11:00 p.m. and Megan never called this late. Then again, Megan was Catholic. She could be calling Agnes before she went to Midnight Mass. Considering that this might be the last time Agnes ever spoke to Megan, she answered the phone.

"Merry Christmas, Agnes."

"Who is this?"

"Barry. Your dad."

"Barry?"

"Sorry to call so late, but this being Christmas Eve got me thinking. I know I totally failed as a father and I have no right to ask you this, but will you give me another chance?"

Agnes looked to Ms. Rat for advice on how to respond, but she was busy eating.

"Another chance to do what?"

"I want to start over. I want to get it right this time."

"I was thinking the same thing."

"That's great." There was tremendous relief in his voice. "This is the best Christmas gift ever."

"I have to go now."

"Yeah sure. I'll talk to you later."

"Goodbye Barry." Agnes hung up.

She slipped the bunny ears inside her jacket. She drove to the North Shore. Red and white strings of lights twined around streetlamps. The store windows were covered with a blizzard of sprayed-on snow.

The Walnut Street Bridge was a pedestrian bridge. It was Claudia and Agnes' favorite place in the city. They loved standing in the middle and watching the river below. Agnes dropped her plan to scatter Claudia's ashes from the bridge when she came up with the idea of saving her instead. As Agnes suspected, the bridge was deserted on Christmas Eve.

Agnes stood by the railing and gazed down at the Tennessee River.

Snow began to fall, not heavily, just enough flakes to add frosting to the park benches. Agnes pulled her jacket tighter as she shivered both from the cold and the anticipation. She set her time destination on the clock. She looked in both directions to make sure no one was coming, and then flipped the switch.

The bridge's aquamarine iron beams melted like sticks of butter in a hot skillet. The city's lights became a universe of tiny white and yellow blobs. She floated in the air as large blobs of blue and orange streaked past her. It dawned on Agnes how much she missed the complete silence of time travel. Being alone with nothing to interfere with her thoughts was comforting.

If only she had thought to bring her stopwatch, she could have timed how long she floated before reaching her destination. On previous time skips, the length of time she traveled affected the amount of time she floated above the normal time stream. A stopwatch would have helped her ascertain how quickly she was traveling.

She floated for what seemed like six hours. When the world returned to normal, she had a sour stomach and her mouth tasted like she hadn't brushed her teeth in a year.

CHAPTER
19

Saturday, October 27, 1990

Agnes had set the Time Tefillin's clock for 6:00 p.m. on Saturday, October 27, 1990. She would verify the date and time at her first opportunity. There was no snow, but the wind from the river chilled her to the bone.

The Walnut Street Bridge was in terrible shape. Weeds covered the sidewalk and the narrow two-lane road had serious potholes. The bridge had recently been added to the National Register, but the city hadn't begun repairs. Agnes took a step on the sidewalk and heard a rotting timber snap. Agnes moved back and grabbed the handrail as the slat she'd put her foot on fell to the river below. Holding her breath, she counted to fifteen before she heard the splash.

"Metaphor, anyone?"

She hadn't come all this way just to fall into the river. Slowly she continued, listening carefully to every creak. At the foot of the bridge, she waited impatiently until she was sure no one was around before she climbed over the barricade.

She had less than seven hours to change history.

So much had yet to happen to North Shore. There wasn't a Coolidge Park with its restored carousel and fountain surrounded by stone animals. Instead, there were sparse patches of grass and a few decrepit industrial buildings. Most striking for Agnes was the absence of the Tennessee Aquarium on the opposite shore. She'd gone there on so many middle school trips she'd named the fish.

Halloween decorations replaced the Christmas decorations in shop windows. The air smelled of soggy wood and dead fish. The only businesses that seemed to be thriving were the dive bars. At the end of the bridge's lane was one such bar, the Coral Reef. The workday hadn't ended and already there was a line of men at the bar creating a cloud of tobacco smoke over their beers.

While waiting at the bus stop, Agnes noticed the cars on the street were boxier with longer trunks. There were more small hatchbacks. The bus arrived. Agnes' antique coins clinked as she dropped them into the farebox. She slid into an empty seat and settled by the window.

The bus was half full. Two Black teenagers with flat top haircuts got on and slouched in their seats. They wore colorful nylon jackets and carried portable CD players. Agnes could hear the music, tinny and relentless, leaking from their headsets. A balding white man with a ponytail wearing a polyester suit looked up from his newspaper at the teenagers, shook his head, and returned his attention to his newspaper.

Riding along Dayton Boulevard, Agnes gazed out the window at her hometown the year before she was born. Many of the same business, like I-Deal Motors, Buddy Ratley Signs, and Echols Furniture, were here, but they looked newer and cleaner. The similarity between 1990 Red Bank and 2008 Red Bank was a stark reminder to Agnes that Chattanooga's coming economic resurgence wouldn't quite reach her neighborhood.

She got off the bus at Memorial Drive and thirty minutes later caught a bus headed for Hixson. The setting sun filled the interior of the bus with an orange haze. A few miles later, Agnes pulled the overhead cord to let the driver know she was ready to get off. The bus didn't go into Allan's neighborhood. She would have to walk the rest of the way and her destination was uphill. Agnes zipped up her bomber jacket.

The winding road was narrow, there were no sidewalks, and the last rays of the sun were disappearing rapidly. Cars came dangerously close as they passed. Agnes heard a heavy rock beat in the distance. It came from the only house lit up at the top of the hill. Costumed teenagers parked their cars on the street and filed inside.

Slipping into the shadows of a tree-filled yard, Agnes took off her jacket and jeans. She removed the Time Tefillin, rolled it up, and stuffed it into the fanny pack. As she returned to the road, she put on the bunny ears and used a car's rear-view mirror to help her apply a smudge of black eyeliner to her nose and lines on her cheeks for whiskers. Except for the pink fanny pack, she looked like Claudia. She crammed her discarded clothes and the tube of black eyeliner into an empty metal trashcan sitting on the curb.

Agnes checked the time. She had five hours left on her time skip and two hours before she needed to stop Barry and Claudia from having sex. That left her three hours to get back to the bridge before her time ran out. She was pleased. Her plan was running smoothly.

Agnes was greeted at the door by a boy dressed as Elvis.

"Welcome to the home of the King," he drawled. "I love bunny rabbits. Later, I might have to hunt you down in the Jungle Room."

"Rabbits don't live in the jungle," Agnes said. "They live in the forest."

"Haven't you heard of the Jungle Room in Graceland? I'm dressed as Elvis, so you see where I'm going with this."

"Rabbits don't live in the jungle."

Other guests arrived, and Elvis turned his attention to them. Agnes entered the house, doing her best to keep the leotard from crawling up her butt. The blaring rock music disoriented her, and she resisted the urge to plug her ears with her fingers. She couldn't understand why the music was so loud. No one could have a decent conversation in this din.

The evening was young and only a few guests were milling about. Agnes was able to explore the house freely and find the best routes for a quick escape. She wished she had her notebook so she could write down this time period's choices of music, hairstyles, and Halloween costumes. She would have filled many pages just on the mysterious attraction of mullets for boys and big hair for girls.

By the time Agnes entered the basement, she'd become accustomed to the environment, and the music no longer bothered her. The basement had been made into a game room. To Agnes' delight, a pool table dominated the center of the room. Since there was no one else around, she racked up the balls.

As she knocked ball after ball into the pockets, she wondered why she didn't play pool more often. The weight and the power of the cue stick felt good in her hands. It would make a good weapon.

Agnes held the stick out in front of her. She still hadn't decided how she was going to stop Claudia and Barry. Whatever she did had to be quick and effective. She gave the stick a practice swing. It was an extreme solution to her dilemma but had an almost flawless chance for success.

"You're perfect," she said.

Agnes left the game unfinished and carried the cue stick with her to the second floor. The party was still confined to the first floor. Below her, she could hear the music and people trying to shout over it. She found the door with the KEEP OUT sign and went inside. The smell of tobacco smoke reminded her of her grandparents.

Agnes studied the bedroom. The mother's closet was crammed full of dresses, pants, blouses, and silk shirts. The father's closet had suits, dress shirts, slacks, and casual shirts, but was much less crowded. Agnes chose it as her hiding place. She pushed aside an assortment of men's shoes to make a place on the floor to sit.

Agnes turned out the lights and waited for her eyes to adjust to the darkness. She made test runs, getting up quietly and sliding open the closet's folding doors. Thankfully, they didn't squeak. After five minutes practice, she was able to get out of the closet and swing the pool cue at an imaginary Barry without making any noise.

Now all she had to do was wait. Agnes checked the time. Barry and Claudia were due to arrive in less than an hour. Nervous sweat trickled down her back. She needed to remain calm if she was going to have a successful mission. She took deep breaths to relax.

She checked the time. Barry and Claudia were supposed to be in the room right now. She didn't hear anything but the ticking of the clock on the bedside table. She peeked outside the closet. The room was empty. She had to find out what went wrong. She left the pool cue in the closet.

An army of costumed teenagers had arrived. A line for the second-floor bathroom snaked along the hallway wall. Agnes hurried past them.

The first floor was even more crowded than the second floor. Agnes pushed her way through the crowd. In the living room, there was a clock over the fireplace mantle. The time was wrong. She worked her way into the kitchen. The clock in there was also wrong.

Agnes found Elvis pouring a drink from a beer keg. She tapped him on the shoulder.

"Oh hey, bunny girl," he said. "Did you ditch the witch so that you could join me in the Jungle Room?"

Agnes' spine tingled. The witch Elvis referred to must be Megan. He had mistaken Agnes for Claudia. Her mother was here somewhere in the house.

"We've already established rabbits aren't indigenous to jungles," Agnes said. "Are you aware that all of the clocks in your house are an hour slow?"

Elvis' beer was mainly foam, but he took a sip anyway, leaving a creamy mustache on his upper lip.

"Yeah. Tomorrow's Daylight Saving Time. I plan to have a horrendous hangover in the morning and the last thing I'm going to want to do is turn all the clocks in the house back an hour. So, I did it this afternoon. Besides, in a couple of hours, all the clocks will be correct."

"I see," Agnes said. "Barry didn't realize the time on the beside clock was an hour early."

"You want me to pour you a beer?"

Agnes left Elvis without answering. She had to get back to the bedroom.

Her mother's laugh stopped her in her tracks. The reverse of time hadn't changed it a bit. In a room off the main hallway, Agnes located Claudia sitting on a couch between Megan and Barry. If Agnes hadn't seen the photos taken this night, she might not have recognized them. They were so young, just children. Claudia was so beautiful it made Agnes's heart ache.

Agnes resisted the temptation to run to Claudia and throw her arms around her. To hold her mother one more time even if she wasn't her mother yet. Her lower lip trembled as she fought back tears.

Claudia looked out at the hallway and locked eyes with Agnes. Time stood still. Agnes wanted to run, but her feet wouldn't move. Claudia turned her head and handed Megan the marijuana cigarette she was holding. Agnes almost fainted.

She circled back through the house so she could approach their room without being seen. She leaned against the wall next to the doorway. A grim reaper passing by handed Agnes a plastic cup. She was about to explain she didn't want anything, but the reaper had already walked away. She cautiously sipped the liquid in the cup. It was beer. Agnes still didn't want it, but it helped her blend in with the crowd.

As Agnes eavesdropped on Claudia, she marveled at her mother's cleverness and easy laugh. Agnes was more familiar with the Claudia who was tired from working long hours and worried about how to pay the bills. Claudia's early pregnancy had destroyed the happy Claudia laughing with her friends in the study. Agnes was more determined than ever to complete her mission.

"I have to pee," Claudia announced. Adrenaline rushed through Agnes' veins. She had to get to Allan's parents' bedroom before Claudia and Barry.

Agnes pushed her way through the crowd and made her way to the second floor. She was hurrying toward the master bedroom when two girls stumbled out of a smaller bedroom and directly into her path. They were dressed as a glam rocker and a cartoon mouse.

"Got any rolling papers?" the glam rocker asked.

"No, I do not," Agnes said.

"You sure?" said the mouse. "We got some killer Mexican."

"If I had rolling papers, I would gladly give them to you."

"You talk funny," said the glam rocker.

The girls giggled and continued with their quest.

Once inside the bedroom, Agnes paused to let her eyes adjust to the dark. She got inside the father's closet and grabbed the pool cue. As she waited, she worried. She worried her hands were too sweaty and the stick would fly out of her hands. She worried Barry and Claudia would hear her breathing in the closet. She worried she'd chicken out and never leave the closet.

"Calm down, Agnes," she whispered. "You are in complete control."

The bedroom door opened, and Agnes covered her mouth to keep from squeaking out loud. The bedroom light clicked on. Agnes scooted tighter into the corner of the closet.

"You're right," Barry said. "Here's a bathroom."

Agnes heard the bathroom door open.

"Someone might see the light under the bedroom door and realize we're in here," Claudia said. "Turn out the overhead light."

"But then I'll be standing here in the dark," Barry said.

"You're a vampire. You're not supposed to be afraid of the dark."

The bathroom door slammed shut and the bedroom light blinked out. Agnes crept out of the closet. Barry faced the bedroom window, silhouetted by moonlight. She could feel her heart beating in her ears as she inched closer to him. She held the stick up, ready to swing.

Agnes paused. As a result of time travel, at this moment in time, she and her father were both seventeen. He had no idea he was about to have sex with Claudia. He had no idea he was going to be a bad father and ruin Claudia's life. At this moment in time, he was an innocent boy. It was unfair to punish him for the mistakes he hadn't committed yet. But it was better to cause Barry pain now than to allow him to cause everyone pain later.

He twirled a ring of car keys on his finger. The keys slipped off his finger and dropped to the floor. As he began to bend down to find them, Agnes called his name.

"Barry."

He straightened and turned around.

"Hey, Claudia. You done?"

Agnes caught the look of horror in Barry's eyes right before she poured every ounce of heartbreak, disappointment, and yearning caused by his absence and broken promises into her swing, and then she whacked his testicles. There was a whistle of air followed by a heavy thud. Barry made a sound like a balloon losing air. He grabbed his groin as he crumbled to the ground and curled into a fetal position.

Kneeling next to him, Agnes gently put her hand on Barry's shoulder. "I'm sorry, but this was the most effective solution. I hope there's no permanent damage, either physically or psychologically."

Barry moaned in response.

A gleam of light on the floor caught Agnes' eye. It was Barry's keyring with the keys to his shiny new car. The same car that almost ran Megan and Claudia off the road on the way to the party. Still feeling some animosity toward Barry, Agnes grabbed the keyring and put it in her pink fanny pack.

The sound of a toilet flushing warned Agnes it was time for her to leave. She hurried out of the bedroom, down the stairs, through the mass of teenagers, and out of the house. It wasn't until she was on the front lawn that she realized she had taken the pool cue with her. Her knuckles were white from gripping the shaft.

The cool night air dried the sweat on her face. She retrieved her jeans and bomber jacket from the trash can. Agnes checked the time. Her miscalculation due to Daylight Savings Time meant she only had an hour left before she would get pulled back to 2008. Her original plan was to take the bus back to the Walnut Street Bridge, but she needed a quicker way to get there.

In the driveway was Barry's red Trans Am. Agnes smiled. Using his car for her escape had a certain poetic justice to it. She took the keys out of her fanny pack, got in the car, and tossed the pool cue into the back seat.

Claudia had taught Agnes how to drive a stick shift, but she still stalled out on her first attempt to get the car started. Normally, Agnes was a slow, careful driver, but she was in a hurry. She took the winding curves dangerously fast and flew down the highway. Agnes had to admit the Trans Am was a fun vehicle to drive. She parked the car in the parking lot behind an art supply store located directly across the street from the Walnut Street Bridge. She left the keys in the ignition and the door unlocked.

Agnes took the Time Tefillin out of her fanny pack and put it on. She didn't need to set the clock. At the end of her seven hours in 1990, she would be pulled back to exactly the moment she left December 24, 2008.

As she turned the corner of the art supply store, she saw a thin man wearing a dirty apron standing outside the Coral Reef bar which was next to the entrance to the bridge. He was smoking a cigarette. Agnes couldn't get on the bridge without him seeing her. He might not care if she was trespassing, but she didn't plan to find out. She hid behind the art supply store until he took his last puff, dropped the butt to the ground, and grinded it with the heel of his shoe.

He entered the bar's back door. Agnes hurried down the alley and across the street. She scaled the bridge's barricade and worked her way to the middle of the bridge.

Agnes checked the time. Five minutes left. She had altered the timeline of Claudia's life. And hers. Once the seven hours of ripples created by Agnes skipping across the river of time ended, her existence would end as well.

She had known all along she was erasing herself and though she was sad and frightened, she didn't regret her decision. If her actions tonight saved Claudia, then her sacrifice was worth it. Agnes breathed in deeply because her last breath could be coming at any moment.

Her seven-hour time limit ended, and Agnes disappeared.

II

SECOND AGNES

CHAPTER
20

Wednesday, July 4, 2007

Agnes took a break from reading her book, *Einstein: His Life and Universe*, to observe the manmade beach. The air smelled of suntan lotion, grilled meat, and lake water. Music blasting from portable radios competed with children shrieking and motorboats roaring across the water. But despite all the activity, Chester Frost Park was far from overcrowded.

"Is this what happens when a holiday lands in the middle of the week?" Agnes asked.

"It's early," Claudia said. "The beach will be packed tonight for the fireworks."

"But we'll be home by then, right?"

Claudia sighed. "Yes, we'll be home by then."

She put on her sunglasses and floppy hat then sprawled out on her towel. Agnes couldn't how understand how her mother could enjoy being exposed to the sun considering she spent her working hours next to hot stoves and sizzling oil. As for Agnes, she would have been perfectly happy

Mickey Dubrow

reading in her bedroom all day, but she understood that limited exposure to the sun was the best method for boosting her body's requirement of vitamin D.

Agnes noticed a boy checking them out. She didn't have to wonder if he was looking at her or Claudia. All males beyond puberty were attracted to Claudia. He did a double take and walked toward them.

"That boy is coming towards us," Agnes said. "I don't recognize him. Do you?"

"What boy?" Claudia said.

Agnes nodded in the boy's direction.

"I've never seen him before," Claudia said.

He was tall with a mop of blond hair. He wore cut-off jeans and tennis shoes with no socks. His hairless chest was smooth and muscular. He stopped at the foot of their towels smelling of boyish sweat and Axe body spray.

"Hey, Ms. Cook," he said. "You probably don't remember me. I'm Josh Hawkins. You used to be part of our carpool when I was in grammar school."

Claudia squinted at the boy.

"You're little Josh Hawkins? Look at you! You're all grown up. I can't believe you remember me after all these years."

"I always looked forward to the days you drove because your car always smelled like hamburgers."

"Sadly, it still does."

Josh gawked at Agnes.

"Agnes? Is that you?" he asked.

Agnes blushed and held her book over her chest.

"Yes. It's me."

"I haven't seen you since fifth grade. You skipped ahead. What grade are you in now?"

Claudia interrupted before Agnes could answer.

"Are you here by yourself?" she asked.

Agnes picked up the agitation in her mother's voice, but Josh was oblivious.

"My family's over there," Josh said, pointing toward the campgrounds. "We spend a week here every summer. Dad loves fishing in Dallas Bay. The fireworks tonight are going to be awesome."

"We can't stay that late, so we'll miss them."

"That's too bad because they're awesome."

"Thank you for stopping by. Goodbye."

Josh blinked a few times before it sank in that Claudia had basically told him to go away. He mumbled a goodbye and hurried away.

Agnes glared at Claudia. "You didn't need to be so mean to him."

"I wasn't mean. Why? Did you want to go out with him?"

"No. That's not the point. He wasn't trying to do anything. Not every human with a Y chromosome…" Agnes was going to say, "Is like my father," but held her tongue.

Agnes put her book down and stood. She brushed the sand off her butt.

I'm going for a walk," she announced.

"Are you going to look for that boy?" Claudia asked.

"I just want to take a walk."

"Don't be gone too long. You want to leave before the fireworks, don't you?"

Agnes wanted to explain she wasn't opposed to fireworks. She had a stack of lab reports she wanted to complete before she returned to school. But there was enough tension between her and Claudia, and she didn't want to add to it.

Claudia dug her phone out of her tote bag and put in the ear buds. Agnes knew from the way her mother smiled that she was listening to her R.E.M. playlist.

Agnes picked her way through the families sprawled on the beach facing Lake Chickamauga to the trail that wound through the trees to Dallas Bay. There was no sand on its rocky shore. Agnes was glad she thought to wear her sandals.

Except for two elderly men fishing, she had the shore to herself. A few boats in the bay floated lazily with fishing lines trailing behind them, while the rest zoomed about sending ripples across the bay and waves lapping the shore.

Watching the speeding boats race past stagnant boats reminded Agnes of Einstein's theory that time is a river with faster and slower boats. She waded into the bay, squatted, and scooped up a handful of rocks. She picked through them, keeping only the flat, smooth rocks and tossed the rest back.

She skipped the rocks across the water. The first few sank after a couple of skips, but soon she was getting five to six skips per rock.

"You're pretty good."

Fear shot through Agnes as she looked for the source of the voice. She spotted Josh Hawkins standing in the shadow of an oak tree. As he stepped out into the sun, she saw that he was pinching the stub of a hand-rolled cigarette between his forefinger and thumb. Agnes recognized the sweet smell coming from the cigarette. Josh held out the joint toward her.

"Want some? There's probably enough for one toke. If I'd known you were coming, I would have waited to light up."

Agnes wrinkled her nose. She'd tried marijuana once and didn't care for it.

"No, thank you. I don't like clouding my mind with drugs."

Josh shrugged. He sucked on the stub and then flicked it into the lake. It sizzled as it hit the water.

"Sorry about earlier," Josh said. "I wasn't trying to hit on you."

"It's okay," Agnes said.

"It's too bad you're not going to be here for the fireworks tonight. Maybe you could talk your mom into staying. Me and some buddies scored a six pack of beer."

As they were talking, Agnes realized Josh was staring at her body. She didn't understand how Josh could possibly consider her attractive. She never gave much thought to her appearance. She kept her unruly brown hair tied in a ponytail and never bothered to wear make-up. Then again, his interest could have been triggered by a combination of teenage male hormones and the marijuana in his system.

"Drink beer with you buddies, huh?" Agnes said. "I thought you said you weren't trying to hit on me."

Josh's face paled.

"No, really. Just a friendly invitation. No big deal."

"Thank you," Agnes said. "But my mother and I must leave before the fireworks."

"I really screwed this up. I should go."

"No, wait." Agnes rubbed the surface of the rock in her hand. "Skip rocks with me?"

Josh grinned.

"Okay."

He splashed into the water and gathered up handfuls of rocks. They went through them together and made a pile of smooth, flat stones. They took turns skipping stones across the water.

"I'm sorry my mom was mean to you," Agnes said. "She doesn't trust men."

"Some guys can be assholes."

They skipped rocks in silence. Agnes couldn't think of anything else to talk about. She hadn't seen Josh Hawkins since she was eight. The only thing she remembered about him was that he always smelled like onions.

"I'm on the basketball team at Red Bank High," Josh said. "Which school are you going to? Please don't say Hixson High. They're our biggest rival."

"I'm about to start my second year at Georgia Tech."

Josh smacked his forehead. "That's right! I read about you in the paper. You're like super smart."

Agnes couldn't help but smile. "Yes, I'm super smart."

"What's your major?"

"I'm working on my doctorate in physics."

"What kind of classes do you take for that?"

"I don't go to class. I work in a laboratory. My lab is studying the possibility of time travel."

"That's cool, but you know what would be really cool? If you built a time machine."

Agnes laughed. Josh was so big and friendly, she felt like she was talking to a Labrador retriever. She wondered if all boys his age were like him.

"Funny you should say that," Agnes said. "Can you keep a secret?"

Josh looked around. The two old fishermen were too far away to overhear their conversation.

"Yeah. I can keep a secret."

"I am building a time machine. I haven't told anybody but you. Even my lab director doesn't know."

Josh tossed a stone and gave Agnes a sidelong glance.

"No, you're not. You're pulling my leg."

"It's not a functioning device yet. I'm missing something and I'm not sure what it is."

Agnes tossed a stone. It skipped seven times before sinking into the lake.

"You've certainly figured out how to skip stones," Josh said.

"You just have to find the magic angle. That's how you get the highest number of skips."

Agnes searched for more stones. She examined them carefully until she found the perfect stone, flat and round. An electric current of excitement spread through her. The answer she was seeking was in her hand.

"Skipping stones," she said. "Time is a river. Downstream is the future and upstream is the past. But when I skip a stone, I don't worry about which way the river is flowing. I only have to find the magic angle, the right combination of hydrodynamics, momentum, and gravity to enter the time stream. Then I can utilize the force of the river to skip from one point in time to the next."

Agnes squeezed the perfect stone in her hand and headed back toward the beach. Josh dropped the stones in his hand and rushed to join her.

"You're leaving?" he asked.

"I must make notes while the theory is still fresh in my mind."

"Hey, if you're not too busy between now and when you go back to school, maybe we could go out. I have a driver's permit and Dad lets me borrow the car."

Agnes stopped. Josh kept going. He caught himself and came back to her.

"My mother and I are different in many ways," Agnes said. "But when it comes to men, we're the same. We don't trust them."

"If you didn't trust me then why did you skip stones with me? Why did you tell me about your time machine?"

"Just because I skipped rocks with you doesn't mean I trust you. And no one would believe you if you told them about my time machine."

"But I'm a nice guy," Josh said. "You can trust me."

Agnes wasn't listening. She continued on her way and didn't look back.

CHAPTER
21

Monday, August 4, 2008

Today was Agnes' seventeenth birthday. Claudia was seventeen when she had Agnes. That would make today the perfect day for Agnes to give birth to a functional time travel device.

Agnes lived on the third floor of the Stein House, the women only residence hall. Her dorm room contained two narrow bedrooms with a shared bathroom. Agnes didn't have a roommate and used the second bedroom as her secret laboratory. Since it was summertime, hardly anyone was in the building, and nobody complained about the chemical burning smells coming from her room.

On her work desk sat an eight-by-eight-by-eight-inch metal box attached to a digital clock. A camcorder on a tripod waited on the other side of the room. After going over her checklist one last time, Agnes decided she was ready to begin the experiment. She set the clock, started the camcorder, and faced the lens.

"Transport solid object attempt number two hundred ninety-six. Goal

is for object to travel sixty seconds forward in time. Begin in three…two…
one."

Agnes flipped the switch activating both the box and the clock simultaneously. Immediately, they disappeared. She started the stopwatch.

Her phone rang. She grudgingly answered.

"Who is this? What do you want?"

"How's my birthday girl doing?"

Agnes gritted her teeth. Of course, it was him. He had an almost supernatural sense of the perfect time to ruin any occasion.

"Now's not a good time, Derrick. I'm in the middle of something."

Agnes studied the stopwatch. Nine seconds had passed. Fifty-one seconds to go.

"You don't have time for your daddy to wish you a happy birthday?"

"I'm doing an experiment that requires my complete attention."

"Don't get all high and mighty with me, little lady."

Twenty seconds passed. Forty seconds to go.

"What do you want, Derrick?"

"It's like this, sweetie. Daddy needs to borrow some money. Just enough to carry me through the next couple of months."

It was early afternoon and Derrick was already slurring his words. Agnes could practically smell the alcohol on his breath through the telephone.

"I don't have any money."

"You're getting paid to go to college. Surely you can spare me some of that scholarship money."

"The money goes directly to Georgia Tech. I don't have access to it."

"You sure about that? Don't hold out on me."

"Most fathers give their children gifts on their birthday, not the other way around."

Forty-six seconds passed. Fourteen seconds to go.

"I'll get you something once I get back on my feet. I promise."

"Goodbye, Derrick."

"Happy Birthday, Agnes."

Agnes resisted the urge to throw the phone at the wall.

At exactly one minute, the time machine reappeared. After months of failed experiments, she successfully sent an object through time. Joy and relief flooded her, but part of her still fumed from her father's phone call. Agnes should have been used to it by now. She'd lost count of the birthdays and holidays Derrick ruined not by his absence, but by showing up and making the event about him.

The phone rang.

"What do you want now?" Agnes demanded.

"I just wanted to wish you a Happy Birthday," Claudia said. "Did I call at a bad time?"

"Mom, I'm sorry. I thought you were Derrick."

"Did he call you for money?"

"How'd you guess?"

"Why else would he call? He called me first and I told him to go to hell."

Agnes relaxed.

"I'm glad you called, Mom."

"Did you do anything special for your birthday?"

Agnes walked over to the desk and picked up the box. The metal felt cool in her hand.

"Yes, Mom. I did."

CHAPTER

22

Saturday, October 27, 1990

"When did it get so damn cold?" Claudia said, shivering in her black dance leotard. "I'm about to freeze my tail off."

"I'm sure it's plenty warm inside," Megan said.

"Oh, look. The redneck is here."

"I hope somebody steals his car."

The red Trans Am that almost run them off the road earlier that evening was parked in the driveway. Standing next to the car, the girls could hear the Halloween party inside Allan's house was going strong.

Elvis greeted the girls at the front door.

"Hey, bunny rabbit. I didn't see you leave. Glad you're back and brought a cute witch with you."

"What are you talking about, Allan?" Claudia asked. "We just got here."

He waved his red cup in a circle.

"I've been tapping the keg all afternoon. I'm starting to see double."

To get to the kitchen, Megan and Claudia squeezed past vampires, pirates, glam rockers, clowns, cats, slashers, bloodied victims, and superheroes. As designated driver, Megan couldn't drink so she shared a joint with four Ninja Turtles instead. Claudia poured a whiskey and soda. Leaving the kitchen, Claudia felt like she was in a sauna heated by costumed teenagers and was glad she wasn't wearing more clothes.

They were about to turn a corner when a boy dressed as Jason, the horror movie killer, leapt out at them.

"Derrick!" Claudia said. "You asshole. You made me spill my drink."

"You should have seen your faces," Derrick said.

He led them to a study where their friends Barry and Neal were waiting for them. Barry was a vampire and Neal was a cowboy. After posing for photos, they settled on couches and smoked Neal's pot. Barry and Derrick took turns going to the kitchen for booze refills.

"Hey, did you see my new car?" Barry said. "I parked it in the driveway so that it wouldn't get scratched."

"Please tell me that red Trans Am isn't yours," Megan said.

"My dad gave it to me as an early graduation present."

"You almost ran us into a ditch on the way here!"

"Sorry. I didn't know it was you."

Claudia was about to pass a joint to Megan when her eyes widened.

"Oh my God!" she said. "I'm so blazed from this weed. I just saw myself."

"Where?" Neal asked.

"Out there!" Claudia pointed toward the hallway.

"Girl, what are you talking about?" Megan said, taking the joint from Claudia.

"I swear I saw this girl who looked like me and was dressed like me. I would have sworn it was me, but she had a pink fanny pack."

The gang scanned the crowd but didn't see a bunny or a fanny pack.

"A fanny pack? You wouldn't be caught dead wearing no fugly fanny pack."

"I know. Fanny packs are so lame."

"Hey," Neal protested. "I sometimes wear a fanny pack."

"Which proves fanny packs are lame," Megan said.

Everybody laughed as Neal blushed.

Thirty minutes later, Claudia announced she had to go to the bathroom and asked Barry to accompany her. Barry put his arm around Claudia's shoulder and guided her through the crowd. They checked every bathroom in the house on both floors and at each one they encountered a chain of people blocking them from their goal. Claudia was certain her bladder would burst.

On the second floor, they came across a room with a KEEP OUT sign taped to the door.

"I bet this is Allan's parents' bedroom," Claudia said.

"You think?" Barry asked.

"I bet they have their own bathroom."

"We can't go in there. It says to keep out."

"But it doesn't say, Keep out, Claudia and Barry."

The master bedroom did have its own bathroom. Claudia almost peed on herself when she saw relief was near. She hurried over and paused before she closed the door.

"Someone might see the light under the bedroom door and realize we're in here. Turn out the overhead light."

"But then I'll be standing here in the dark," Barry said.

"You're a vampire. You're supposed to be able to see in the dark."

Once inside, Claudia lowered the toilet, wiped it down with toilet paper, then wiggled out of her leotard. With immense relief, she emptied her bladder. As she was peeing, she thought she heard something fall on the floor but figured the noise came from downstairs.

Claudia didn't put her leotard back on. She wanted to have sex with Barry for a long time and now that she had him alone, she was determined to do it. She turned off the bathroom light and cracked the door open. Her bare skin tingled.

"Barry?"

He didn't answer.

Claudia opened the door a bit more and poked her head out to make sure he hadn't left. She was horrified to see him on the floor in a fetal position. She struggled back into her leotard before hurrying to his side. He moaned when she put her hand on his shoulder.

"Barry? What happened?"

"Why'd you do it?"

"What are you talking about? I was in the bathroom."

"You said you were sorry, but I don't believe you."

Barry cried so hard, he hiccupped. Claudia tried to roll him over to see where he was hurt but he wouldn't budge.

Panic stricken, Claudia rushed downstairs to the study where Neal, Derrick, and Megan were sharing a joint. The three friends' eyes were red as they stared at Claudia. She was shaking, her rabbit ears were on crooked, and her whiskers were smeared.

"Something happened to Barry," Claudia said. "He's hurt really bad."

"Hurt?" Megan said. "How?"

"I don't know." She gestured with her hands. "You have to come with me."

Megan, Derrick, and Neal followed Claudia as she hurried up to stairs, past people waiting to pee, and past the KEEP OUT sign into the master bedroom. Barry lay on the carpeted floor where Claudia had left him. They looked at each other, unsure what to do. Derrick sprawled on his stomach so that his head was level with Barry's.

"Barry. Where you hurt?"

"I want to go to the hospital," Barry said. "I think there's permanent damage."

Derrick peered up at the others. "I've seen this before. Somebody kicked him in the nuts. Must have kicked him pretty hard if he wants to go to a hospital."

Derrick, Megan, and Neal looked accusingly at Claudia. She shook her head as she backed away from them.

"I was in the bathroom when it happened."

Barry moaned and whimpered as Neal and Derrick helped him to his feet. He wouldn't stop cradling his crotch. The journey down the stairs was a slow delicate descent. Elvis approached them in the living room.

"Please tell me he's not driving," Elvis said, pointing at Barry.

"He's not drunk," Megan said. "He was attacked."

"Attacked?"

"She did it," Barry said, pointing at Claudia.

"I swear it wasn't me," she said.

Elvis chuckled. "Sounds like a lover's quarrel."

"We'll take it from here," Neal said. "By the way, great party."

Megan ran to get her car while Neal and Derrick walked Barry to the driveway. Claudia followed close behind.

"My car!" Barry bellowed.

"Dude, you're in no condition to drive," Neal said.

"It's missing. Somebody stole my car."

The driveway was empty, and Barry's Trans Am was nowhere in sight.

"You're having the worse night of your life," Derrick said.

Megan pulled up in her car and parked where Barry's Trans Am had been. Neal and Derrick eased Barry into the back seat. Neal walked around the car and got in next to Barry. Claudia was about to get into the front seat, but Megan held up her hand.

"It's probably better if you don't come," she said. "I'll swing back here to get you later."

Barry rolled down the back window and leaned his head out.

"Call the police. Tell them to find my car."

"I'll call them," Derrick said. "It's an orange Yugo, right?"

"Don't mess around, Derrick. I need my car back."

"Chill out, dude. I'll take care of it."

Claudia and Derrick watched Megan's car disappear down the hill.

"I need another drink," Claudia said.

"I hear you," Derrick said.

They parked themselves in the kitchen so that Claudia could drink whiskey without interruption. Derrick poured mostly foam from the dregs of the beer keg.

They spent the next two hours drinking. Claudia only spoke when

Derrick asked her a direct question. Except for the diehards, the house was empty. Claudia and Derrick had the kitchen to themselves.

"Where are they?" Claudia said, her voice slurring. "I hope Barry's okay."

"I'll call the hospital," Derrick said.

"Did you call the police about Barry's car?"

"Damn. I forgot. I'll do that right after I call the hospital."

Derrick left in search of a telephone.

Claudia couldn't believe her plan to have sex with Barry had gone so terribly wrong. She'd only had sex once before. It happened this past summer when her family went to Destin. She'd met a cute boy on the beach. He was nice and knew more than she did, but she wanted the next time to be special. She wanted Barry to be her boyfriend. There didn't seem to be much chance of that happening now.

The image of Barry curled up on the floor kept repeating in her head. She forced that image aside and another took its place. Something she saw for a brief moment.

Derrick returned.

"It was that girl, the one dressed like me," Claudia said. "She attacked Barry. It had to have been her."

"I thought you said she was just a figment of your stoned imagination."

"No. She's real. Maybe she's still here."

Claudia stood. The room spun and she sat back down.

"I talked to Megan," Derrick said. "Barry's going to be okay. Megan's taking him home."

"What about Neal? His car's here."

"She's taking him home, too. He'll pick up his car tomorrow. I told her I'd carry you home. It's on my way."

"No, it's not. Besides, I'm staying at Megan's tonight."

"Whatever. I told her I'd take you so come on. Let's bounce."

Claudia wanted to wait for Megan to come back, but she was too depressed and wasted to argue. She could barely feel her feet as they made their way down the hill to Derrick's Dodge Rampage.

Claudia and Megan had joked behind Derrick's back that his car couldn't decide if it was a sports car or a pick-up truck. The cracked fiberglass camper mounted to the truck bed added another level of confusion.

"Your car always smells like a dead rat," Claudia said as she attempted to buckle her seatbelt. She finally succeeded on the third try.

Derrick hung his hockey mask on the rear-view mirror.

"I might have hit a squirrel or something on the way here," Derrick said.

"Not just tonight. I smell it every time I get in your car. Do you keep dead animals under the seats?"

Derrick chuckled. "On the engine. They cook up nice and tender once she gets hot. Makes for good eating."

"God, you're gross. What did the police say?"

"Police?"

"About Barry's stolen car?"

"I gave them Barry's phone number. They'll call him if they find it."

Derrick turned on the radio and Guns N' Roses' "Welcome to the Jungle" blared out of the speakers. Claudia turned the heater on full blast. The air from the vents intensified the stench of rotting rodent, but she endured the smell because she was freezing. Claudia hugged herself for extra warmth and drifted off to sleep before they got to the bottom of the hill. Derrick shook her awake.

"Are we at Megan's already?" Claudia mumbled. She had a sour taste in her mouth.

Derrick reached across Claudia and unbuckled her seatbelt. Instead of pulling his hand back, he put it on her thigh. Despite being pig-eyed from sleep, Claudia could see they weren't at Megan's house. There were no houses at all. They were in a gravel parking lot next to a two-lane road. Claudia knew where they were. White Oak Park. She'd attended countless birthdays and middle school picnics in the park's pavilion. Fog hung over the grassy fields completely hiding the baseball diamond. The hairs on the back of her neck stood up as Claudia sensed she was in danger.

"Why'd you stop here?" she asked.

"Why did you think?" Derrick said, wiggling his eyebrows.

He tried to kiss her. Claudia turned her head aside. His hand snaked down between her legs. She shifted in the seat, facing the window.

"Come on," Derrick said. "You know you want it."

"No, I don't," Claudia said. "I want to go home."

He pulled her towards him while she pushed him away. He tried to kiss her again, but she ducked her head. He grabbed her breast. Pain shot through her, and she elbowed him. Derrick leaned back with his hand on his jaw. They glared at each other, then he smirked.

"You like to play rough? So do I."

Derrick climbed out and came around the front of the car. Claudia tried to lock her door before he got to it, but she was too flustered. He yanked the door open and dragged her out. The sudden movement left her head and stomach reeling. Derrick opened the hatch to the camper. He winked before taking her hand. He tried to lead her to the camper, but Claudia dug in her heels and pulled away from him.

"Stop it, Derrick," Claudia said. "This isn't funny."

Like an animal with its paw stuck in a trap, Claudia was seized by a blind panic. Escape was the only thing on her mind. She managed to twist her hand free of Derrick's grip, lost her balance, and landed on the hard asphalt.

"Please, Derrick. I don't feel good. I'm just going to walk home from here, okay?"

He stood over her and smiled crookedly.

"You don't have to play hard to get."

Claudia looked around frantically. One side of the road was the park and on the other was a thicket of woods.

"Somebody's going to see us," she said.

"Nobody comes around here this late at night. But just to be on the safe side, we're going to do it in the camper."

Derrick got behind her and dug his hands under her armpits. He lifted her to her feet, then pushed her. She stumbled toward the car. Her bunny ears fell off and were trampled underneath Derrick's boots. He tried to stuff her into the camper, but she wiggled away and ran toward the road.

"Help! Somebody please help me!"

Claudia ran on the center line, praying a car would come. She looked over her shoulder just as Derrick tackled her. She landed on her stomach with him on top of her, knocking the air out of her lungs.

She was trying to catch her breath when Derrick grabbed her hair. She screamed in pain as he forced her to her feet. She scratched at his arm as he pulled her by the hair to the car.

When they got to the camper, fear overtook Claudia and she went limp, her body like a ragdoll. She felt like she was having out of body experience watching herself from far away. Derrick struggled to lift her dead weight but managed to get her into the camper. He climbed in and yanked the hatch shut.

Often before classes, Derrick would park in the far corner of the school parking lot and the gang would climb into the camper to smoke pot. At the sound of the first class bell, the camper door would open up and they would emerge from a dense marijuana cloud. The sweet smoky smell had seeped into the fiberglass. Claudia used to savor the smell in this cramped space, but now with Derrick pressing his weight on top of her, she knew she would never again equate the camper or the smell with friends gathered for a shared high.

Derrick's hand frantically yanked and scratched at her crotch unable to understand a leotard was a one-piece outfit without a zipper. He tried to pull the fabric between her legs to one side, but the elastic was too tight.

"How about a little help?" he mumbled, his breath hot and sticky on her neck.

Claudia couldn't speak or move. She had trouble keeping her eyes open. Sleep was overtaking her, offering a type of escape when she felt something cold and solid on her neck.

"Take it off or I cut it off," Derrick said, his voice eerily calm.

He held a knife to her neck. Claudia didn't doubt for a second that he would slit her throat. Instead of prompting her into the action, the fear made her shut down even more. When it became obvious that she wasn't going to move, Derrick slipped the knife under her leotard at the crotch. The cold blade stung her skin. She heard a ripping sound and then felt cool air on her skin. With the leotard no longer an obstacle, Derrick pushed her limp legs apart.

Claudia gritted her teeth in anticipation. The boy in Destin had tried to enter her when she was dry, a painful lesson for both of them. The metallic buzz of Derrick pulling down the zipper to his coveralls seem to go on forever, but then once it stopped, nothing happened. Instead, she heard a rhythmic slapping sound. With great effort, Claudia lifted her head and peered between her legs. Derrick was hunched over, frantically pumping his flaccid penis.

"Just give me a fucking second," he said

"You can't get it up because you know you shouldn't be doing this," Claudia said.

Derrick grabbed his knife and lunged on top of Claudia. He held the sharp blade against her throat again.

"I can get a hard-on if you'd just shut the fuck up!" Derrick shouted, flecks of spit landing on her cheeks.

The stink of urine filled the camper as Claudia emptied her bladder. Urine ran down the valleys in the steel bed. Derrick pulled the machete away from her throat. She realized she'd been holding her breath and she gasped for air.

"See," Derrick grunted. "I told you I could do it!"

Claudia felt searing pain as he plunged into her. He slammed into her four times then groaned like a dying animal.

Derrick climbed out of the camper. She could hear him zipping up his coveralls and his footsteps crunching on the gravel. Something soft hit her face. It was her bunny ears. He slammed the hatch down. Moments later, the engine started, and the car began to move. Claudia's crotch was sticky with urine and sperm. Finally able to move, Claudia found an oil-stained towel and wrapped it around her waist to cover herself.

The Claudia she'd been earlier that evening, the one sat with Megan on her bedroom floor and glued cotton balls onto the backside of her leotard, that Claudia was gone. She escaped into a safe corner of her mind. The Claudia in the camper was a new person. A ruined person.

Fifteen minutes later, the car stopped. The camper hatch opened, but she couldn't see Derrick. He jumped into view. He wore his hockey mask and held his costume machete like he was about to attack. Flinching, Claudia covered her face with her hands.

"Gotcha!" he said.

Claudia waited until Derrick stepped aside before she inched her way out. They were parked outside her house. She didn't care that she had asked him to take her to Megan's house just as long as she got away from him.

The air was frigid. She was barefoot. Her shoes had come off sometime during the attack. Hugging the bunny ears to her chest, she hobbled toward her house.

"No kiss goodnight?" Derrick said from behind the mask.

She didn't dare answer. The predator had released his prey. She didn't want to do anything to make him change his mind. She heard his car drive away before she reached the front door.

CHAPTER
23

Friday, December 7, 1990

Derrick didn't see Claudia until he reached his car in the school parking lot. She sat on the hood with her backpack in her lap. She wore her R.E.M. Green World Tour T-shirt because it was her favorite, and she felt she could tackle anything when she had it on. Today, she wasn't so sure.

"We need to talk."

Five weeks had passed since the Halloween party. Claudia had avoided the gang during that time. The others figured she felt bad about kicking Barry in the nuts.

"Barry's still pissed at you," Derrick said.

"I didn't do anything," Claudia said angrily, but then she softened her tone. "How is he?"

"His dick isn't purple anymore. The doctor told him he'll have a normal sex life and have kids, but Barry acts like he's ruined forever."

"I saw his car in the parking lot. I guess the police caught whoever stole it."

"They found it behind a store in North Chattanooga with the keys in the ignition."

Claudia hugged her backpack.

"We need to talk."

"You already said that."

"I'm pregnant."

Derrick smirked. "Who knocked you up?"

"Who do you think, asshole?"

Derrick looked around the parking lot. It was a busy beehive of kids leaving for the day.

"Let's talk in the car."

"Why? So, you can rape me again?"

"Keep your voice down and get in the fucking car."

"I'm never getting in that car again as long as I live. We can talk just fine right here."

Derrick sat on the hood next to Claudia.

"You keeping it?" he asked.

"I wasn't going to considering the circumstances, but then I figured it wasn't the baby's fault how it was conceived."

"I'm glad to hear it."

Tears ran down Claudia's face. She pulled a tissue out of her backpack and blew her nose.

"Why did you do it? I thought we were friends?"

Derrick shifted his butt on the hood so that he faced Claudia.

"I like you. I mean really like you. I have for a long time, but you didn't see it because you were into Barry."

Claudia felt a wave of nausea that wasn't morning sickness.

"You have a funny way of showing it. You held a knife to my neck."

Derrick hung his head. "I'm sorry," he mumbled. "I was hurt you chose Barry over me. I got a little rough with you."

"Derrick, you assaulted me. That's more than getting a little rough."

He slid off the car and paced back and forth.

"I have a drinking problem. Okay, there I admit it. Now you know my terrible secret. I get drunk and I do stupid things."

"How can you have a drinking problem? You're only seventeen."

"Sometimes you're so naive. I started drinking when I was fourteen. I wouldn't have actually cut you. I love you, Claudia. Let's get married and raise our child together."

Claudia hopped off the hood and stared at Derrick.

"Married? Are you kidding me?"

"You're keeping the baby. I'm the father. It makes sense."

Claudia felt dizzy.

"Are you going to slit my throat if I say no?"

"I promise, Claudia. I'll never hurt you again. I'll stop drinking. I'll do everything in my power to be a good husband and father."

Claudia slung her backpack over her shoulder.

"I don't believe you."

"Then why did you tell me about the baby?"

"I wanted you to know your actions have consequences."

Claudia walked away.

CHAPTER

24

Saturday, October 4, 2008

Agnes wasn't sure who was more confused, her or the boy sitting in the booth across from her. She had been sitting by herself in a booth at the Varsity on September 6, 2008, when she was suddenly transported back to October 4, 2008. But she hadn't activated the Time Tefillin.

"How did you do that?" he asked.

A girl wearing too much make-up and too tight pants came to the table and glared at Agnes.

"Who the hell is this?" she asked the boy.

"She came out of nowhere, like a ghost."

"Ghost, my ass. I leave for five minutes to go the bathroom and come back to find you flirting with another girl."

"I wasn't flirting with her. She appeared out of thin air."

"Excuse me," Agnes said. "I have to go now."

She stumbled out of the booth. As she hurried away, she could hear the angry girlfriend cursing her confused boyfriend. Once outside the Varsity,

Agnes checked the time and date. She had returned to the exact time that she had left.

In her dorm room, she played back the video she'd recorded on her camcorder. In the video, Agnes squatted next to a concrete wall as she faced the camera.

"Transport living test subject attempt number fourteen in progress. Second report," she said. "Primary scientist has been in past now for five hours and twelve minutes. Primary scientist will observe and record her past self as she buries transport living test subject attempt number one in the ravine below my position. For details on the rodent's demise, please refer to my notes from that day. Primary scientist of September sixth is unaware I have traveled back in time to observe myself. If the experiment proceeds as planned, she will remain unaware."

The camera spun around and zoomed in on the other Agnes as she approached the ravine. Agnes paused the video and grinned. She had definite proof she had traveled to the past.

Equally important was the discovery of the seven-hour time limit. She'd been in the past conducting her experiment when at the end of seven hours, she was thrust back to her starting point. Agnes would have to plan future trips more carefully. She didn't want to suddenly appear in a stranger's booth like she did today.

Agnes stripped off the raincoat and baseball cap she'd worn for her journey, and then carefully removed the Time Tefillin from her head and arm. Taking the lid off a cardboard box, she placed the Time Tefillin inside. After putting the box under her bed, she made a cup of tea.

Enough experiments had been done to prove the Time Tefillin worked. As soon as she put together a proper presentation, time travel wouldn't be a secret anymore. First, she would show her invention to Professor Levin and then together they would share it with the scientific community. There was plenty more work to do, but first Agnes wanted to celebrate. This called for something truly special, a blatant waste of money on something deliciously decadent.

Agnes ordered a pizza.

CHAPTER

25

Friday, January 19, 2001

Agnes was working on her homework when Claudia entered her bedroom.

"How much did you get done?" Claudia asked.

"Just finished," Agnes said closing her math book.

"All of your classes?"

"Yes."

"Even English?"

Agnes nodded. Claudia sighed.

"Then what are you going to do this weekend?"

"I have the ninth-grade physics textbook my science teacher lent me," Agnes said. "I've been wanting to read it."

"Good. Come on. It's almost six.

Claudia grabbed the pink duffel bag sitting on Agnes' bed. They'd packed it together the night before with clothes, toiletries, books, note-books, pens, juice boxes, granola bars, fruit, her stuffed animal, Ethel Owl, and a mobile phone. It was a ritual they'd been doing for years. They used to pack for every other weekend, but Derrick decided he was too busy and cut the visits to once a month.

They went to the living room. Claudia dropped the duffel bag by the door and handed Agnes two twenty-dollar-bills folded together.

"In case of emergency," Claudia said. "Hide it or he'll take it."

Agnes handed the money back.

"I still have the money you gave me last time. I hid it in my shoe."

They sat on the sofa. In her head, Claudia scolded herself again. She should have known Derrick would sue for visitation rights. Not because he was eager to be part of Agnes' life but so he could continue to exert control on Claudia's life. Since she'd never reported the rape, she couldn't claim he was unfit to see his daughter.

Claudia looked at her watch. "He's late. As usual."

"Maybe he won't make it this weekend," Agnes said.

"We should be so lucky."

As they waited, day crossed into night. Streetlights came to life. The HVAC hummed as warm air blew through the vents. There was a lingering scent of spaghetti and meat sauce they had for dinner the night before. Agnes took the physics textbook out of her duffel bag and Claudia turned on the TV.

Derrick arrived at 6:45 p.m. Claudia opened the door, and he blew in smelling of cold air and body odor. He wore a Carhartt coat over oil-stained coveralls.

"Hey, sport," Derrick said, ruffling Agnes' hair. "Ready for a super fun weekend with your dad?"

"I guess," Agnes said.

"She's not going anywhere until I smell your breath," Claudia said.

Derrick glared at Claudia.

"I'm not doing it this time."

"Let me smell your breath or Agnes stays home this weekend."

"I'm telling you I haven't had a drop all day."

"Do it."

Derrick opened his mouth wide and exhaled into Claudia's face. She grimaced and waved her hand. Derrick laughed.

"I ate a slice of pizza with extra onions and garlic."

Claudia helped Agnes into her coat and knit cap. Agnes slipped on her gloves. Derrick lifted Agnes' duffel bag and pretended it was super heavy. "Did you pack everything you own?" Derrick asked. "Maybe you want to live with Daddy permanently because I'm more fun than Mommy."

Agnes didn't respond. Claudia knelt and hugged her tightly. Agnes felt a twinge of guilt that she enjoyed the look of worry and longing on her mother's face.

"I'll miss you," Claudia said.

"Geez," Derrick said. "She'll only be gone a couple of days."

Claudia stood and faced Derrick.

"Bring her home on time."

"Don't I always?"

No, he didn't always bring Agnes back home by six on Sunday, but Claudia didn't say anything. She and Agnes had learned the hard way that saying anything negative would set him off on a defensive tirade.

"Okay," Derrick said. "Let's get this show on the road."

He leaned in to kiss Claudia goodbye, but she pushed him away. Grumbling, Derrick barreled out the door with Agnes following him. Opening the trunk of his car, he tossed Agnes' duffel bag inside. He got behind the wheel and started the car. Agnes tried the passenger door. It was locked. She knocked on the window. Derrick unlocked the door and put the car in gear at the same time. As Agnes reached for the door, he lurched forward. She chased the car and when it stopped, she tried again. Derrick lurched forward again. Agnes could hear him laughing inside the car.

On her third attempt, Derrick kept the car still, and Agnes was able to get in. He roared down the road before she could get her seatbelt on. The car smelled of cigarettes, beer, and intestinal gas. Empty beer cans rattled across the back seat floorboard.

"Claudia talk about me?" Derrick asked.

"No," Agnes said.

"Don't lie to me. What'd she say?"

"Nothing."

"She's been badmouthing me, hasn't she?"

The heater in the car blew out lukewarm air. Agnes zipped up her coat.

"I think Mom avoids talking about you. You're not exactly her favorite subject."

Derrick let that sink in.

"She'd better not badmouth me. Part of the joint custody agreement states that I have the right to be free of unwarranted derogatory remarks. That means it's against the law for her to badmouth me."

"You are aware that it works both ways," Agnes said.

"What's that supposed to mean?"

"Mom has the right to be free of unwarranted derogatory remarks from you."

Derrick almost ran a stop light, slamming on the brakes at the last second. Agnes lurked forward.

"Did you tell her I said something?" Derrick asked. "Because if you did, you're in big trouble, little lady."

"I didn't say anything," Agnes said.

"Better not. Because if you did, it was a lie. And you shouldn't lie."

Derrick lived in a two-story apartment building built in 1974 on the side of a steep hill. One side had a pleasant view of Red Bank. The other side faced the ranch houses across the street. Derrick's two-bedroom apartment was on the ranch house side.

When they got to the door of Derrick's apartment, he flipped through the keys on his key ring.

"I can't find the key to the apartment. Looks like we're going to have to sleep in the woods tonight. Hope no bears eat us."

"Or we could stay in a hotel," Agnes said.

"I can't afford no hotel. Maybe we should go back to Claudia's."

"Okay. Take me home and you can sleep in the woods."

Derrick held up a key.

"Here it is."

He unlocked the door. The smell of cigarettes and beer was heavier in the apartment than in his car. Derrick walked past his bedroom and dropped Agnes' duffel bag on a single bed in the second bedroom. The bed was against the wall opposite a curtain-less window. Next to the bed was an old dresser. In the center of the room was a Bowflex exercise machine with Derrick's dirty laundry draped on it.

As Agnes put her clothes into the dresser, Derrick went to his bedroom and slammed the door. He was still in there when Agnes finished unpacking.

She went to the kitchen and turned on the light, causing the roaches to scatter. On the counter was a box of cereal, an off-brand Agnes had never seen before. The freezer contained stacks of frozen dinners. In the refrigerator, she found Muscle Milk, half a block of Velveeta cheese, a pizza box containing one mummified slice of pizza, a carton of milk, and a twelve pack of Pabst Blue Ribbon tall boy beers. Agnes opened the spout to the milk carton, sniffed, and grimaced. Emptying the carton into the sink, globs of spoiled milk poured out. She washed it down the drain and tossed the carton into the garbage can which wasn't full for once.

Derrick came out of the bedroom. He had changed from his coveralls to sweatpants and a sweater.

"You hungry?" he asked.

"Yes," Agnes said.

Derrick peered into the freezer.

"What's your poison? I got chicken, steak, or turkey."

"Turkey," Agnes said.

Derrick took two frozen dinners from the freezer, roast turkey with dressing and Salisbury Steak, removed them from the cardboard box, and placed them into a microwave crusted with spills from past meals. As the dinners rotated, Derrick set up two TV trays in the living room, one in front of an ugly orange loveseat and the other in front of a pea green recliner with strips of duct tape to cover the tears.

Agnes wasn't surprised Derrick didn't have napkins but was impressed he had more than one roll of paper towels. She tore off two sheets, folded them, and put one on each tray. She washed and dried two forks and two knives and put them on top of the folded sheets.

Agnes didn't like to watch TV when she ate. She rarely watched TV at all, but Derrick expected her to eat her meals with him and he always ate in front of the TV. He owned a dining room table but used it as a storage shelf for cigarette cartons, toilet paper, jumbo bags of chips, and cases of soda.

The microwave dinged. Derrick used a ratty dish towel to protect his hands as he carried the dinners to the trays. He opened the refrigerator and got his first tall boy of the night.

"Where's the milk?" Derrick asked.

"It was spoiled," Agnes said. "I threw it out."

"Then what the hell are you going to drink with dinner?"

Agnes wrinkled her nose. Milk with dinner was something parents gave little kids.

"I'll drink water."

"Suit yourself."

Derrick popped open the beer and drank deeply. He sighed contentedly. Agnes knew from experience that he would consume the entire twelve pack tonight without showing any signs of inebriation. After he finished the beer, he would start drinking something harder like whiskey or gin. That was when he would become noticeably drunk. At the end of the evening, he would either stumble to bed or pass out in his easy chair. If he fell asleep in the chair, Agnes made sure he wasn't holding a lit cigarette.

Derrick plopped into the recliner and pressed the TV remote. He flipped through the channels until he found a fishing show. With his attention of the screen, he shoveled food into his mouth in between sips of beer. Though steam rose from Agnes' roast turkey with dressing dinner, the turkey was half frozen. She picked around it.

After Derrick ate the last bit of Salisbury Steak, he lit up a cigarette and used the dinner's plastic container as an ash tray. When he tapped his cigarette, the ashes landed with a hiss in the leftover brown sauce.

Agnes stood to carry her plastic container to the garbage can.

"While you're up, get your old man a beer," Derrick said.

She threw away her container with the frozen turkey then got Derrick a beer. The fishing show had ended, and he was watching a game show where people faced their worst fears for cash prizes. Agnes considered the show voluntary torture and couldn't understand why anyone would agree to participate. Still hungry, she went to her room and got a granola bar and a juice box along with the ninth-grade physics textbook.

After moving sodas and chips aside to make space for herself on the dining room table, Agnes read the textbook while eating her granola bar.

"What are you doing in there?" Derrick called.

"I was still hungry, so I made myself a snack," Agnes called back.

"Why aren't you in here?"

"I want to read my book."

"You'd rather read a book than watch TV with your old man?"

"I did watch TV with you. Now I'm reading a book."

Derrick didn't respond. He watched TV and Agnes read. She was so engrossed reading about the basic principles of physics that she didn't notice when he walked past her on the way to get another beer. The sound of him popping open his beer caught her attention. Looking up, she saw him leaning against the doorway between the kitchen and the dining room.

"You're always reading books," Derrick said before taking a long sip of beer.

"I like to read," Agnes said.

"You think reading books makes you better than other people? Better than me?"

"No. I just like to read."

Derrick snatched the textbook before Agnes could react. Fear spiked in her. The principal had trusted it with her. She'd get in trouble if something happened to it.

"What are you reading that's so damn interesting?" Derrick said, peering at the cover. "Physicals? Aren't you too young to be reading about sex?" Agnes tried to grab the book back from Derrick. He held it too high for her to reach.

"Not physical," Agnes said. "Physics. It's a science book."

"Reading a science book didn't keep you out of trouble," Derrick said, grinning. "Thought I didn't know about you getting suspended for a week, didn't you?"

Agnes lunged for the book again, but Derrick kept it away from her. "How did you find out?" Agnes asked.

She didn't think Claudia told him. Claudia wouldn't think it was any of his business.

"School called me," Derrick said. "Asked me to come in, but I was too busy. Told them Claudia could stand in for me. This time."

Agnes should have known the school would have called both parents.

"What'd you get in trouble for?" Derrick asked.

"Didn't the school tell you?"

"I want you to say it."

Agnes figured the school had told Derrick, but he'd forgotten.

"I set a trap in a boy's locker so that when he opened the door, he got hit in the face with a water balloon," Agnes said.

"That's it?" Derrick asked.

"The water balloon was also a stink bomb. For two weeks, he smelled like rotten eggs."

Derrick chuckled.

"Not bad. Sounds like something I would do. Why this particular boy?"

Agnes clenched her fists and glared at Derrick.

"His name is Trey Dobbs. He's a bully. He kept picking on me and the school wouldn't do anything to stop him."

"You must have done something to make him angry," Derrick said.

"I didn't do anything. He pushed me around because I was smaller and weaker than him. But I was smarter. He doesn't bother me anymore."

Derrick glared at Agnes.

"Sounds to me like you're the bully," he said. "One week suspension wasn't enough punishment. You still haven't learned your lesson."

Agnes paled.

"What are you going to do?"

Derrick stormed into the bathroom. Agnes chased after him. The lid on the toilet was up. He held the textbook over the bowl.

"Don't do it!" Agnes pleaded. "It's not my book. It belongs to the school."

"You should have thought of that earlier," Derrick said.

He dropped the book into the toilet. It landed with a splash. Agnes reached for it. Derrick slammed the lid down, just missing her fingers. He carried her out of the bathroom, shut the door, and locked it. Agnes banged on the door. Then she heard the toilet flush. She imagined the book spiraling down the drain and the disappointment on Principal Milligan's face when she told him she'd lost the book. He would never trust her again. Agnes stood helpless outside the bathroom and sobbed. She hated crying. Derrick came out, went to the dining room for the tallboy he'd been drinking. Agnes rushed into the bathroom and pulled the soaked book out of the toilet. The pages were already beginning to warp. Not only would she get into trouble for ruining the book, now she had nothing to read. Holding the dripping book in her hands, she stood outside the living room. Derrick had settled back into the recliner.

"Why did you do it?" Agnes asked.

Derrick shook his finger at her.

"I wanted you to know your actions have consequences."

CHAPTER
26

Sunday, October 26, 2008

Claudia started her car and turned the heater on full blast, glancing in the rear-view mirror at the closed garage door before switching on the radio.

"Good morning!" shouted the deejay. "Our classic rock weekend continues with another thirty minutes of uninterrupted music from your favorite classic rock artists. Let's kick this Sunday off with thirty minutes of R.E.M."

The opening chords of "Talk About the Passion" played through the car's speakers. Claudia loved too many R.E.M. songs to have a favorite, but she was rather fond of this one. She agreed with Michael Stipe that not everyone could carry the weight of the world. She could barely carry herself. Claudia shut her eyes and let the music sooth her.

CHAPTER
27

Monday, October 27, 2008

Agnes forced herself to remain calm as she set up the conference room for her presentation. She couldn't wait to see the look on Professor Levin's face when she explained to him time travel was not only possible but was a reality. At first, he wouldn't believe her but then she would show him the videos of her successful time travel experiments.

She hooked her computer up to the overhead projector and tested the video playback. She kept the Time Tefillin in a box, so she could dramatically reveal it at the end of the presentation. Everything was ready. Agnes checked the time. Professor Levin was running late. That was so unlike him. How could he be late today of all days? It was her fault. Because she wanted the invention to be a surprise, she hadn't made Levin aware of the historic importance of her presentation.

Agnes sat at the table with her computer in front of her and waited. The room was too warm and smelled like artificial pine trees because of the cleaner they used on the floors.

Professor Levin entered the room. Agnes grinned, but then she saw he wasn't alone. Megan Wallace was with him. Her eyes were watery. Alarm bells went off in Agnes' head. She calculated the possibilities of why she was here without Claudia and all of them ended with something that couldn't be fixed.

Megan held out her arms. "Come here," she said.

Tears filled Agnes' eyes as they hugged.

"Is she hurt or is she dead?" Agnes asked.

"I'm so sorry, Agnes. Claudia's dead."

Megan held Agnes as she sobbed.

"The police tried to call you," Megan said. "When they couldn't reach you, they got my number on Claudia's phone."

"How did it happen?" Agnes asked

"She was found in the garage with the car running and the garage door closed. The cause of death was carbon monoxide poisoning."

Agnes couldn't believe it. Claudia would never leave her alone.

"I'm sorry," Professor Levin said.

"The police tried to call me?" Agnes said. "I never got the call."

She rummaged in her backpack and took out her phone. It was off. She had turned it off during the weekend, so she could concentrate on getting her presentation ready. Agnes turned the phone on. There were two messages from an unknown number, three from Megan, and one from Claudia. She listened to Claudia's message.

"Agnes, it's Mom. I miss you. Call me when you get this message. Love you."

Agnes put her hand over her mouth. Not only had she lost her mother, she'd lost her last chance to talk to her.

"I came to take you home," Megan said. "I'll help you pack."

Agnes ripped the connection out between her computer and the overhead projector. She stuffed the computer into her backpack and crammed the box holding the Time Tefillin in next to it. At this moment, she hated her invention. If only she hadn't been so obsessed with this damn thing, she wouldn't have missed Claudia's call.

Levin walked Megan and Agnes out of the building.

"Take as much time as you need," he said. "If you need anything let me know."

Agnes gave Levin a quick hug.

"I'm sorry I wasn't able to do my presentation, Professor Levin, but history will have to wait."

CHAPTER

28

Saturday, November 1, 2008

The Fellowship Hall at Red Bank United Methodist Church always smelled like vinegar to Agnes. Maybe the cleaning staff used vinegar to clean the large room or maybe the cooks in the attached kitchen used tons of it to cut through their mayonnaise-heavy dishes.

Claudia's friends and co-workers hugged Agnes as if they were related to her. Everybody told her how sorry they were for her loss. Those who had lost a mother said the pain was like a hole in the heart that never heals. The reverend's sermon got positive reviews from the mourners. The response to the musicians who sang the R.E.M. song "I'll Take the Rain" was more mixed.

Agnes was especially pleased to see Denise. She'd worked with Claudia at Wendy's for many years and the two of them had been close. Denise hugged Agnes tightly.

"If you're not having Claudia buried, then where is she?" Denise asked.

"She's in a box in the living room at home," Agnes said.

Denise's eyes widened, and she looked sick.

"Claudia wanted to be cremated," Agnes explained. "She said it would be cheaper. If you don't provide an urn, the crematorium puts the remains in a cardboard box. Claudia would be furious if I bought an expensive urn."

"Yeah, but she can't stay in a box. I'll take up a collection at work and see about getting Claudia a nice urn."

Megan came with her husband, Steven, but thankfully didn't bring their three boys. Neal came all the way from New Orleans with his wife, Susan. Barry came with his fiancé, Lucy, a dumpy woman who reminded Agnes of her lab animal Ms. Rat. They were Claudia's closest friends and sat together at the same table.

Mourners ate and talked. Agnes drifted from conversation to conversation, answered questions with as few words as possible, listened politely, and then moved on to the next group that pulled her into their small circle.

After leaving a circle of Wendy's employees, Agnes heard someone say, "What is he doing here?" She knew without seeing him who they meant. Her stomach clenched with dread. Derrick staggered through the crowd. What hair he had left stuck out in all directions. The suit he wore looked like he'd slept in it. He probably had. Sobbing loudly, he tried to hug people only to have them duck under his arms or push him away.

"She was the love of my life," Derrick wailed. "But I messed up and lost her. I thought someday we'd get back together, but now that's never going to happen."

He found the beverage table and filled half a cup with iced tea. Making no effort to hide his actions, he took a flask from his jacket pocket and filled the glass to the rim. Taking a healthy gulp, Derrick made an unsteady beeline for Claudia's friends and collapsed in a chair beside Barry. Agnes maneuvered through the crowd so that she could listen to their conversation.

"Glad to see the gang's all here," Derrick said. "Can't believe it took Claudia dying to get us together."

"We've gotten together many times before now," Megan said.

"Really? I don't remember being invited?"

"That's because we didn't invite you," Neal said.

Derrick glared at Neal. "Why the hell not?"

"We had to choose between you and Claudia." Megan said. "It wasn't much of a contest."

Derrick took a big gulp and shuddered.

"Well, now you can invite me. Claudia is gone, God bless her. I can't believe she did herself in. I didn't think she had the balls to do it."

"Killing yourself doesn't take balls," Steven said. "Suicide is a coward's way out."

Megan nudged her husband and shook her head to indicate she didn't care for his assessment of Claudia.

"Claudia wasn't a coward," Neal said. "She was one of the strongest people I know."

Neal stared at his hands. His wife, Susan, rubbed his shoulder.

"I think she couldn't live with the guilt anymore," Barry said.

Agnes didn't know much about Barry. Claudia hardly ever mentioned him and whenever the group got together, he and Claudia were cordial to each other, but there was obviously tension between them.

"Claudia didn't have anything to feel guilty about," Megan said.

"Really? You don't think she felt guilty for ruining my life?"

Megan groaned. "Come on, Barry. She didn't ruin your life."

"You can't begin to understand what I went through. In college, I had the ultimate babe magnet car. Hot girls threw themselves at me. But every time I was alone with a girl, I freaked out. Claudia scarred me for life. It took years of therapy before I could be intimate with a woman."

Lucy took Barry's hand and smiled sadly at him.

"She swore it wasn't her," Neal said. "I didn't believe her at the time, but she never changed her story. I think she might have been telling the truth."

"You really cared about her, didn't you?" Susan said.

Neal blushed. "She was one of my best friends. Of course, I cared about her. There's no reason to be jealous."

"I'm not jealous. Should I be jealous?"

Neal patted Susan's knee. "No. To be perfectly honest, all the guys had a crush on Claudia."

"Tell me about it," Megan said. "I loved Claudia, but when we were around guys, it was like I wasn't there."

Derrick leaned over and leered at Susan.

"And all these guys are jealous of me because I'm the one Claudia wanted to be with."

Susan recoiled from his boozy breath.

"You sure about that?" Megan asked.

"It's why she attacked Barry," Derrick said. "He put the move on her, and she didn't want nothing to do with him, because she was saving herself for me."

"That is not at all what she told me."

"Well, it's the truth."

"If Claudia loved you so much, then why wouldn't she marry you?" Neal asked. "I know you asked."

Derrick downed the remainder of his drink and crushed the plastic cup in his hand.

"She never said how much she loved me because she was a liar! She was always spreading lies about me even though part of our joint custody agreement was she wasn't supposed to say derogatory things about me."

Megan sprang to her feet and threw her lemonade in Derrick's face.

"How dare you!" she said. "Telling lies about her at her own funeral. It's like you're raping her all over again."

Everyone stood still as statues as Megan's words sank in. They didn't notice Agnes had joined them until she spoke.

"What did you mean by that?" Agnes asked. "Did Derrick rape Claudia? Is that how I was conceived?"

Megan's lower lip trembled. "I'm sorry, honey. I didn't mean for that to come out."

"It makes sense. There didn't seem to be any chemistry between Mom and Derrick. In fact, she always acted like he made her flesh crawl. I don't know why I never guessed. The only way she would have had sex with him was if he physically forced her."

"I'm sorry you found out this way."

"It's okay. In fact, it's a relief. I used to feel bad I didn't love my father."

Derrick got out of his chair, tottered, and grabbed the chair to keep from falling. He used his sleeve to wipe Megan's drink off his face.

"I didn't rape Claudia!" Derrick shouted. "I didn't make her to do anything she didn't want to do."

People turned and stared at him. The reverend made his way over to the table.

"Is that an admission you forced my mother to have intercourse?" Agnes asked.

"Don't start with me, little lady. I'm still your father."

Red splotches had bloomed on Derrick's face, and he shook his finger at her. When Agnes was younger, that finger and the threat it carried frightened her. He never hit her and as far as she knew, he never hit Claudia, but the potential violence was always there just below the surface, ready to erupt. But looking at him now as an aging alcoholic who had never shown any inclination to improve his lot in life, she almost felt pity for him.

"Sadly, it's true," Agnes said. "You are still my father. I think everyone here will agree that you've caused enough suffering for one day. Please leave."

"She's right," the reverend said. "You should leave."

Derrick positioned himself in front of Agnes. He grabbed her arm and squeezed. She ignored the pain.

"Don't make me do something you'll regret," Derrick said.

Neal and Steven moved behind Derrick.

"Is this the only way you can get a woman to do what you want?" Agnes asked. "By physical intimidation?"

Derrick was oblivious of the concerned men circling him. His focus was entirely on Agnes.

"I only use force when they give me no other choice."

"How many times did you want to hit me, but Mom stood in the way?"

"More times than you can ever imagine."

"The feelings mutual. Does it make you happy that I hate you?"

Derrick let go of her arm. Agnes rubbed where he held her.

"All I ever wanted was for you and Claudia to understand how much I love both of you." Derrick said.

"Then prove it," Agnes said. "Leave. Now."

Derrick flinched as if she had struck him. He hung his head. He started to leave and found himself face to face with the reverend. He turned and pushed past Neal and Steven.

"What an asshole."

Everyone spun around to see who had spoken. It was Barry's fiancé, Lucy. She'd been so quiet Agnes had wondered if the woman was capable of speech.

CHAPTER
29

Saturday, December 6, 2008

Barry took a bite of his sandwich and nodded as he looked around the restaurant.

"I like this place," he said. "Decent food, nice atmosphere. Good choice, Agnes."

Agnes ordered a small pizza and regretted it. She had smelled rich tomato sauce when they had walked in and was fooled into believing that meant good pizza.

The restaurant was a scruffy, hipster place in Chattanooga's trendy North Shore. Barry had picked a table by the front window, so he could watch the tourists shopping for Christmas gifts. Agnes found the constant parade of people distracting. They were close to the entrance so whenever someone opened the door, a gust of chilly wind whipped around her legs.

"Thank you for meeting with me," she said. "I hope Lucy doesn't mind I didn't invite her along. I wanted to have a private conversation with you."

Barry stuffed potato chips into his mouth. "She's cool. She doesn't get jealous." He crunched loudly before swallowing the chips. "Not that there's anything to be jealous about. I mean I'm old enough to be your father, and we're just having lunch."

Agnes stared at him blankly and wished he didn't talk with his mouth full.

"That was a pretty crazy scene at Claudia's funeral," Barry said. "Have you talked to Derrick since then?"

"He hired a lawyer. He claims he has the right to full custody of me now that Claudia's deceased."

Barry stopped eating his sandwich in mid-bite and dropped it on his plate.

"You're kidding me?"

"What he really wants is Claudia's house, which I inherited."

"Can he really do it?"

"He's the surviving parent. But Derrick is an alcoholic. He can't hold down a job, which means he won't be able to afford to pay the mortgage on the house."

"I don't get it. Why does he want the house if he can't afford it?"

"Isn't it obvious?" Agnes asked. "He wants to sell it."

"Then what happens to you?"

Agnes took a deep breath.

"Claudia was the responsible parent and now that she's gone, I'm on my own."

"Is that why you asked me to have lunch with you?" Barry asked. "For money? I'd help you if I could, but I'm barely getting by myself."

"That's not why I asked you to meet me." Agnes took a notebook out of her backpack and opened it to a clean page. She took out a pen and held it ready. "Do you mind if we begin?"

Barry finished his beer. "This looks serious. I better get another beer."

Agnes waited while he flagged down the waitress. Barry was a handsome man. Agnes could understand why Claudia was attracted to him when they were in high school. Claudia was lucky they didn't have a long-term relationship. Barry wasn't a complete dullard, but he wasn't very interesting. Claudia would have tired of him quickly.

The waitress brought Barry another beer and refilled Agnes' glass of iced tea. Barry took a swig of his beer and then picked up his sandwich.

"Okay," he said, taking a big bite. "What did you want to see me about?"

"I want to ask you some questions about the Halloween party you and Claudia attended on October 27, 1990."

Barry choked on his sandwich and sipped his beer to clear his throat. "I can't talk about that," he said. "I spent years in therapy trying to forget that night."

Agnes wondered how much of the time with the therapist was for dealing with his trauma and how much was simply dedicated to his ego. She sipped her tea and dapped at her lips with her napkin.

"Can you at least try? If I ask something too painful, we can skip the question and move on to the next one."

"Why do you want to know about that night?"

Agnes had anticipated this question and had come up with a variety of reasons other than the truth. She tried the false reason she felt would appeal to Barry's ego.

"I can't accept Claudia chose Derrick over you until I find out exactly what happened that night."

Barry sipped his beer and stared out the window. The sun was bright and sharp. There was a feeling in the air that winter would arrive soon. A minute passed and Agnes worried that Barry would get up and leave at any moment.

"Let me think about it," he said.

For the next half hour Barry talked about Lucy, their upcoming wedding, and college football. Agnes pretended to be interested while she bounced her leg impatiently under the table.

They finished eating. The waitress cleared their plates and brought the check. Barry didn't try to stop Agnes from paying. She was annoyed. Not at his lack of chivalry. After all, she had invited him. She was miffed she had bought him lunch and didn't get any information.

But then, he surprised her.

"Are you sure you want to hear about that night? You're going to hear some awful things about Claudia. It might be more than you can handle."

Agnes resisted the urge to roll her eyes. "Yes, I'm sure."

"Ask your questions."

Agnes held her pen over her notebook.

"How exactly did Claudia attack you?"

"She hit me with a pool cue." Barry leaned forward and lowered his voice. "In a very personal area. Very personal."

"Were you playing pool?"

"No. We were in a bedroom."

"Why was there a pool cue in the bedroom?"

Barry picked at the label on his beer bottle.

"I don't know. There was a pool table in the basement, but we were on the second floor. We didn't bring it with us. I guess Allan's dad put it in the bedroom."

"Who is Allan?"

Barry explained that a Red Bank High School classmate named Allan had the party at his house while his parents were out of town.

"Claudia asked me to help her find a bathroom. We weren't supposed to go into Allan's parents' bedroom, but it had its own bathroom. There was a line for all the other bathrooms in the house."

"Why did Claudia ask you to escort her? Wouldn't it have made more sense for her to go with Megan?"

"Everybody knew Claudia had a crush on me. She wanted to be alone with me."

"Do you think she wanted to have sex with you?"

Barry hesitated before answering.

"She did, but then she changed her mind. She could have just told me. I wouldn't have tried anything. She didn't have to ruin my life."

The last sentence came out loudly. Barry caught himself and glanced around the room to make sure nobody had noticed.

"I'm sorry," he said. "I told you that you were going to hear some awful things about your mother."

"It's okay. I really appreciate this," Agnes said as she scribbled down notes and flipped to a new page. "Let's talk about something else. It's my understanding you and Derrick were close friends in high school. Are you still close friends?"

"We were best friends, but we've drifted apart over the years."

"Did he talk to you about taking Claudia home from the party?"

"Not just me. He bragged about it to everybody."

"What did he say?"

Barry squirmed in his seat.

"It's kind of graphic. I'm not sure I should repeat it."

"I may only be seventeen, but I am a very mature seventeen."

"Really? So, you've already had sex and all that?"

"No. I'm a virgin. But I understand how the human body works."

Barry shrugged.

"This is the story Derrick told everybody at school. After Megan and Neal took me to the hospital, he and Claudia stayed at the party and got shit-faced. Sometime after midnight, Claudia asked Derrick to drive her home. She was supposed to wait for Megan to come back and pick her up, but she begged Derrick to take her."

Agnes wrote down "after midnight" and underlined it.

"Do you know if Megan returned to the party?" Agnes asked.

"Yeah. After my parents took me home from the hospital, Megan drove back to Allan's to get Claudia and to drop off Neal. He had driven his car to the party. Megan couldn't understand why Claudia had left."

"Meanwhile, Derrick has driven Claudia home?"

"Well, not straight home. Derrick said that as soon as they got in his car, Claudia came on to him hot and heavy. She rubbed on him and said she wanted to do all kinds of crazy sex stuff to him. Derrick was like sure. Who wouldn't want to make it with Claudia Cook? She suggested they stop at White Oak Park, so Derrick drove to the park. Derrick's car had this crappy camper on the back. We used to smoke dope in the camper before school in the morning. Man, I used to be so baked when I went to class."

"That's fascinating, but let's get back to the park that night."

Barry nodded.

"Derrick said Claudia dragged him into the camper, stripped her clothes off, and pulled his pants down. He said he had no choice but to do her."

Agnes remembered when she was around six or seven a classmate invited her to a birthday party at White Oak Park. Claudia wouldn't let Agnes go. Agnes didn't think much about it at the time because she didn't like going to birthday parties. The kids in her class were boring, especially at birthday parties. All they wanted to do was run in circles and eat cake. Now Agnes understood why Claudia wouldn't let her go. The ground at White Oak Park was cursed. Evil things took place there.

"This makes me so angry," Agnes said. She bore down on the pen so hard it tore through the page.

"I warned you it was graphic."

"Derrick's story is an absurd boy's fantasy. What makes me furious is that by spreading those lies, he in essence assaulted Claudia again."

Barry peeled the label off his beer and crumpled it up into a soggy ball. "I didn't know Derrick raped Claudia until Megan told us at the funeral. Megan wouldn't lie about something like that."

"That's true. Megan wouldn't lie."

"I don't understand why Claudia kept it a secret."

Agnes realized Barry was a victim in this situation as well. When Derrick told Barry his fabricated story, he wasn't just covering his crime. He wanted to hurt Barry by bragging he had gotten Claudia instead of Barry. Derrick had to hurt people, especially those closest to him, to alleviate his own pain. Agnes almost felt pity for him.

"There was a girl in my dorm who was raped," Agnes said. "At first, nobody believed her. Eventually, it went to court. The judge let the boy who raped her go free because in the judge's words it would have ruined his life. No one considered how it ruined the girl's life. I can understand why Mom never said anything."

"Yeah. Something like that happened when I was in college," Barry

said.

Agnes turned to a new page in her notebook.

"What else do you remember about the Halloween party?"

"Somebody stole my car," Barry said.

"That's unfortunate. Is it because you left your car at Allan's house overnight?"

"No. They stole it before I left the party. My dad gave me this awesome cherry red Trans Am as an early graduation present. I parked it in Allan's driveway. When Derrick and Neal helped me out of the house, I saw someone had taken it."

Agnes wrote down "red Trans Am" and underlined it.

"The car was stolen while you were inside at the party. That's very interesting. Did the police ever find the car?"

"Yeah. The next day. It was in the parking lot of a store a block that way." Barry pointed out the window.

Agnes knew the store. It was an art supply store directly across the street from the Walnut Street Bridge. She wrote "Art supply store parking lot."

"You were lucky," Agnes said.

"I sure was. They left the keys in the ignition and the door unlocked. But that's not the weird part. The police found a pool cue in the back seat. That really freaked me out, you know, for obvious reasons."

Agnes couldn't help it. She rolled her eyes.

"Barry, did it ever occur to you that the pool cue in your car was the weapon used to attack you?"

Barry's forehead knitted as he thought it over.

"I suppose. After she hit me, Claudia went downstairs to get the other guys to help me. She could have put the pool cue in my car first. You know that makes sense. She hid the pool cue in my car."

"In your car? That was probably already gone by then."

"I don't know if it was gone. Claudia could have given the stick to whoever stole the car."

"That would suggest she and an accomplice planned the attack in advance."

Barry stared out the window. Agnes could see that reasoning on this level was an extreme challenge for him.

"Yeah, you're right," he said. "She probably didn't put it in my car."

"Haven't you ever thought about this before? In all those years of therapy, the pool cue in your car never came up? Your therapist never talked about it?"

"We talked about my dad more than anything else."

Agnes wrote down "Barry equals idiot. Barry equals passive. He would have avoided fatherhood. Must be a factor for why he was eliminated."

"I have a very difficult question to ask you," Agnes said. "But it's extremely important to me you try to answer it."

"Okay," Barry said as he sunk back into the booth.

"Describe how it happened."

"How what happened?"

"You know. In the bedroom. That Halloween night."

Barry took a dramatic deep breath. Agnes realized he was enjoying this. He was getting a free therapy session that included lunch.

"Claudia went into the bathroom. She told me to put out the lights and wait for her. I put out the lights. I was standing in the bedroom with my back to the bathroom door when I heard her say my name. I turned around and saw her holding the pool cue. And then she hit me. I fell on the floor. I don't remember much after that because I was in so much pain."

"Where were your car keys?"

"In my hand. No, I dropped them."

"Are you sure it was Claudia who hit you? The lights were off. The room was dark. Whoever hit you probably took your car keys, and we know Claudia didn't drive off in your car."

Barry gritted his teeth as he thought about what Agnes had said. She was sure it wasn't the two beers he drank that kept him from coming to the logical conclusion someone other than Claudia attacked him. Besides, it wasn't something Claudia would have done. She was never afraid to speak her mind. If she decided not to have sex with Barry, she would have said so. Someone else attacked Barry with a pool cue and Agnes was almost certain she had figured out the identity of the assailant.

"It had to have been Claudia," Barry said.

"What makes you so sure?" Agnes asked.

"Bunny ears."

"Bunny ears?"

"Claudia was dressed as a rabbit. She wore these fluffy white bunny ears." Barry held his forefingers on either side of his head and wiggled them. "Even in the dark I could see them."

Agnes smiled as she wrote "bunny ears" and underlined it twice. What a clever detail. It was the kind of detail she would have come up with.

"Okay, Barry. One last thing. Do I sound like Claudia?"

Barry rubbed his chin.

"A little bit. You talk the same way she did, but your voice is higher."

"I would like to try an experiment. I want you to close your eyes and I'm going to say your name."

Barry laughed. "You're going to do what?"

"Say your name."

"Okay, that's weird. This whole lunch has been weird, but that's the weirdest. I can't wait to tell Lucy about this."

"Feel free to tell Lucy whatever you like, but let's do my experiment. Close your eyes."

Barry closed his eyes.

Agnes spoke in a clear voice, not a shout nor a whisper. "Barry," she said.

Barry gasped and clutched his stomach. He opened his eyes and stared at Agnes like a rabbit caught in a trap.

"You sound more like Claudia than I realized," he said.

Agnes wrote down, "I am certain beyond all doubt I'm not the first."

CHAPTER
30

Wednesday, December 24, 2008

Agnes stood in the doorway between the kitchen and the dining room. In the kitchen was the phone mounted to the wall by the refrigerator. On the dining room table was the box containing the Time Tefillin. Agnes checked the time. It was 10:45 p.m. She was convinced an Agnes before her had time traveled back to the night her parents created her and stopped them from having intercourse. This had reset her timeline but probably not in the way she anticipated.

To figure out how the "first" Agnes had accomplished this, Agnes considered how she would have done it. She would have chosen a time and location where there was the least chance of anyone seeing her disappear in 2008 and reappear in 1990. And vice versa.

By her calculations, the most optimal time and place in 2008 was some time before midnight on Christmas Eve. Deciding the location for the time skip was easier. It would need to be somewhere where there was no chance of anyone seeing her leaving or arriving. Many locations would work, but it had to be the Walnut Street Bridge. It was Agnes and Claudia's favorite place.

If the phone didn't ring by midnight, it meant her theory about a first Agnes was incorrect and she would proceed with her plan to travel back to 1990. She was going to stop Derrick from raping Claudia. By Agnes' logic, Claudia wouldn't have committed suicide if Derrick hadn't assaulted her. Raising a child as a single mother would have been difficult enough, but Derrick had made it unbearable by forcing his way into their lives.

The phone rang. Agnes answered on the first ring.

"Hello?"

"Merry Christmas!"

Agnes groaned.

"Derrick, I don't have time to talk to you."

"I'm your father. Make time."

"What do you want?"

"What are you doing up so late? Santa won't come unless you go to bed."

Agnes rubbed her forehead. She had always hated Derrick, but now that she knew what he'd done to Claudia, his voice was like acid in her stomach.

"If you don't tell me why you called, I'm going to hang up," Agnes said.

"I called to wish you a Merry Christmas and to tell you I love you. I know I don't give you as much attention as you probably deserve, but that doesn't mean I'm not thinking about you all the time."

His false sincerity was enough to make her skin crawl, but he made it worse by using the same silly singsong voice adults use when speaking to small children.

"I don't have time for this. What's the real reason you called?"

Derrick chuckled. "Never could get anything past you. You're just like me. You have a great bullshit detector. I wanted to let you know I'm moving in tomorrow."

"Moving in?"

"You're a minor. I'm your parent. You can't live alone."

Agnes gazed at the box with the Time Tefillin. She yearned to put it on. The sooner she got back to 1990, the sooner she would erase Derrick from Claudia's life.

"On Christmas day?" she said. "That's a new low even for you."

"I would think having your father come live with you after losing your mother would be a wonderful Christmas gift. There should be a Hallmark movie about us."

"You can't move in. Not until your case goes through family court."

"To hell with them. I've already given my lawyer way too much money to make it legal for me to live with my own flesh and blood. I'm moving in tomorrow."

"I know what you're doing. It won't work."

"Okay, Miss Smartypants. What does that big brain of yours think I'm doing?"

"I turn eighteen in August," Agnes said. "At which point, you'll have no legal claim on me or anything I own. You're trying to move in before then and sell the house."

"Sell the house?"

"This house is my inheritance and you're determined to steal it from me."

Derrick didn't respond. Agnes could hear music and people talking in the background. He was in a bar.

"You're so pathetic!" Agnes said. "You only thought you'd get a free house and a chance to move out of your terrible apartment?"

"No," Derrick said defensively. "I wasn't thinking any of those things you said."

"You're not stepping foot in this house until I have a legal document stating I must let you in."

"We'll see about that."

Derrick hung up. Agnes checked the time. It was 11:00 p.m. She sat in the living room and tried to read, but she couldn't focus on the words.

Midnight came, and the phone didn't ring. She went to the dining room and opened the box on the table. The light bounced off the Time

Tefillin's silver cubes. Agnes picked up one of the cubes. The metal was cool. She could sense the power inside. Putting the cube back, she decided to wait another hour just to be sure. The phone rang.

Agnes stared at the phone too frightened to move. The phone continued to ring until the call went to the answering machine. A shiver ran through her when she heard the caller's voice.

It was her voice.

"Mom? Are you there? It's me, Agnes."

Agnes picked up the phone. "Mom's not here, Agnes. Where are you? I'll come pick you up."

"Who's this?"

Agnes took a deep breath.

"You know who this is. Where are you?"

For fifteen seconds, they listened to each other's breathing. Finally, the caller responded.

"You know where I am. I'll be waiting for you."

Agnes checked the time. It was ten minutes past midnight, the start of a new day.

Snow flurries swirled around the car as Agnes drove toward the North Shore. The flakes melted as soon as they landed on the windshield. She could count on one hand the number of cars she saw on the road. The city was deserted as everyone waited for Christmas day. Agnes parked on Frazier Avenue at the entrance to the Walnut Street Bridge.

She was waiting on the stone retaining wall. She got up and walked around the car, her hands in her jacket pockets as she bent down and peered inside. Agnes rolled down the window, so they could both get a better look at each other.

Agnes marveled at her outfit, stonewashed jeans, a bomber jacket, a pink fanny pack, and puffy tennis shoes. Snowflakes stuck to her frizzy brown hair. She walked around to the passenger door, got in the car, and sniffed.

"Everything is the same," she said. "The same car. The same smells. You're wearing the same clothes I wore. Nothing changed. I should have guessed, but I'm still surprised."

"You must be the first Agnes," Agnes said.

"That would make you Second Agnes," she said.

Second Agnes put the car in gear and headed toward home.

"A lot did change. Is Barry Plunkett your father?"

"Yes. Who's your father?"

"Derrick Whitlow."

First Agnes frowned.

"That awful man? I'm sorry. I only met him once. I thought he was most unpleasant. I can't believe Mom had sex with him."

"He didn't give her a choice. He waited until after Neal and Megan took Barry to the hospital."

"The hospital? I didn't hit him that hard."

"I've only been around Barry a couple of times, but he seems the type to act like an injury is worse than it is. After they left, Derrick convinced Mom to let him drive her home. He stopped at a park and raped her."

First Agnes glanced at her watch.

"I created the situation that allowed him to take advantage of her. I made her life worse than it was before."

They drove through a tunnel. The only light came from the dashboard. Second Agnes could barely see First Agnes.

"Is Mom dead?" First Agnes asked.

"Yes, she is." Second Agnes said.

"When?"

"In the garage on Sunday, October 26?"

First Agnes sniffed and quickly progressed to sobbing.

"I wasn't able to save her. The entire trip was a failure. Now I'm going to die for no reason. It's like I committed suicide just like Mom, only slower. I'm such an idiot."

Second Agnes got a lump in her throat. She didn't know what to say. First Agnes was right. Her mission had failed. Second Agnes reached over and found First Agnes' hand. They felt a tingling of electricity, but no one blew up and the space-time continuum didn't rupture.

     Mickey Dubrow

They came out of the tunnel. Second Agnes glanced at her passenger.

"You have something on your face other than tears," Second Agnes said.

First Agnes pulled down the sun visor and checked her face in the vanity mirror. She groaned as pulled a hanky out of her jacket pocket. She rubbed a black smudge off her nose and streaks of black on her cheeks.

"I copied Mom's Halloween costume," First Agnes said.

"Do you still have the bunny ears?" Second Agnes said.

First Agnes unzipped her jacket and felt around inside.

"I must have left them in Barry's car. How did you know about them?"

"During my research, I found out about the attack on Barry Plunkett at the Halloween party. I interviewed him for details. He remembered the bunny ears. Your costume fooled him into thinking you were Claudia."

"I needed a way to get close to him."

"I surmised someone wanted to stop Claudia from having sex with Barry, just as I want to stop her from having sex with Derrick. That meant a plan almost identical to mine had already been executed. The only person who would want to do this was me, which meant I wasn't the first Agnes. This timeline we're in now is not the original timeline."

Knowing they were in an altered timeline would have been thrilling if Claudia were alive. First Agnes glanced at her watch again.

"You're planning on going back to 1990? You must have a time machine."

"I call mine a Time Tefillin."

"So, do I. You're in Professor Levin's laboratory?"

"I came to his office one morning and he had the tefillin on."

"So much is the same," First Agnes said as she watched the snowflakes hit the windshield. "And so much is different."

When they got to the house, First Agnes followed Second Agnes inside and did a quick tour of the rooms.

"I can still smell Mom," First Agnes said. "I miss her so much."

"Me too," Second Agnes said.

Second Agnes made hot tea and they sat at the dining room table.

"I'll show you mine if you show me yours," Second Agnes said.

First Agnes blushed as she unzipped her pink fanny pack and pulled out her Time Tefillin. Second Agnes got the box she kept her Time Tefillin in and took it out. They traded time machines. They carefully examined each other's device, gently running their fingers over them and testing the digital clocks.

"Your stitching on the straps is straighter than mine," First Agnes said.

"Your soldering on the cubes is cleaner," Second Agnes said.

First Agnes glanced at her watch yet again.

"How much time do you have left?" Second Agnes asked.

"Five hours and thirty-two minutes."

"How long were you in 1990?"

"Seven hours and then I was pulled back."

"The seven hour ripple. I've experienced it as well. Maybe coming here was the end of your ripple. Maybe you're here to stay."

"We'll know for sure in five hours and thirty-two minutes. My theory is since my timeline no longer exists. I started a new ripple when I arrived in your timeline. At the end of seven hours, I'll cease to exist."

"You knew this would happen."

"The same will happen to you if you go back and stop Derrick."

"I know." Second Agnes stood and put her hands on her hips. "Okay, if these are your final hours, is there something you'd like to do? Somewhere you'd like to go?"

First Agnes shrugged. "Sitting here drinking tea is fine. I'm home. I don't want to be anywhere else. The only thing I would change is for Mom to be here."

Second Agnes got a box of chocolate chip cookies, their favorite, to go with the tea. She adjusted to First Agnes' presence quickly. It was like seeing her twin sister after many years apart. They discussed their experiments. They talked about Professor Levin. They agreed if Claudia had decided to remain a virgin until she got to college, she would have met someone much better than Barry or Derrick and none of this would have happened. They talked about Claudia and then talked about her some more.

They discussed the difference between Barry and Derrick as fathers.

"I'm truly sorry," First Agnes said. "Derrick is much worse than Barry. At least, Barry occasionally tried to be a good father, even if he had no clue where to begin."

After the cookies were gone, they put on their jackets and went outside. They stood in the back yard. The snow had stopped. The wind made the limbs of the oak trees sway as if waving hello. The sky was clear. They gazed at the stars.

"I was going to change history," First Agnes said.

"You did," Second Agnes said. "Just not the way you expected."

"There are two theories represented by our standing here together. The first is nature versus nurture. Despite our different upbringing, we are both above average intelligence, studied physics, and invented time machines. This would seem to prove nature is more important than nurture."

"Perhaps. But then, if it hadn't been for Claudia's nurturing, we might not have reached our full potential. She protected us, encouraged us, and sacrificed her own happiness so we could become who we wanted to be."

First Agnes sighed. "True. However, studies show that children in single parent households don't excel as well as those in two parent homes."

"Those studies never met our fathers."

They laughed.

"What was the second theory you were thinking of?" Second Agnes asked.

"The Grandfather Paradox."

According to the Grandfather Paradox, if a time traveler went back in time and killed his grandfather before he produced children, then the time traveler would cease to exist. However, the grandfather always managed to survive any attempt by the time traveler to murder him.

"You went back in time and stopped your father from getting your mother pregnant," Second Agnes said. "But then, she got pregnant by another man."

"And though I will soon cease to exist, you will continue to exist. The

Grandfather Paradox has proved to be a paradox."

"How much longer do you have?"

First Agnes checked the time.

"Forty-five minutes. I'm cold. Let's go inside."

They stamped their feet to loosen the snow on their shoes before going inside. Second Agnes filled the kettle with water and put it on the stove. As she put teabags in the two ceramic cups, she remembered when Claudia bought them at a yard sale. They were beautifully designed with green vines looping around. The people selling them only wanted a dollar each, but Claudia haggled them down to both cups for a dollar.

It was a random association but seeing the two cups made her realize Claudia had died twice. Somehow that made her death even sadder. Of the many theories she and First Agnes discussed, there was one they hadn't covered. The theory of fate, there were some things that were meant to happen. Perhaps a gifted child named Agnes was meant to invent a time machine. The child's mother, Claudia, was meant to get pregnant on October 27, 1990. And perhaps the mother was meant to die on October 26, 2008.

Second Agnes refused to accept Claudia's death as fate. If First Agnes could change their father, then Second Agnes could save their mother.

The kettle whistling brought Second Agnes out of her thoughts. She poured the steaming water into the cups and carried them into the dining room. First Agnes was putting on her Time Tefillin. She saw the confusion in Second Agnes' face.

"I feel better with it on," First Agnes said. "Besides, I might need it."

Second Agnes nodded.

"The tea is ready. I'm afraid we're out of cookies."

They sat at the table and sipped their tea.

"Don't do it," First Agnes said.

Second Agnes didn't need her to explain what she was talking about. They were essentially the same person.

"I have to go back," Second Agnes said. "You see what you did as a failed experiment. We never consider an experiment a failure."

"Yes, I know," First Agnes said wearily. "By definition, an experiment is a test performed to learn about something not yet known. What I know now is that there are some things you cannot change."

"I can't give up. I have to try."

"Even if you save Mom, you'll end up like me."

Second Agnes gazed at the steam rising from her cup.

"Then the next Agnes will benefit from my success."

First Agnes sipped her tea. She shook the box of cookies to see if any were left, but the box really was empty.

"I should've said yes," she said.

"Yes to what?"

"When Josh Hawkins asked me out on a date. I should've said yes."

"Who is Josh Hawkins?"

"Last year on the Fourth of July at Chester Frost Park. He was in our grammar school carpool."

"The boy we skipped stones with? I understand that without him we might not have come up with the time skip theory or gone searching for the magic angle, but does that truly warrant a date?"

"It would have been nice to go out with a boy. I never went on a date. He's the only boy who ever asked me. I should have said yes. I should have kissed him that day by the shore. I've never been kissed. Now I'll never know what it's like." First Agnes touched her lips. "I can feel it. It's time."

And then First Agnes was gone.

Second Agnes stared at the space where First Agnes had been. It was as if she never existed. Second Agnes didn't think the house could feel any emptier without Claudia. She was always talking to herself. It was nice to have someone talk back. She wiped away tears before she put the cups in the sink. Outside, the birds were chatting, and the first hints of dawn crept along the edge of the horizon. Soon, children would be getting up to see what their parents left them under the Christmas tree. Second Agnes went to bed. Tonight, she was going on a long journey, and she needed her rest.

CHAPTER
31

Saturday, October 27, 1990

Second Agnes arrived on the Walnut Street Bridge at 11:00 p.m. on Saturday, October 27, 1990. She was dressed warmly in a winter coat and a knit cap. First Agnes warned her the bridge was in bad shape, but it was worse than she expected. At every step, she feared her foot would break through the rotting wood, and she would plummet to the rushing river below. It took her ten minutes to get to the barricade.

Across the street was the art supply store. The Halloween decorations in the store's window of witches and Jack-o-lanterns were handmade, charming, and not scary at all. The building was on an incline. Second Agnes walked uphill to the parking lot behind the store. She had passed the building hundreds of times but had never paid much attention to it. The art supply store was just one of several small businesses in the block long building, each with their own back entrance. Second Agnes descended a short stairwell that brought her eye level with the parking lot. It was 11:25 p.m. There was nothing for her to do now except wait for First Agnes. Her

Mickey Dubrow

stomach growled. She scolded herself for not bringing something to snack on while she waited. She knew from past journeys that skipping across lengthy time periods made her hungry.

At 12:15 a.m., headlights lit up the parking lot. Second Agnes ducked down, and the light passed over her head. She heard the car door open and close. She rose enough to peek. First Agnes stood next to the red Trans Am. She was putting on her Time Tefillin. Second Agnes lowered herself and waited.

Second Agnes was happy to see First Agnes again but resisted the urge to speak to her. She decided not to let First Agnes know she was here. Other than complicating her mission by having to explain how she knew about First Agnes and the car and so on and so forth, she didn't want First Agnes to try and talk her out of stopping Derrick.

Footsteps went by and then stopped. Second Agnes climbed the stairs and took another peek. First Agnes was at the corner of the building, spying down the hill. Second Agnes knew First Agnes was waiting for the dishwasher to finish his cigarette before she could cross the street to the bridge without anyone seeing her.

Minutes crawled by. Finally, First Agnes disappeared around the corner of the building. Second Agnes hurried over where First Agnes had been standing. First Agnes had reached the bottom of the hill and was crossing the street.

Second Agnes walked over to the car. The hood was warm. She opened the door, climbed in, and sank comfortably into the driver's seat. She'd never been in a new car before. The dashboard sparkled. The new car smell of plastics, adhesives, and sealants was intoxicating, though probably not good to breathe for an extended period of time.

She located the pool cue lying across a back seat that must have been designed to only accommodate small children and legless adults. As she was moving the pool cue to the passenger seat, she found First Agnes' discarded bunny ears headband on the floorboard. Second Agnes grinned as she ran her finger over the soft, white material lining the wire ears.

The motor roared to life without the prodding she had to do with Claudia's car. Second Agnes shifted into reverse, backed up, shifted to first gear, and drove out of the parking lot. When she reached the bottom of the hill, there were no signs of First Agnes and the dishwasher. She turned right and headed toward Red Bank. She checked the time. It was 12:40 a.m.

The car was fun to drive. She'd only driven a stick shift a couple of times and preferred automatics, but the gears changed so smoothly she could see why people loved sports cars. Feeling total control over a powerful engine was exhilarating. Speeding came naturally.

Second Agnes zoomed through the tunnel connecting Cherokee Boulevard to Dayton Boulevard. As she emerged, a police car passed her going in the opposite direction. She eased off the gas and shifted down to first gear. The last thing she needed was to get pulled over for speeding in a stolen car without a driver's license from this decade.

She thought about ducking onto a side street, but when it became clear that the policeman wasn't going to turn around and chase her, she relaxed. She made sure to not go over the speed limit again.

The road to the park went through a neighborhood of ranch houses built far apart with overgrown lots filling in the space between them. Inside the park, the road bisected rolling hills and lush forest.

Second Agnes passed a gravel parking lot. Derrick's car wasn't here. That didn't surprise her. His logical choice would be the lot on the other side of the park. It was off the main road at the top of a hill and hidden by trees.

She drove through the park. Fog hung over the grassy fields completely hiding the baseball diamond. At the back entrance, a side road led up the hill to the second parking lot. Second Agnes' pulse quickened when she passed a cluster of pine trees and got a full view of the lot. Derrick's car wasn't here either.

Second Agnes checked the time. According to her calculations, Derrick and Claudia should have been here by now. Had Derrick gotten the name of the park wrong? He was drinking heavily tonight. Maybe he only thought he was at White Oak. That meant they could be in any secluded area where no one would hear a girl yelling for help. She got out of the car, leaving the car idling, and listened to the pine trees swaying in the wind as she contemplated her next move. She needed to approach the situation logically. The problem was her target was illogical. Derrick was unpredictable even when alcohol didn't blur his reasoning.

And that was the answer. A logical person would have chosen this parking lot because of the privacy it afforded. Derrick would have been drunk enough and stupid enough to use the lot that was right next to the street where anybody could drive by.

Second Agnes scrambled back into the car and drove toward the other side of the park. She rolled down her window. A short distance from the gravel lot, she heard a girl screaming. Agnes stepped on the gas.

The car was in the gravel lot. Second Agnes positioned the sports car behind Derrick's Dodge Rampage. Her headlights shone directly on the camper mounted to the back. She waited a minute and when nobody came out, she laid on the horn. The extended honk echoed through the surrounding trees.

The camper door swung upward, and Derrick climbed out. His face was flushed either from anger, alcohol, or both. His coverall was unzipped to his navel. From where she was sitting, Second Agnes could only see Claudia's bare feet inside the camper. The rest of her was covered in darkness as if an animal was in the process of devouring her.

Second Agnes wanted to frighten Derrick as much as Claudia was frightened at this moment in time. She took off her knit cap and put the bunny ears on. If the bunny ears didn't scare him, they would at least confuse the hell out of him.

"Hey," Derrick said, shielding his eyes from the glare of the headlights with his hand. "This ain't no business of yours, so you best just move along."

Second Agnes got out of the car, clutching the pool cue.

"Hey? Is that a Trans Am?" he asked. "Where'd you get that car?"

She strode toward him. Her footsteps crunched on the gravel.

"Where'd you get that thing on your head?" Derrick didn't sound as confident now. "Who the hell are you?"

Second Agnes reared back to swing the pool cue at Derrick's head. He held up his hands to deflect the blow. Second Agnes anticipated this. She reasoned he would try to grab the pool cue away from her. She also reasoned he was too intoxicated to expect a counter move.

Instead of swinging the pool cue high, Second Agnes brought it down low and whacked Derrick's groin. He groaned as he sank to his knees. Second Agnes swung for his head and smacked his left ear. Derrick yelped and clutched the side of his head.

That should have been enough, he was in pain and Claudia had plenty of time to escape, but a fury overtook Second Agnes.

She hit him for all his lies.

Whack!

She hit for the time he flushed her physics textbook in the toilet.

Whack!

She hit him for all the misery he caused her and Claudia. The pool cue whistled in the wind when she swung it down on his prone body.

Whack! Whack! Whack!

She hit him for raping Claudia and ruining her life.

CRACK!

The pool cue broke in two. Second Agnes tossed the splintered stick into the woods. Derrick was curled up into a ball on the ground.

"Please stop," he whimpered. "I don't why you're doing this to me, but I'm sorry for whatever it is you think I did. Just please stop hurting me."

Second Agnes breathed heavily as sweat rolled down her face. Looking down at Derrick, she felt empty. She heard stirring coming from the camper. Claudia was climbing out. Second Agnes didn't want Claudia to see her. There was no way to explain her presence here.

She knelt beside Derrick.

"Why'd you hit me?" Derrick asked.

Agnes leaned close to his ear.

"I wanted you to know your actions have consequences."

Second Agnes raced for the car, climbed inside, and slammed the door shut. Claudia was out of the camper and stood on unsteady feet. Her face was puffy from crying and a bruise was forming on her forehead. Her hair stuck out in all directions and her feet were bare. She looked back and forth between Derrick on the ground and the car in front of her. She squinted against the glaring headlights to try and get a better look at the driver.

Second Agnes wanted desperately to rush to Claudia and hold her. To feel her, smell her, say goodbye, all the things she didn't get a chance to do. Instead, Second Agnes backed up and drove away. In the rearview mirror, she could see Claudia watching the car. Soon, Second Agnes couldn't see her at all.

She didn't check the time until she reached the art supply store's parking lot. She had a little less than three hours left before the end of her seven hour time limit. She put the Trans Am in the same spot First Agnes had used earlier. The pool cue was gone, but she still had the bunny ears. She left them on the passenger seat as a souvenir and put on her knit cap.

Second Agnes didn't need to put on her Time Tefillin because she had never taken it off. She leaned against the car's warm hood and gazed up at the stars. She had traveled back in time and beaten the snot out of her deadbeat father. All in all, a major scientific accomplishment.

She wished she could have taken Claudia home and made sure she was okay. An odd realization came to her. As of this moment, Derrick was no longer her father. Claudia was no longer her mother. Technically, Second Agnes no longer existed.

Would there be a third Agnes? So far, fate decided that no matter what happened on this night, nine months from now, an Agnes would exit Claudia's womb. Had Second Agnes defeated fate? There was a way to find out. Second Agnes checked her digital clock. There was plenty of time before her seven hours ran out. She wouldn't wait until then. She wanted to return to 2008 at a time of her choosing rather than the moment she left. But first, she wanted to deal with her groaning stomach. She never got a chance to eat, and she was starving. There was a Krystal hamburger restaurant two blocks away. They were open twenty-four hours a day.

III

THIRD AGNES

CHAPTER
32

Wednesday, July 4, 2007

Agnes dropped to her knees in the sand next to Claudia and rummaged in her beach bag for her notebook. She sat cross-legged on her towel and flipped to a clean page. With her full attention on what she was writing down, she didn't notice her mother watching her.

"You saw him, didn't you?" Claudia said. "That boy, Josh Hawkins. I can tell just looking at your face. When I was your age, I had the same look for a boy at school."

Agnes blushed.

"Yes. I ran into him."

"Then what?"

"Mom!"

"I'm serious. This is the first time I know of that you've spent any time with a boy. It must have been amazing for you to immediately write it down in your diary."

"This is not a diary. It's my lab notebook."

"So even your dates are scientific experiments?"

Agnes stopped writing and glared at Claudia.

"It was not a date. We happened to be in the same place at the same time. We skipped rocks and while we were skipping rocks, I had a major breakthrough on my science project. I'd like to write it down while it's still fresh in my mind."

"Oh please, don't let me stop you."

Agnes started to write, but then paused with her pen poised above the page.

"Besides, I haven't seen Josh Hawkins since grammar school. The only thing I remembered about him was that he smelled like onions."

"Does he still smell like onions?"

"No. He smells much better now."

Claudia's eyes widened.

"Oh, did he?"

Agnes blew a strand of hair out of her eyes.

"Mom. Please. Not now. I have to make notes."

Claudia slathered sunscreen on her arms as Agnes filled page after page with her revelation that time was a river, and time travel could be achieved the same way a stone skipped across the water. Downstream was the future and upstream was the past. She just needed to find that right combination of hydrodynamics, momentum, and gravity to enter the time stream. She needed the magic angle.

Around them, families enjoyed the hot sun and cool lake on Chester Frost Park's manmade beach. Children splashed in the lake while their parents watched. Hot dogs and hamburgers sizzled on grills. Cold beers were popped open, and foam dribbled over sweaty hands. It was a perfect Fourth of July.

When Agnes finished her notes, she shut her notebook and put it back into her tote bag. She put on her sunglasses and lay on her back.

"I can't wait to get back to the lab."

Claudia turned over on her stomach and poked Agnes' shoulder.

"Tell me, pumpkin," Claudia said. "Do you have any interest in boys?

Or girls for that matter?"

Agnes wrinkled her nose.

"I suppose if I had to classify my sexual preference, it would be hetero-sexual. However, at this moment in my life I would have to say I'm asexual. I have been completely absorbed in my project. Sex is the last thing on my mind."

"Is this going to be a permanent condition? Will you ever want to have a relationship with a human being instead of test tube?"

Agnes sat up, took her mother's plastic bottle of suntan lotion, and squeezed a glob into her hand. As she smoothed it over her shoulder, she looked at the R.E.M. logo tattoo on her mother's left shoulder blade. Agnes didn't care for tattoos, but she appreciated her mother loved something so much she had a symbol of it marked on her skin.

"Someday I'd like to have a boyfriend, but not now."

"Don't wait too long. If you don't make time for boys, then the right one might come along, and you'll miss him."

Agnes felt a stab in her stomach. She hated talking about boys with Claudia. The conversations always left them both feeling sad because they eventually ended up being about Agnes' father.

"You're right, Mom. But I'm still not going out with Josh Hawkins no matter what he smells like."

CHAPTER
33

Saturday, October 4, 2008

To her surprise, Agnes left rainy Saturday, September 6, 2008, and returned to sunny Saturday, October fourth without flipping the switch on the Time Tefillin. She was still seated in the Varsity booth where she had been taking notes, but now there was tray of food in front of her and a very confused boy seated across from her.

"Have we met before?" he asked. "You look familiar."

A girl wearing tight clothes came to the table and gawked at Agnes.

"Where did she come from?" she asked the boy.

"I have no idea. She appeared like magic."

The girl crossed her arms and tilted her head at Agnes.

"I know you from somewhere," the girl said. "Where do I know you from?"

"There's been a mistake. I don't know you," Agnes said. "Please excuse me."

She bolted out of the booth. As she hurried away, she glanced over her shoulder. The couple was watching her. Agnes slipped into the crowd and made her way out of the restaurant.

In her dorm room, she played back the video of her spying on September sixth Agnes burying Mr. Rat. This was definite proof Agnes had traveled into the past. She turned on her voice recorder.

"Transport living test subject attempt number sixteen. Conclusion. Primary Scientist observed and recorded her past self as she buried living test subject number one, also known as Mr. Rat, in the ravine behind my dorm. Primary Scientist made the decision to remain in September sixth for further observation. However, at the end of seven hours, Primary Scientist returned to October fourth at the exact time of original departure. What I find troubling is the Time Tefillin acted on its own accord. Based on this observation, Primary Scientist theorizes there is a limit to how long a test subject can travel to a designated time before being forced to return to the original departure time."

Agnes clicked off the recorder.

She made a cup of tea and spent the rest of the afternoon writing more detailed observations of her time skip. She checked the Time Tefillin for any damage it may have suffered during her journey to the past. When she was satisfied it was in good shape and fully operational, she put it away in a metal box.

Standing up to stretch, Agnes glanced out of her dorm window. Night had fallen and she was hungry again. Technically, she hadn't eaten in a month. She didn't feel like eating at the Varsity again. Besides, she should be celebrating. She had the proof time travel was possible. She should do something special.

Agnes picked up her phone and ordered a pizza.

CHAPTER
34

Tuesday, October 7, 2008

As Agnes rode the elevator, which always smelled like French fries, she worried about her meeting with Professor Howard Levin. He hadn't told her the purpose of their meeting. She felt like she was in trouble but wasn't sure what she'd done wrong.

Well, she had invented a time machine behind the professor's back, so there was that.

Agnes' footsteps echoed in the empty halls as she approached Professor Levin's office. She thought back to the early morning she'd come to ask him a question about their research and saw him praying and wearing his tefillin. It was pure chance she'd come by when she did. If she hadn't, she might never have been able to create her time machine. She was too dedicated to science to call it fate but had yet to come up with a better explanation.

Professor Levin rose to his feet when she entered his office and gestured for her to take a seat in his visitor's chair.

"Agnes," he said. "How are you?"

"Fine. How are you?"

Once she was seated, he sat down.

"Good. Good. You're probably wondering why I asked you to meet with me today."

"Is there a problem with my lab work?"

"Not at all. You've been exemplary as always. Your mother called me. She thinks I'm working you too hard. She claims that every time she calls, you tell her you're too busy to talk. She says this even happens on weekends. She reminded me that you may be a genius, but you're still only a seventeen-year-old girl who should be out doing the kinds of things normal seventeen-year-old girls do."

Agnes' cheeks burned with embarrassment.

"I can't believe Mom called you without telling me. I'm sorry, Professor Levin. I promise I'll make sure she never does it again."

Levin waved his hand.

"It's okay, Agnes. Because of your special circumstance, we gave your mother direct access to my office. Claudia can call me any time she wants. After our conversation, I became concerned and scheduled this time for us to talk."

"I still wished she had spoken to me first."

Levin stroked his thick beard.

"Just because you have twenty-four-hour access to the lab doesn't mean you have to be here day and night."

"I'm aware of that Professor Levin."

"I don't believe I've given you more work than my other assistants."

"You haven't. And I don't come here on the weekends. You can check with the security guards."

"That isn't necessary. I believe you. Normally, I wouldn't pry into a student's private life, but you're younger than the average student. You're gifted, but you're still a young girl. You may be taking on more than you can handle and not realize it."

Agnes stared at her tennis shoes. She was wearing two different socks.

She considered matching socks a waste of valuable time.

"I'm fine, Professor Levin. Honestly, I am. This is just something between me and Mom. She tries not to be too clingy, but sometimes she can't help herself."

"Well, it's understandable. She's a single mother and her only child is away at college."

Agnes knew it was more than that, but she didn't want to talk to Professor Levin about Claudia's reasons for clinging so tightly. It wasn't that she didn't trust the professor, but she wasn't going to talk about Claudia behind her back even if she thought it was okay to talk about Agnes behind her back. However, Claudia had unknowingly given Agnes a reason to discuss her secret project with Professor Levin.

"Actually, I have been busier than normal," Agnes said. "I came up with an alternate theory about proving the existence of time travel. I didn't mention it to you earlier because it was just an idea, and I wanted to have more to go on."

Levin leaned forward and rested his elbows on the desk.

"I'm always open to new ideas. Tell me about it. I don't care how rudimentary it is."

"Instead of talking about it now, I'd like to make a formal presentation, so I can better defend my theory."

"You make it sound so mysterious. Okay, Agnes. When would you like to make your presentation?"

"Can we do it at the end of the month?"

Levin smiled.

"I'm looking forward to it."

Once Agnes was out of Levin's office, she did a giddy dance. She had been afraid he'd somehow found out about the Time Tefillin. She was tempted to tell him she had a functioning time machine in her dorm room, but a proper presentation would be much more satisfying.

As for Claudia, Agnes would try to call her more regularly like she used to do when she first arrived at Tech. The truth was she did miss talking to her mother.

　　　

CHAPTER
35

Saturday, October 27, 1990

"Are we at Megan's already?" Claudia mumbled. The massive amount of alcohol she drank at the party left a sour aftertaste in her mouth.

Derrick reached across Claudia and unbuckled her seatbelt. Despite being pig-eyed from sleep, Claudia could see they were in the gravel parking lot of White Oak Park.

"Why'd you stop here?" she asked.

"Why did you think?" Derrick said, wiggling his eyebrows.

He tried to kiss her and get his hand between her legs. She squirmed away from his advances.

"Come on," Derrick said. "You know you want it."

"No, I don't," Claudia said. "I want to go home."

She avoided his advances then elbowed him. Derrick rubbed his jaw. They glared at each other, then he smirked.

"You like to play rough? So do I."

Derrick left the car and dragged her out so roughly she almost vomited. He opened the hatch to the camper and winked at her. As she fought his attempts to get her into the camper and he ignored her pleas to let her go, a part of Claudia couldn't believe this was happening. Derrick was supposed to be her friend. He'd always been a bit of a jerk, but she'd never seen him this cruel before. How did she allow herself to be here? Where there warning signs in the past she had missed?

Breaking free from another attempt to stuff her into the camper, Claudia wiggled away and ran toward the road.

"Help!" she shouted, "Somebody please help me!"

Derrick huffed behind her, but Claudia didn't dare turn back to see how close he was. She almost made it around the bend in the road before he tackled her. She landed on her stomach with him on top of her, knocking the air out of her lungs. He grabbed her hair and forced her to her feet. Like a rabbit caught in a snare, ready to chew her arm off if it meant freedom, Claudia scratched at Derrick's arm as he pulled her by the hair to the car.

When they got to the camper, fear overtook Claudia, and she went limp as a ragdoll. Derrick struggled to get her into the camper then climbed in and shut the hatch. Claudia prayed it would be over quickly. Derrick tried to pull her leotard away from her crotch, but the elastic was too tight.

"How about a little help?" he mumbled.

Claudia couldn't help. Fear had rendered her unable to move or speak. Her mind wanted to escape by falling asleep and she felt herself drifting off. Something cold and hard pressed against her neck. Derrick had a knife against her throat.

"Take it off or I cut it off," he said.

They heard a car approaching. Derrick twisted around. Blinding light filled the camper's window.

"Keep quiet or I'll slit your throat," Derrick hissed.

The driver of the mystery car laid on the horn. The blaring echoed off the surrounding trees.

"Don't move. Don't speak. Don't breathe. I'll be right back."

Derrick opened the hatch and light from the headlights poured in. The car idled like an impatient beast. Derrick climbed out of the camper and faced the car.

"Hey," he said. "This ain't no business of yours. You better just move along."

The driver got out of the car. Claudia couldn't tell if it was a man or a woman. She could make out two long oblong shapes on the driver's head. Claudia couldn't believe it. Bunny ears. The driver wore bunny ears.

"Hey? Is that a Trans Am?" Derrick asked. "Where'd you get that car?"

Panic seized Claudia. That was Barry's stolen Trans Am. She wasn't sure how she knew, but she was certain it was. This was the girl she'd seen at the party in a bunny outfit identical to hers. First, she attacked Barry and now she was after Derrick. No sane person would do that, which could only mean one thing. A maniac was stalking Claudia and anyone near her. Her heart raced as she listened to the maniac's footsteps getting closer.

"Where'd you get that thing on your head?" Derrick asked. "Who the hell are you?"

The maniac swung a long stick at Derrick. He raised his hands to stop her, but she was too fast. Claudia heard a whistling sound followed by a heavy thud. Derrick groaned as he sank to the ground. The maniac struck him with the stick again and again until it broke in two, the wood splitting with a loud crack.

"Please stop," Derrick blubbered. "I don't know why you're doing this to me, but I'm sorry for whatever it is you think I did. Just please stop hurting me."

Claudia had heard enough. She couldn't cower in the camper any longer. Whatever was going to happen to her, she wanted to face it head on. Her blood pounded in her ears as she forced her aching body to climb out of the camper.

By the time she got out, the maniac was back in Barry's car. Claudia shielded her eyes and tried to see the driver's face, but the headlights were too bright, and the interior of the car was too dark. The Trans Am reversed then drove away. Claudia watched the car disappear around a bend in the road.

Derrick rolled onto his back. His face was a bloody mess.

"I'm hurt real bad."

Claudia touched her neck where he'd held his knife.

"Good."

Worried he might have the strength to get up, Claudia ran barefoot on the center line of the asphalt road. The air was frigid, and her shoes had come off sometime during Derrick's attack. The first house she came to sat on a grassy hill. A bare bulb cast a weak light on the porch. Claudia banged on the door.

"Help!" she shouted. "Someone tried to rape me! Call the police."

No one answered. She banged on the door harder.

A man's voice inside shouted, "Go away!"

"But he tried to rape me!"

"You probably asked for it. Now get off my property."

Claudia hurried back to the road. She didn't stop at any more houses. She ran until she reached Dayton Boulevard. Her lungs burned as she slowed down to a walk. The frigid wind chilled the sweat on her face and legs. Pain shot through her each time she stepped on a sharp rock. Every passing car made her flinch for fear it was Derrick's Dodge Rampage or Barry's Trans Am.

Her heart jumped when a car driving in the opposite direction screeched to a halt and made a U-turn. She hurled herself down an embankment and hid in a cluster of trees. The car pulled onto the side of the road. The driver got out and stood at the top of the hill. Claudia crouched down and prayed he didn't find her.

"Claudia? Is that you?"

It was Neal's voice. Claudia came out of the woods.

"Neal! Oh my God. Yes, Neal. It's me."

He scrambled down the hill. Claudia threw her arms around him.

"I was driving home, and I saw you walking on the other side of the road," Neal said.

"It was terrible," Claudia said. "I was so scared."

"Come on, let's get in the car. It's freezing out here."

Neal held Claudia's hand as they climbed the hill. He opened the car door for her where it was warm. Claudia felt safe for the first time in hours. "Megan freaked out when we got back to the party and you weren't there," Neal said. "She didn't know where you'd gone."

"Derrick said he talked to Megan at the hospital. He said she told him to give me a ride home."

"We didn't get any phone calls at the hospital. I'm not even sure how you'd call somebody if they're not a patient."

Claudia examined her arms and legs. She was covered in scrapes and bruises. Her feet were bleeding.

"Derrick lied so he would have an excuse to get me in his car. He tried to rape me."

"He did what? Where the hell is he? I'm going to kick his ass!"

"Somebody beat you to it."

"Who?"

The entire evening was a nightmare with many bizarre twists and turns. Claudia didn't know where to begin.

"You can tell me what happened later," Neal said. "I'll take you home."

He headed in the direction of Claudia's neighborhood. She grabbed his arm.

"I don't want to go home."

"Okay, I'll take you to Megan's."

"No. I don't want anybody to see me like this. I can't deal with it now."

At the first intersection, Neal made another U-turn.

"You can stay at my place tonight. My bedroom is in the basement. It has its own entrance. I have my own bathroom. It's messy, but it's private. My parents won't even know you stayed over. How does that sound?"

"Good. Let's do that. Thank you, Neal."

In his cowboy costume and his white cowboy hat in the back seat, Neal looked every bit the young hero who saved a poor damsel in distress. He turned off Dayton Boulevard and drove up sloping hills to a pleasant neighborhood of older but well-maintained homes. In every other drive-way, bicycles were parked next to minivans. Neal's home was a two-story beige house with a wraparound porch on the top floor, twice as big as Claudia's house. A minivan and a sedan were parked in the garage. Neal put his car behind the minivan. Except for the porch light, the house was dark. Claudia felt like the whole neighborhood was asleep.

As soon as they stepped out of the car, an enormous German Shepherd bolted out of the garage and barked at them. Claudia squealed and grabbed Neal's arm.

"Calm down, Rosie," Neal said. "It's okay. She's a friend."

The dog gazed at Neal with baleful eyes then sniffed Claudia.

"You can pet her," Neal said. "She's really sweet once she gets to know you."

Claudia rubbed the thick fur on Rosie's neck. The dog wagged her tail.

"It's a pleasure to meet you, Rosie," Claudia said.

Rosie licked Claudia's hand and then trotted to her dog bed at the back of the garage. She circled three times on the bed before settling down and closing her eyes.

Neal led Claudia into the garage. It smelled like motor oil and dog food. They walked in single file between the minivan and the sedan. The entrance to the house was between Rosie's dog bed and a freezer, but instead of going in, Neal turned right. A small concrete walkway led to a door on the side of the house. Neal unlocked the door, and they entered his bedroom.

"Welcome to my humble abode," Neal said as he flipped on the lights. Claudia was immediately jealous. It was a basic finished basement, but Claudia would have loved to have this much space. It took up most of the ground floor. Her bedroom was tiny and directly across the hall from her parents' bedroom.

Neal's bedroom definitely belonged to a boy. On the wall was a poster of a baseball player holding his bat ready for a pitch. On another wall was a poster of a buxom woman in a bikini leaning seductively on a fancy sports car. A shiny guitar was propped next to a ratty couch. A set of dumbbells sat on the floor at the foot of a single bed.

Claudia was pleasantly surprised Neal's place wasn't messy as he claimed. It was neat and clean. She expected a boy's bedroom to smell like a locker room after a ball game, but his room smelled freshly scrubbed. She walked over to a bookshelf and explored Neal's CD collection. She pulled out R.E.M.'s *Murmur* and held it up.

"This is my favorite album of all time."

"Do you want to borrow it?"

"I have it. I have all their music."

"We can listen to it in the car when I take you home tomorrow." Neal pointed to a door on the other side of the room. "There's the bathroom. You probably want to get cleaned up."

Claudia inspected the bathroom. It was small, but it had a sink, toilet, and a shower. All three were clean. She examined her torn and muddy leotard.

"I'd love to take a shower, but then I'd have to put this disgusting thing back on."

Neal rummaged through a dresser next to the bed.

"You can wear these to sleep in. They're clean."

He offered her a faded blue T-shirt with the logo for the Chattanooga Lookouts and a pair of striped boxer shorts. Claudia wasn't sure she was comfortable wearing his clothes, but it would be better than sleeping naked. She took the T-shirt and shorts then entered the bathroom.

Claudia stripped off her leotard and her underwear. She faced the mirror. The scrapes on her arms and legs had stopped bleeding. Her feet were sore but had stopped bleeding as well. Her hair had bits of gravel embedded in the tangled strands. An ugly bruise blossomed on her forehead. There were black smears across her cheeks from the make-up she'd used to create a bunny nose and whiskers. She lifted her chin to examine the broken skin across her neck where Derrick held the knife. She felt a flush of embarrassment Neal had seen her looking so messed up.

In the shower, she made the water as hot as she could stand it. Steam rose around her. The water stung her wounds, but as it sluiced down her back, she could feel the pent-up tension of the night melt away.

As she washed her hair, Claudia thought about how her parents were going to freak out when they saw her. Though Claudia was the victim, she would ultimately be the one held responsible. She hadn't waited for Megan to return. Yes, Derrick lied to get her to ride with him, but Claudia hadn't questioned him. She drank too much and made herself vulnerable. She got into his car voluntarily. What did that awful man say, the one who wouldn't open his door? When Claudia told him someone tried to rape her, he said she probably asked for it. As much as she'd love to see Derrick arrested for assaulting her, Claudia knew she could never tell Mom and Dad about it. At sixteen, she already knew women were blamed for getting raped.

Claudia rinsed her hair and soaped her body. Then, she stood under the hot water and let it rinse away the dirt and the pain. When the hot water started to run out, she turned off the shower, got out, and toweled herself dry.

Tomorrow morning, she would have Neal drop her off at Megan's house. She and Megan would come up with a story for why she was bruised. Maybe she'd say she had too much to drink and tumbled down a hill. Her parents would ground her, but worse things had already happened.

Neal's T-shirt came down to her knees. The elastic on the boxer shorts kept them from sliding off her hips. She wiped the steam off the bathroom mirror. She still looked terrible, but much better than before.

While she was in the shower, Neal changed into sweatpants and a T-shirt. He'd put a blanket and a pillow on the couch. But what was really cute was he'd made his bed. Claudia distinctly remembered it was unmade when they arrived.

"I'll take the couch," Neal said.

"That's okay. I can take the couch."

"You're my guest. I insist. Besides, I've slept on this couch many times."

"Good, because I'm exhausted."

Claudia climbed under the covers. The bed felt like heaven. Neal turned off the lights and settled in on the couch. Claudia closed her eyes and listened to the ticking of the alarm clock on the bedside table.

"Are you asleep?" she asked.

"No," Neal said.

Claudia told him the whole story. It felt good to say it out loud and to hear how incredibly crazy the entire night had been. Her journey started out when she went to the bedroom with Barry and ended with Neal picking her up off the side of the road.

"Even though he's my friend, I've always known Derrick was an asshole," Neal said. "But I never guessed how big an asshole. I never thought he'd do what he did tonight. If I'd known what he was capable of, I wouldn't have been friends with him."

"Well, he's definitely not my friend anymore. And I still have to see him every day at school."

"Report him to the police."

"He'd just deny it. It would be my word against his."

They were propped up on their elbows facing each other across the room. Claudia felt like she was at a sleepover, sharing secrets and telling horror stories. The moonlight came through a slit in the window curtain and fell across Neal's face. Claudia wondered why she never noticed Neal was very good looking. He was one of her closest friends, but she'd been so in lust with Barry, she had ignored him.

Neal wasn't as tall or athletic as Barry, but he was seriously cute. He was much smarter and more considerate than Barry. He was that intelligent, down to earth, nice guy that girls ignore, so they can date bad boys, but then end up marrying.

"I'm sorry," Neal said.

"For what?"

"At the party, you said you saw a girl dressed like you. You thought she was the one who attacked Barry. I didn't believe you. I thought you made her up as an excuse for what you did. But then, she shows up out of nowhere in Barry's car and beats up Derrick. It had to have been the same girl."

"You believe me now?"

"Yeah. It's so bizarre it must be true. But who is this mystery girl? How'd she know what you'd be wearing to the party? Why was she following you?

I'm tempted to look outside and see if she followed you here."

"Maybe you should," Claudia said, pulling the blanket up to her chin.

"Don't worry, if anybody was out there, Rosie would let us know."

"This is going to sound crazy, but I think the mystery girl was trying to protect me."

"While wearing bunny ears?"

Claudia giggled and then burst into tears. Neal left the couch and sat on the edge of the bed.

"I'm so sorry," he said. "I didn't mean to make you cry."

Claudia shook her head.

"It wasn't you. I feel like I was in a pinball machine getting knocked around from one thing to the next. I was trying really hard not to cry, but I couldn't keep it in anymore."

"Do you want me to hold you?"

Claudia nodded. Neal put his arms around her, and she leaned into him. He hugged her as she sobbed. They reclined on the bed as he continued to hold her. She put her arms around him and finally felt safe. And then, he kissed her. Not a hard kiss, but his lips gently pressing against hers. Claudia wasn't sure if she should push him away or kiss him back. She decided to go with her instincts. She kissed him back.

As they kissed, Neal got under the covers with her. Their bodies pressed together. He began to put his hand under her T-shirt and froze.

"Is this okay?" Neal asked.

Claudia smiled.

"Yes. It's okay."

She had planned to make love to a boy tonight, but she never would have guessed it would end up being this one.

* * *

Neal parked in front of Megan's house and turned off the engine. The music from Neal's *Murmur* CD turned off as well. Claudia leaned across the seat to kiss him. Already she was addicted to his kisses.

"You look so much better in my clothes than I do," he said when their lips finally parted.

Claudia wore a sweater over a Lookouts T-shirt, sweatpants, and a pair of thick socks. She wore no shoes. Neal's shoes were too big for her feet. She carried her dirty leotard and underwear in a plastic bag.

"I like your clothes," Claudia said. "I just might keep them."

Neal took her hand and rubbed her knuckles with his thumb.

"About last night," he said. "I hope it was the start of something."

Claudia pushed a strand of hair behind her ear. A pleasant shiver ran through her.

"I think so."

They kissed until a sharp rap on the car window made them jump apart. Megan stood beside the car with her arms crossed.

"Do you mind?" she said. "My neighbors are Baptists. They don't appreciate these public displays of affection."

Neal rolled down his window.

"Hey, Megan. Heard anything from Barry?"

"Not yet."

"I'll see you at school tomorrow," Claudia said as she climbed out of Neal's car.

She and Megan watched Neal drive away.

"Good thing you called me this morning when you did," Megan said. "I was about to go by your house to make sure you got home."

"Good thing you didn't. The less my parents know the better."

"I want to hear every detail. Leave nothing out. Including the dirty parts. Especially the dirty parts."

While preparing and devouring a breakfast of sugary cereal, bacon strips, and apple juice, Claudia told Megan about her long, strange adventure. The telling took a long time because Megan peppered her with questions. When Claudia was done, she was exhausted as if she'd lived through it again.

"Well, let's see what we can do about those bruises," Megan said.

They cleaned their breakfast dishes then went to Megan's room. She applied make-up to Claudia's face.

"I can't mask the purple bruise on your forehead completely," Megan

said.

Claudia looked in the mirror. "Maybe my parents won't notice if I comb my hair over it."

She changed into the clothes she'd worn to Megan's house the day before, putting Neal's clothes in the bag with her leotard. She thought about asking Megan to take her by White Oak Park to look for her shoes, but quickly rejected the idea. Claudia never wanted to see the park again.

It was late Sunday afternoon when Megan dropped Claudia off at her house. Before going inside, she threw her leotard and underwear into the trash bin. Like White Oak Park, she never wanted to see them again.

Her parents were doing their usual Sunday afternoon activities, her father was watching a football game on TV and her mother was doing laundry. By keeping her head down when she spoke to them, they didn't notice her bruises. Once she was in the safety of her bedroom, Claudia stashed Neal's clothes in the bottom drawer of her dresser under her winter sweaters.

She stretched out on her bed and thought about Neal. She imagined holding hands with him as they walked down the hall at school. She wondered if they got married would their children have his blue eyes.

Claudia didn't remember falling asleep. When her mother woke her up to see if she wanted dinner, the sun had gone down, and her room was dark. She told her mother she wasn't hungry and slept until her alarm woke her the next morning to get up for school.

CHAPTER
36

Thursday, October 31, 2002

The doorbell rang. Claudia opened the door and was greeted by a princess, a vampire, and Spider-Man.

"Trick or treat!" they shouted.

The costumed children's adoring parents hung back as Claudia tossed miniature Milky Ways, Snickers, and Baby Ruths into the children's bags. With her task completed, Claudia rejoined Agnes on the living room couch.

"You have to get the door next time," Claudia said.

"Sure," Agnes said.

She took a handful of popcorn from the bowl she and Claudia were sharing. They were watching Agnes' favorite movie, "The Time Machine," the 1960 version. They watched it every Halloween. They were at the movie's most frightening scene according to Agnes, Weena taking George to an ancient library. He picked up a book and it dissolved in his hands. The thought of all that lost knowledge sent an icy chill through Agnes.

"You're not too old for trick or treating," Claudia said. "Throw on a costume and I'll drive you around the neighborhood. We could score a lot of candy."

"I don't care for candy," Agnes said. "I prefer cupcakes and cookies."

The doorbell rang. Pausing the movie, Agnes went to the front door with Claudia following behind her. The trick or treaters this time were a caveman, a Powerpuff Girl, and a cowboy.

"You don't see a lot of cowboys these days," Claudia said.

Agnes put a candy bar in each sack. As she closed the door, she realized Claudia was missing. She found Claudia in her bedroom, dapping her eyes with a tissue.

"Sorry," Claudia said. "Halloween is not my favorite holiday."

"Mine either," Agnes said.

She didn't need to ask why her mother was crying. The photograph of Claudia posing with three boys at a Halloween party was mounted on the living room wall in a silver frame. It was the best photo of Neal that Claudia owned. In the photo, he was a handsome cowboy with his hat tipped back, holding his six-shooter raised and ready to fend off cattle rustlers and horse thieves. Over the years, Agnes had memorized Neal's face. She looked for evidence of his features in her own face but had yet to find any.

Agnes and Claudia returned to the living room and "The Time Machine." The Morlocks captured the Elois and carried them back to their subterranean lair.

"I can't believe my eleven-year-old girl is in college," Claudia said. "You're growing up so fast."

"My brain is growing quickly, but not the rest of me. I'm still a kid."

"A kid who doesn't want to dress up for Halloween."

Agnes shrugged. She was used to Claudia teasing her. She never let on how much she enjoyed it. That would ruin the game.

"Before you know it, you'll be going off to graduate school," Claudia asked. "What am I going to do here without you?"

The doorbell rang before Agnes could answer.

CHAPTER
37

Sunday, October 26, 2008

Claudia Cook started her car and turned the heater on full blast, glancing in the rear-view mirror at the closed garage door before switching on the radio.

"Good morning!" shouted the deejay. "Our classic rock weekend continues with another thirty minutes of uninterrupted music from your favorite classic rock artists. Let's kick this Sunday off with thirty minutes of R.E.M."

The opening chords of "Talk About the Passion" played through the car's speakers. Claudia thought about the morning when she and Neal listened to R.E.M. in his car. Best day of her life. She closed her eyes and let the music sooth her.

CHAPTER
38

Saturday, November 1, 2008

Agnes listened to the phone message Claudia left her six days earlier. She'd listened to the message more than a dozen times.

"Agnes, it's Mom. Tried calling you earlier but got your voicemail. Is your phone working? I always feel blue this time of year. I know I should get over it, but that's easier said than done. Call me when you get this message. Love you."

A motion outside the car caught her attention. Agnes was parked outside Red Bank United Methodist Church. Megan stood in front of the car waving at her. Agnes rolled down the window.

"Agnes, honey?" Megan said. "I know you're hurting, but there's a lot of people inside who want to share your grief with you."

"I'm not very good with people," Agnes said.

Megan reached through the window and put her hand on Agnes' shoulder.

"I know," Megan said. "But try anyway."

Agnes climbed out of the car. Megan hugged her.

"It was a lovely funeral," Megan said.

"I forgot the anniversary was coming up," Agnes said. "I was completely absorbed in getting my presentation ready on time. I turned off my phone so I wouldn't be disturbed. If only I hadn't, then I could have talked her out of it."

"You don't know that. You can't blame yourself."

"Yes, I can."

Agnes tugged at the hem of her black dress. The dress belonged to Claudia. It belonged to her now. She didn't want the dress. She wanted her mother.

"You look so much like her," Megan said, putting her palm on Agnes' cheek.

"Thank you," Agnes said. "But I'm not as beautiful as she was."

Megan hugged Agnes again.

"If nothing else, come in and eat something," she said. "There's enough food in there to feed an army."

Claudia's friends and co-workers milled about the Fellowship Hall. They hugged Agnes as if they were related to her and told her how sorry they were for her loss. Megan led Agnes to one of the round tables covered with paper tablecloths and a vase holding a single silk flower set in the middle. They sat next to Megan's husband, Steven.

"Steven," Megan said. "Would you get Agnes something to eat?"

"Be happy to," he said. "What would you like, Agnes?"

"Food," Agnes said.

"I'll see if they have any."

He headed for the buffet table.

"What was your presentation about?" Megan said.

"I'd rather not talk about it," Agnes said.

Megan nodded.

A tall man with a buzz cut and a voluptuous blonde approached their table. Megan's face lit up. She jumped to her feet and gave him a hug.

"Barry! I haven't seen you in ages."

"I don't believe you've met my wife," Barry said, turning to the blonde. "Stacy, this is Megan. Megan, Stacy." The women shook hands. Barry peered down at Agnes. "And you must be Agnes. Hello, Agnes. I'm Barry Plunkett. I knew your mother in high school."

Agnes shook his hand. He had a firm grip. Studying his face, Agnes realized she'd seen him before. He was one of the three boys posing with Claudia in the Halloween photo hanging in the living room. He was the vampire.

As Barry and Stacy joined the table, Steven returned with a plate filled with finger sandwiches and carrot slices, and an iced tea in a plastic cup.

"Barry, Stacy," Megan said. "This is my husband, Steven."

"Pleasure to meet you," Barry said, shaking Steven's hand.

Agnes picked at the food while Megan and Barry reminisced about their high school days, telling funny stories about each other and Claudia. Their spouses pretended they had a clue what the two of them were talking about.

A man plopped down in the chair next to Barry. Agnes had never seen such an ugly person. His face was pockmarked, his hair was greasy, his suit was wrinkled, and he reeked of alcohol. Megan and Barry glared at him with undisguised repulsion.

"Well, looky here," he said. "It's the whole gang. At least those still walking the earth."

"I'm surprised to see you're not six feet under," Megan said. "How did you manage not to drink yourself to death?"

The ugly man showed Megan his middle finger.

"Who are you?" Agnes asked.

He looked at the others and then at Agnes. "Claudia never mentioned her old buddy, Derrick Whitlow?"

Agnes narrowed her eyes at him. He was the third boy in the Halloween photo, the one in dirty overalls holding a machete.

"Did you go to school with my mother?"

"Yeah. We all hung out together. Didn't we?" He stared at Barry and Megan as if daring them to contradict him.

"Yeah, we did," Barry said. "How you been, Derrick?"

"Getting by. Looks like you made out all right."

He ogled Stacy's breasts. She crossed her arms over her chest.

"I see you haven't changed since I last saw you," Barry said. "You're still an asshole."

Derrick chuckled.

Agnes wished he hadn't come. She couldn't believe her mother had ever been friends with such a disgusting human being.

"Megan," Agnes said. "I enjoyed the stories you told about Claudia. Do you have any stories about Neal?"

"Neal was a great guy," Megan said.

"He was the kind of guy you could depend on if you needed help," Barry said.

Derrick rolled his eyes.

"Oh, for God's sake!" he moaned. "You make Neal sound like he was Jesus H. Christ! He pointed at Agnes. "You want to know what your dad was really like? He was a wimp. A loser. He's lucky he died before you were born because he would have been a lousy father."

Before anyone else could respond, Agnes sprang to her feet.

"If you say one more negative thing about my father, I will insist you leave immediately."

Derrick chuckled.

"You'll insist? Oooh. I'm scared."

Agnes didn't back down. She could feel the others watching her.

"I will have you removed. Your actions have consequences."

Derrick paled, and he sank low in his chair.

"It's you. You'd said you'd come back." He grabbed Barry's arm and pointed at Agnes. "Can't you see it's her?"

Barry pulled his arm free. "Just how wasted are you, man?"

Derrick kept staring at Agnes.

"Where are your rabbit ears?"

Agnes put her hands on her hips. The gesture made Derrick flinch.

"I assure you, Mr. Whitlow," she said. "I have never seen you before in my life. I would not be disappointed if I never laid eyes on you again."

Derrick fell out of the chair and scrambled to his feet.

"I have to go."

He rushed out of the hall.

"Okay that was weird, right?" Steven said.

"Even for Derrick that was weird," Megan said.

"You must have reminded him of someone," Stacy said.

"I can't imagine who," Agnes said.

She returned to her chair and attacked the food on her plate. Suddenly, she was quite hungry.

"We all agree Derrick's an asshole," Barry said. "But he's right about one thing. We've been putting Neal on a pedestal. It's not fair to his memory if we don't tell Agnes what he was really like." He glanced at Megan to make sure she wasn't angry and then he faced Agnes. "Neal was a regular guy. He liked to play baseball and he did okay in school. We hung out and drank beer on the weekends. I was telling the truth when I said you could depend on him to show up if you needed help."

"What did Claudia tell you about him?" Stacy asked.

Agnes sipped her iced tea.

"Mom told me he died before I was born. He was the sweetest man she'd ever known. That he would have been proud of me. That she loved him very much and missed him. But that's it. No details. No stories. She never told me how they met or how long they dated. The only thing I know about his death is that he died in a car accident."

Steven put his hand on Megan's knee.

"You might as well tell her."

Megan dabbed her eyes with a napkin.

"Not now."

Though Agnes had never pushed Claudia for more information about her father, it didn't mean she wasn't curious. In fact, she was very curious but had forced herself not to dig into his past out of respect to her mother. But now, there was a chance to find out more about her father.

"Now is as good a time as any," Agnes said.

"She's right," Barry said.

Megan stood.

"Okay, fine. Come on, Agnes. Let's go somewhere we can talk just the two of us."

Agnes followed Megan to an empty table in the corner of the hall.

"Claudia was going to tell you," Megan said, "but kept putting it off. First, she didn't feel you were old enough and then you were too busy being a genius and dealing with college. It all started when Claudia and I went to this Halloween party. I remember it so clearly. How could I not after everything that happened? I dressed as a witch and Claudia went as a bunny rabbit."

Agnes thought about the costume Claudia wore in the Halloween photo.

"She wore bunny ears," Agnes said. "Derrick said something about bunny ears."

"Derrick is full of crap," Megan said. She looked at the ceiling to make sure she wasn't going to get hit by lightning for cussing in a church. "At the party, Claudia and I meet up with Barry, Derrick, and Neal. Back then Derrick was a jerk, but not the slime ball you saw today. The five of us were our own little tribe and hung out together all the time."

Megan stared at Barry. Agnes recognized the faraway look. Claudia used to get it from time to time. They missed their little tribe.

"What happened after you and Mom got to the party?" Agnes asked.

The question brought Megan back to their conversation.

"We were having a great time then things got…weird."

"Weird?" Agnes asked.

"Really weird."

Megan told Agnes everything that happened on Saturday, October 27, 1990, from when Barry and Claudia went looking for a bathroom until Neal dropped Claudia off at Megan's house on Sunday. Agnes listened carefully and refrained from asking questions until Megan was done.

"Did you ever find out who the mystery girl was?" Agnes asked.

"The mystery girl is still a mystery," Megan said.

"How soon after this weird night did Neal die?"

Megan twisted her wedding ring on her finger.

"When we came to school on Monday, there were a bunch of grief counselors on campus. The principal announced over the PA system Neal Fisher had died in a car accident. I couldn't believe it. I had just seen Neal the day before."

"Did the school say how the accident happened?" Agnes asked.

"Only that the accident wasn't Neal's fault. I didn't know the details until I read it in the paper. After Neal left Claudia at my house, he headed back home. The police were chasing this guy driving a stolen car. He was going over ninety miles an hour when he crashed into the side of Neal's car. Neal died before the ambulance arrived."

Agnes' eyes widened.

"Mom and Neal were only together for one night?"

"Yeah. And you're the result."

Agnes rubbed her chin.

"I suppose it's not unexpected. Mom and Neal probably didn't use protection, her chances of pregnancy were increased."

Megan shook her head.

"No. They used a condom. But condoms don't always work. Apparently, you were destined to be born."

"Apparently," Agnes said.

"Considering all the weird things that happened that night, Claudia's pregnancy was perhaps the only non-weird thing. The car the guy was driving that killed Neal was Barry's car. Somebody stole it at the Halloween party. Derrick claims he saw the mystery girl driving it, but she wasn't in the car when it crashed into Neal."

Agnes glanced over at Barry.

"How did Barry react to the news his car was used to kill his friend?"

"He was devastated. In a twisted way, it was the best thing that ever happened to him. He was floating along in life. His dad gave him anything he wanted, like that fancy car. After Neal died, he was a different person. He stopped smoking pot and drinking beer. He began studying and his

Mickey Dubrow

grades went up. He got into college and later got a good job on his own without help from his dad. I think he's been trying to honor Neal by being the best person possible."

Agnes leaned back in her chair. There was so much information to process. She wished she had brought a notebook to take notes.

"I still don't understand," Agnes said. "The way Mom talked about Neal made it sound like they were together forever. How could he have been the love of her life after such a short period of time? Does love really work like that?"

"Keep in mind," Megan said. "Claudia had just been through this incredibly long and terrifying night. And then Neal came along and rescued her. He was her knight in shining armor."

"He died before he could do anything to disappoint her."

Megan grabbed Agnes' hand.

"Claudia was smarter than that. She knew Neal wasn't perfect. She knew they might not have stayed together. But he gave her one perfect night before everything fell apart. Not only did Neal die, but our tribe died as well. Claudia dropped out of school. Barry went off to find himself. None of us would have anything to do with Derrick. Two years later, I went to college and Claudia stayed here to raise you as a single mother."

"When Mom talked about feeling blue on the anniversary of Neal's death, she wasn't just grieving the loss of my father."

"That's right."

"What if he had lived?"

Megan looked at the ceiling as if Neal would come down from heaven and tell them.

"I think he would have been a great dad," she said.

"Would he have stayed with Mom? Or would she still have been a single mother?"

"Oh God, what a question," Megan said, but then she saw Agnes was serious. "Neal would have stuck around. He was that kind of guy."

"And Mom would have been much happier."

"That's one of those what if things that can drive you crazy. You start thinking if only you could go back in time and change things, then every-thing would work out. But you can't, the past is the past."

"But what if I could go back in time and save Neal? Mom would still be alive."

Megan held Agnes' hand.

"Like I said, those kinds of thoughts will drive you crazy."

Agnes stared off into the distance.

"It's only crazy if you can't do it."

CHAPTER
39

Monday, November 10, 2008

Agnes sat at a secluded table on the third floor of the Chattanooga Public Library and scrolled through *Chattanooga Times* archives on reels of microfilm. She started her search with Sunday, October 28, 1990. When she didn't find anything about Neal's death, she switched to a reel containing *Chattanooga News-Free Press* archives starting with the same date. The story she wanted was on the front page.

MAN CRASHES STOLEN CAR, KILLING ONE, IN RED BANK POLICE PURSUIT

One person was killed when a man driving a stolen car crashed into another vehicle during a Sunday morning police chase in Red Bank.

The two-vehicle crash occurred around 10:30 a.m. at the intersection of Dayton Boulevard and Memorial Drive.

Red Bank Chief of Police Bert Keyserling stated the suspect allegedly stole the car in North Chattanooga and later fled at the estimated speed of 90 mph when Red Bank Police began to pursue. The suspect in the vehicle was traveling northbound striking the motorist heading southbound on Dayton Boulevard.

Police were unable to identify the man at the time of the arrest. The victim's name has not been released.

Agnes searched for more newspaper stories in the days following the accident. She found a story about Neal which included a photo of the memorial created in his memory near the intersection where the crash happened. Bouquets of flowers and teddy bears sat at the foot of a wood cross with his name on it. The story mentioned he was a student at Red Bank High School. A yearbook photo of him wearing a suit, a tie, and a big smile was next to the roadside memorial photo.

Taking notes as she tracked down more stories, Agnes pieced together the events leading up to Neal's death. Around 3:00 a.m. on Sunday, October 28, Vincent Parnell, age twenty-four, finished his shift as a dishwasher at the Coral Reef Tavern. He started out on foot toward his apartment, four blocks from the tavern. His route took him past the parking lot to a group of shops on Frazier Avenue. There was a red Trans Am in the parking lot. Parnell stopped to admire the car and noticed the keys were in the ignition. On further investigation, he discovered the door was unlocked.

Though Parnell already had a criminal record that included petty theft and drug possession, he decided to take the car. He drove for hours on US 27 at speeds exceeding 100 mph. He came off the highway, stopped for breakfast at a Waffle House, filled the gas tank, and was driving on Dayton Boulevard when a patrol car tried to pull him over for speeding. The police chased Parnell until he lost control of the car and smashed head on into Neal's car traveling in the opposite direction.

Agnes found a photo of the crash. Looking at the mangled vehicles, she couldn't believe anyone survived. Barry's prized red Trans Am was reduced to a heap of twisted metal. Somehow Parnell survived with minor injuries. Later, he was found guilty of car theft and vehicular homicide.

None of the stories Agnes found in the archives speculated as to how Barry's car managed to get from the Halloween party in Hixson to the parking lot in North Chattanooga. Once the justice system found Parnell guilty and put him safely behind bars, the case was closed and forgotten.

After finishing her research at the library, Agnes drove to North Chattanooga then to Neal's house. She parked on the street at the edge of the property. Neal's family no longer lived there, having moved away three years after his death. Agnes supposed the house had more memories than they could handle.

While going through Claudia's things, Agnes found an old diary. The entries began on Claudia's first day of high school and ended shortly before Agnes was born. There were many empty pages in the back of the diary. As a single mother, keeping a diary would have been a luxury of time Claudia couldn't afford.

Most of the early entries were about Claudia's obsession with Barry. She described every encounter with him in minute detail. The entries convinced Agnes that hormones made people stupid and was relieved she made it through puberty without doing anything foolish. After the Halloween party, the entries were about Neal and what life might have been like if only, if only. Agnes was stunned when she got to the entries about Neal's parents.

When Claudia informed them she was pregnant with their son's baby, she thought they would be happy to know part of Neal would live on after his death. At first, they didn't believe her and accused Claudia of trying to take advantage of their grief. But once she told them how and when she'd gotten pregnant, they blamed her for his death. The way they saw it, if Neal hadn't taken Claudia to Megan's house that morning, he wouldn't have been on the road when Vincent Parnell ran into him. Agnes finally understood why Claudia never talked about Agnes' paternal grandparents.

Agnes wrote down the mileage from North Chattanooga to Neal's house and made notes about the route. The present owner of the house came out to check his mailbox. Agnes drove away before he noticed her.

When she got home, Agnes warmed up a can of tomato soup and made a grilled cheese sandwich. As she ate, she reviewed all the notes she had taken so far. On a legal pad, she wrote down a list of supplies she would need. She drew a star next to the most important item, pre-1990 money. She had the phone number of a coin collector in East Ridge. After she finished eating, she planned to call him to see if he had what she needed.

Agnes took a bite of her sandwich. The cheese oozed out the sides and dripped to the plate. She could never figure out how to make a grilled cheese sandwich as good as Claudia's. Agnes pushed her notebook and legal pad aside and opened her calendar. She counted the days between today and December 24. She couldn't think of any reason she wouldn't be ready by Christmas Eve. That was the best day to travel because it afforded the lowest chance of anyone seeing her disappear into the past. And when she got back, it would be the most wonderful Christmas Day of her life.

CHAPTER

40

Wednesday, December 24, 2008

Agnes gazed at herself in the mirror. She wore a V-neck sweater over a turtleneck shirt, stonewashed jeans, and a red plaid coat, clothes she'd found in her mother's closet. Claudia wore them as a teenager and had hoped in vain to fit into them again. Agnes hoped they would help her blend into the world of 1990.

She left the house and drove to the North Shore. Red and white strings of lights twined around streetlamps. Store windows were covered with a blizzard of sprayed-on snow.

The Walnut Street Bridge was Claudia and Agnes's favorite place in the city. They spent many afternoons standing in the middle and watching the river below. As she suspected, the pedestrian bridge was deserted on Christmas Eve.

Agnes stood by the railing and gazed down at the Tennessee River. Snow began to fall, not heavily, just enough flakes to add frosting to the park benches. She set her time destination on the clock. She looked around to make sure she was alone and was surprised to see the bridge wasn't deserted after all.

A girl walked toward her. She wore a winter coat and a knit cap. Her hands were buried in the pockets of her coat while her head was tilted down. Agnes was annoyed she'd have to wait until the girl passed before she could flip the switch on the Time Tefillin. She gripped the railing, exposing the strap wrapped around her left middle finger, and stared straight ahead. As the late night stroller's footsteps got closer, Agnes' heart beat faster.

She wondered if this was the mystery girl. Like Claudia, Agnes believed she was real and had a theory about her identity. And that theory frightened her. It would mean Agnes was not as unique and special as she thought she was, and she didn't know how to deal with that.

She shivered when the footsteps stopped beside her. The girl gripped the railing next to Agnes, their fingers almost touching. Wrapped around her middle finger was a strap identical to the one wrapped around Agnes' middle finger. Agnes looked at the girl's face. It was like looking in a mirror.

"It's about time you got here," she said.

"I suspected you were the mystery girl," Agnes said. "So apparently I'm not the first Agnes."

"You're not even the second Agnes. I'm Second Agnes. You're Third Agnes."

"Third Agnes?"

"Come on, let's go home. We have a lot to talk about and I want to warm up. I about froze my butt off waiting for you."

Confused and curious, Third Agnes fell in step with Second Agnes as they walked toward the entrance to the bridge. Third Agnes couldn't help but stare at Second Agnes.

"Are those blood stains on your pants?" Third Agnes asked.

Second Agnes paused under a light and examined the brown stains that started at her knees and trickled down her jeans. There were a few specks on her tennis shoes.

"Don't worry," Second Agnes said. "It's not my blood."

"Something else we can talk about when we get home?"

"Certainly."

When they got to the car, Second Agnes pulled a set of keys out of her pocket.

"You can drive," she said, "but I'd like to see if my key fits." It slid in smoothly and Second Agnes unlocked the door. "Apparently, Mom was destined to buy this particular car."

The streets were deserted. Even the police seemed to have stayed home to wait for Santa Claus. Third Agnes drove while Second Agnes watched the snowflakes melt on the windshield.

"Barry Plunkett was First Agnes' father," Second Agnes said. "My father was Derrick Whitlow."

"Derrick? Ew."

"I take it you've met him."

"Once."

"Once is enough. However terrible you can imagine he would be as a father; he was much worse. Who's your father?"

"Neal Fisher."

"Really? Neal seems like such a nice guy. Why do you want to stop him from having sex with Claudia?"

"I don't want to stop him. I want to save his life."

Second Agnes stared at Third Agnes.

"Okay, this is different."

They arrived at the house. When Second Agnes entered, she breathed in deeply and sighed.

"Still smells like Mom. I suppose you should make the tea since I'm the guest in this timeline. Do you have any cookies?"

"Second cabinet, bottom shelf," Third Agnes said as she carried the kettle to the sink and filled it with water.

As they waited for the water to boil, they compared Time Tefillins. Other than the choice of stitching and the brand of the digital clock, their time machines were identical. The kettle whistled and Third Agnes filled their ceramic cups with hot water. They sat across from each other at the dining room table. While their tea steamed, they shared a plate of chocolate chip cookies.

"How much time do you have?" Third Agnes asked.

Second Agnes checked her watch. "Four hours and thirty-two minutes."

"Not near enough time for all the questions I have."

"Or mine. Let's begin."

Second Agnes started with First Agnes' journey to prevent Barry from becoming her father and ended with Second Agnes' journey to prevent Derrick from becoming hers. Third Agnes picked up the story of Neal rescuing Claudia on the side of the road and ended with Neal's death.

"Barry's damn Trans Am," Second Agnes said. "I'm sorry. I figured the police would find it the next day. That's what happened after First Agnes used the car to get to North Shore. I didn't factor in the possibility of someone who wasn't an Agnes taking the car."

"Both you and First Agnes stole the car," Third Agnes said angrily. "Why not a third person?"

"You're right. But there's no way I could have predicted the car would be the instrument of Neal's death any more than I could have predicted he and Claudia would end up together."

Third Agnes' sudden anger faded away just as quickly.

"You're right. There were several incredible coincidences that night."

Second Agnes chewed on a cookie.

"Still, I should have predicted Neal would be the third father. Claudia had three close male friends. She had an Agnes with two of them, so it only stands to reason that after the first two were eliminated from the timeline, she would have an Agnes with the third."

"It almost makes you believe in fate."

Second Agnes grabbed another cookie.

"I rarely eat this many cookies, but since the end of my existence is mere hours away, I'm not worried about overeating."

Third Agnes took a cookie and broke it in half. She ate one half and left the other on her plate.

"You're very calm considering the circumstances."

"First Agnes spent her final hours with me. When I went back to deal with Derrick, I knew exactly what was going to happen to me."

Third Agnes went to the kitchen to make them more tea. When she got back, Second Agnes had eaten the rest of the cookies, including the half Third Agnes had left on her plate.

"How much time?" Third Agnes asked.

"Two hours. How do you plan to save Neal?"

"I'm going to steal Barry's car before Vincent Parnell does. If that doesn't work, then I will save Neal with this." Third Agnes took a tire pressure gauge out of her pocket.

Second Agnes leaned across the table to get a better look at the chrome tube with the bulbous head.

"You're going to let the air out of Neal's tires?"

"Exactly. I hope I don't have to because first I'd have to walk all the way to Neal's house. It's not that far, but as you've informed me, October 28, 1990 was a very cold night."

"Would you let the air out of all four tires?"

"Of course. That should delay Neal long enough that he's not on the road when the police chase Parnell."

"But then Neal's parents will find out Claudia spent the night in his room."

"Better they get in trouble than Neal gets killed. Their punishment will become a charming story they tell on their wedding anniversary."

Second Agnes snatched the tire gauge out of Third Agnes' hand.

"Don't do it," Second Agnes said. "It's a waste of time. You said earlier you almost believe in fate. Admit it, our situation is beyond science. Will we keep making the same mistake over and over again? Will we have to get to One Hundred Agnes before we admit there are certain things we cannot change?"

Third Agnes took the tire gauge back and put it in her pocket.

"It's different this time. I can save Neal. I can save Mom."

Second Agnes rubbed her forehead.

"Don't you get it? Just as there will always be an Agnes, she will always grow up without a father. Claudia will always die in the garage on October 26, 2008. But because Agnes is too stubborn to accept this and move on, Agnes' life will always stall before the end of 2008 because she's too busy screwing up 1990."

"You're wrong!" shouted Third Agnes. "You're just jealous because you know I have a chance to be happy. I'll have a good father who will love Claudia and live with us. And Claudia won't kill herself!"

Second Agnes sipped her tea. Third Agnes used a napkin to dry her tears.

"I'm sorry," Third Agnes said. "I shouldn't have said that."

Second Agnes shrugged.

"It's okay. It's just me. You know what First Agnes told me shortly before her time ran out?"

"She wished she had more time?"

Second Agnes snorted.

"Everybody wishes that, not just time travelers. First Agnes said she should have said yes when Josh Hawkins asked her out on a date."

"I forgot about Josh. He was cute."

"She said he was the only boy who ever asked her out on a date. She wished she said yes and that she kissed him because she'd never been kissed."

Third Agnes touched her lips. "I've never been kissed."

"Neither have I. He asked me out too."

Third Agnes nodded. "Me too."

"When he asked me, I should have said yes. Do me a favor. You're obviously determined to keep this stupid time loop going, so please pass this message on to the next Agnes. Tell her if she doesn't try to save Claudia and makes it to 2009, call Josh Hawkins and ask him out on a date. And when she's on that date, kiss him right on the lips. Will you do that for me?"

"I'll tell her."

Second Agnes checked her watch.

"Will you look at the time? It's later than I thought."

And then she disappeared.

Third Agnes stared at the empty space where Second Agnes had been. It was if she'd never been here at all. Yet, she missed her. It was like discovering she had another family member and then losing them right away. Third Agnes gathered her things. Second Agnes was wrong. She would be the last Agnes because she would succeed where the first two had failed.

CHAPTER
41

Sunday, October 28, 1990

Third Agnes arrived on the Walnut Street Bridge at 2:00 a.m. on Sunday, October 28, 1990. She was more nervous than she thought she would be, and the dilapidated bridge made her even more so. When she reached solid ground, she took a moment to catch her breath before crossing the street to the art supply store.

The Trans Am wasn't in the parking lot. Not yet. At this moment in time, Second Agnes was beating Derrick senseless with a pool cue. Agnes descended a short stairwell that brought her eye level with the parking lot. She checked the time. It was 2:30 a.m. There was nothing for her to do now except wait.

Her stomach growled. She pulled a plastic bag containing two chocolate chip cookies out of her pocket and ate them while she waited.

At 3:00 a.m., headlights lit up the parking lot. Agnes ducked down and the light passed over her head. A car door opened and closed. She rose for a peek. Second Agnes leaned against the hood of the red Trans Am and stared up at the stars. Agnes lowered herself and waited.

She didn't want Second Agnes to know she was here; certain she would try to talk her out of saving Neal like she tried to do in 2008.

Footsteps came in her direction. Agnes crouched lower in the stairwell. The footsteps passed by her and receded into the distance. When Agnes could no longer hear the footsteps, she peered at the parking lot. There was no one around.

But then, she heard footsteps approaching.

Agnes scrunched down. For some reason, Second Agnes had returned.

"Hot damn! Look at you."

That was definitely not Second Agnes' voice. Agnes peeked to see who it was. A skinny man with a mullet stood next to the Trans Am. A cigarette dangled from his lower lip. Agnes recognized him from his mug shot in the *Chattanooga Times* archives. He was Vincent Parnell, the dishwasher and car thief who crashed into Neal Fisher and caused his death.

Agnes shot out of the stairwell.

"Hey! Get away from that car."

Parnell spun around.

"Where the hell did you come from?"

Agnes pointed at the Trans Am.

"That's my car. You were going to steal it."

Parnell leaned down and peered into the car window.

"How do I know this is your car?"

He flipped his cigarette butt. It landed in the stairwell Agnes had been hiding in.

"It's my car because I say it is," Agnes said.

"You're going to have to do better than that. Either prove it or do something to convince me to take you with me."

He took a step towards Agnes. She moved back.

"I don't have to prove anything," Agnes said. "If you don't leave now, I'm going to call the police."

Parnell quickly reached out and grabbed Agnes' arm. He pulled her to him and pressed his sweaty body against hers. His breath stank of cigarettes and beer.

"Go ahead and call 'em," he sneered. "This ain't your car. I watched the owner drive up here then I seen her walk down the hill. I came by just to have a look and saw she left the keys in the ignition."

"That was me," Agnes said weakly. "I forgot my keys and came back for them."

He flung Agnes away from him. She lost her balance and fell, scrapping her hands on the ground.

"You know what I think?" Parnell said. "You were going to steal the car. But then I came along, and you got scared and hid. You should've pinched it when you had the chance because this baby's mine now."

He climbed in. The engine roared to life. The sports car flew into reverse, spraying gravel in its wake. Agnes climbed to her feet and ran over to the car.

"Don't take the car," she said as she banged her fists on the hood.

Parnell sped past her. The tires squealed as he turned the corner. Agnes chased the car down the hill.

"When the police come after you, don't try to get away!" she yelled. "You're going to kill Neal!"

The Trans Am ran through two red lights in a row before picking up speed and zooming down the road. Out of breath, Agnes sat on the sidewalk and listened as the roar of the car receded into the night.

She rolled back her pants and saw her knees were scrapped as badly as her hands. Her body ached as she got to her feet. She tested her arms and legs to make sure nothing was broken. Her wounds were more emotional than physical.

Agnes checked the time.

She'd been in 1990 for less than two hours and already her first attempt to save Neal had failed miserably. She wasn't ready to give up. Neal's house was an hour walk away. She would arrive at his home with plenty of time to deflate the tires on his car.

Agnes leaned into the wind as she trekked toward Red Bank. Despite wearing a coat over a sweater, the frigid gusts burrowed through and chilled her skin. The wind was bad enough, but whenever a car zoomed by an even colder blast of wind engulfed her. The wake of passing trucks almost knocked her off her feet.

An hour later, Agnes scaled the hills of Neal's neighborhood. Her legs complained with every step. When she reached his street, she leaned against a pine tree and took a short rest. When she felt a little better, she approached Neal's house.

Except for a porch light, the two-story beige house was dark. A minivan and a sedan were parked in the garage. A small two-door car was parked in the driveway behind the minivan. Neal's car. Agnes shuddered as she remembered how it looked after Parnell smashed into it.

Agnes scanned the neighborhood. All the houses were dark and silent. There was a feeling everyone living on this street was asleep. Even the crickets seemed to be slumbering. She took her tire gauge out of her pocket and crept toward Neal's car.

When she reached the car, she took a moment to gaze at the house. She wondered if Claudia and Neal were awake. Maybe they were making love right now. What would they think if they knew the child they created was in the driveway?

Agnes shook away those stray thoughts and squatted next to the rear passenger side tire. Before she could release any air, a large dog came rushing toward her. In a panic, Agnes dropped the tire gauge and ran. The dog barked loudly as he chased her to the edge of the Fisher's property. Once Agnes had crossed the invisible boundary between houses, the dog stopped. Agnes put one hand on a pine tree and the other on her racing heart.

"Please don't bark," Agnes whispered. "You'll wake everybody up."

The dog answered by lowering its head and growling at Agnes. In all her research about Neal's house, there was never any mention his family owned a dog. Agnes scolded herself for not considering the possibility of a watchdog.

The dog watched Agnes for two minutes before deciding she was no longer encroaching on its property. Uttering a short woof, the dog turned, trotted across the lawn, and into the garage.

Agnes sat in the neighbor's yard and leaned against the pine tree. She checked the time. It was 6:00 a.m. She had three hours before her time ran out and she returned to 2008. That meant she had three hours to come up with an alternate plan to save Neal. Certainly, that was plenty of time for a genius such as herself.

The simplest solution would be to knock on Neal's door and talk to him and Claudia. She'd warn them about the danger awaiting Neal a few short hours from now. The plan was absurd on so many levels. She might interrupt Neal and Claudia having sex, thus destroying Agnes' existence. Neal's parents might hear her knocking and refuse to let her speak to Neal. They might even call the police and have her arrested for trespassing. Most likely, the dog would rip her to shreds before she ever reached the door.

There was only one option left. Agnes had to get to Neal and Claudia when they came out of the house. She would have to tell them she was their daughter from the future. Or she could tell them she was the mystery girl who had been stalking Claudia all night. Or an alien from outer space. They didn't have to believe her. She just had to delay them long enough to throw off the timeline that led to Neal's death. Whatever she did had to be done before her time ran out.

As Agnes waited, the night's toll caught up with her. She had survived two confrontations, first with Parnell and then with the dog. She'd walked three miles on a cold and windy night. She was going to have to talk to her parents before they were her parents. No wonder she was exhausted. Agnes closed her eyes and listened to the wind.

The sound of a car engine rumbling to life woke her up. She saw to her horror Neal and Claudia were in his car and the car was backing out of the driveway. Scrambling to her feet, Agnes ran toward them. The car was out of the driveway and on the street.

"Claudia! Neal!" Agnes shouted, waving her hands. "Stop! Don't go!"

She was less than a yard away from them and couldn't understand why they didn't hear her. The car started forward and Agnes ran as fast as she could to catch it.

"It's me, Agnes! Your daughter! I need to warn you! Wait for me! Wait for me!"

As the car slowed down for a stop sign, Agnes doubled her efforts to reach them. When she got within three yards of the car, she could hear music playing on the car's stereo. The volume was turned up so high the car throbbed. When she was a few feet away from the car, Agnes recognized the music. They were listening to R.E.M.

Neal did a rolling stop at the sign and drove through the intersection.

"Wait! Wait!" Agnes yelled.

She got within inches of the car. Her fingers almost touched the trunk. She could see Neal's eyes reflected in the rearview mirror. For a second, their eyes met.

And then, her seven hours ran out.

The road melted under her feet and the trees lining the road became flowing tubes of green and brown. The car dissolved. Agnes screamed, but no sound came out of her mouth. She floated in the silence of the time skip for what felt like hours. It was more than enough time for her heart to break.

When her journey finally ended, Agnes stood in the middle of the road in Neal's old neighborhood. It was Christmas Eve 2008. Snow fell, making the world as silent as a time skip. Agnes trudged toward home. She had nowhere else to go.

* * *

Neal hit the brake and twisted around in his seat.

"Did you see that?"

"See what?" Claudia asked.

They looked out the rear window at the empty road.

"I swear I saw somebody chasing the car. Our eyes met for just a second. Or at least, I thought we did."

"There's nobody there now. What'd he look like?"

"It was a girl."

Claudia grabbed Neal's arm.

"It wasn't her, was it? Was she wearing bunny ears?"

Neal's forehead knitted in concentration.

"No. Definitely no bunny ears. Unless she's hiding in the woods, there's nobody there."

Claudia nervously scanned the woods.

"You sure about that?"

"You got me thinking about the mystery girl, and I must have imagined I saw her."

Claudia leaned across the seat and kissed Neal's cheek.

"Halloween's over," she said. "No more spooky stuff."

CHAPTER
42

Friday, December 26, 2008

Agnes almost didn't answer the phone. She'd already gotten phone calls from Denise, Megan, and Barry asking how she was holding up on her first Christmas without her mother. Every day was torture. The agony was no different on holidays.

"Hello, Agnes? It's Howard Levin."

"Professor Levin?"

"I would have called sooner, but I figured you were busy with family what with the funeral and then the holidays."

Agnes walked from the living room to her bedroom and plopped down on her unmade bed.

"It has been intense these past weeks."

"I just wanted to let you know how sorry I am for your loss. I'm aware there is nothing I can say to lessen the pain you're feeling."

There were many reasons why Agnes liked Professor Levin, and she added that last comment to the list.

"I'm glad you called, Professor."

"This may not be the appropriate time to discuss this, but if and when you decide to return to school, your position in my lab is waiting for you."

"How soon do I have to make a decision?"

"Take as much time as you need."

"Thank you."

The sun was shining through the bedroom window. Agnes wanted to close the blinds but was too depressed to get up.

"Okay, I'll let you go," Levin said. "Let me know if there is anything I can do for you."

"Please don't hang up. Not yet."

Agnes hadn't intended to ask him to stay on the line. The words just came out.

"I'll stay on the line as long as you like."

"I can't think of anything to talk about."

She expected him to be annoyed, but he wasn't. She wondered whom he had lost that made him so understanding.

"When you return, the first thing I'd like you to do is reschedule your presentation," Levin said. "I'm very curious to hear what you discovered about time travel?"

The tears Agnes had been holding back came pouring out.

"It didn't work," she said, "I'm sorry, Professor Levin. I tried so hard, but I couldn't make it work. No matter what I do, Mom always dies in the garage on Sunday, October 26, 2008."

"Are you home alone? Do you have any relatives nearby? I could drive up there."

Agnes pulled out a tissue out of a tissue box on her nightstand and blew her nose.

"I wish I could tell her how much I love her."

"You're not the first person who wished they could go back in time to say the things they wanted to tell the people they love. Or do the things they meant to do for their loved ones but never got around to it."

Agnes jumped out of bed. The answer had been there all along, but she

     Mickey Dubrow

had been too blinded by grief to see it.

"You're right, Professor! I don't care what Second Agnes says. I can save Mom."

"Agnes are you sure you don't want to me come up there?"

"I went about it the wrong way. As did First and Second Agnes, especially First Agnes. Instead of trying to stop Mom from getting pregnant, she should have just rescued Mom from the garage. It's so obvious."

"I can cancel my classes and be there in two hours."

"I can do it, Professor Levin. I can save Mom. And once I do, I'll convince her to never try to kill herself again."

Agnes got on her knees and pulled the box containing the Time Tefillin out from under her bed.

"That does it, Agnes," Levin said. "You need help right away. I'm going to call Claudia's friend to come take care of you. What was her name? Margaret? Miriam?"

Agnes put the box on the bed and flipped open the lid. She picked up one of metal cubes and held it in her palm.

"Megan. You can tell her to come over, but I won't be here. I'll be in the past."

"Please, Agnes. You have a brilliant mind, but you need help. Let us help you."

Agnes took a deep breath. She had hope in her heart again.

"Professor Levin. If I succeed, then chances are you won't remember this conversation because in the new timeline it never happened, so please listen carefully. Time is a river. Once you bind your mind, heart, and deed to the flow of the river you can travel upstream to the past or downstream to the future by skipping across time like a stone across water. I have traveled forward and backward minutes, hours, days, months, and years. I have proof my time machine works. I was going to show it to you at my presentation, but then Mom died and that changed everything. I think perhaps I wasn't supposed to share my invention with the world."

"Now you listen to me, Agnes. Everyone processes grief in their own way. You're suffering from delusions caused by a combination of pressure in the lab and the sudden loss of your mother."

"It's probably best you don't believe me. I have to go now. Thank you so much for calling, Professor Levin. Thank you for everything."

Agnes hung up before Levin had a chance to reply. She put on her tennis shoes and then she put on the Time Tefillin. She set the time on the digital clock for 6:30 a.m. on Sunday, October 26. Next, Agnes needed a place to arrive. She didn't want to freak out Claudia by appearing out of thin air.

Agnes looked around her bedroom and decided to use this location. There was an infinitesimal chance Claudia would have any reason to enter Agnes' room that morning, but Agnes felt it was worth the risk since she would be exactly where she needed to be to stop Claudia from killing herself. She closed her door and tried to think of anything else she needed to do before she flipped the switch.

The phone rang. Whoever it was, Agnes didn't want to speak to them. The only person she wanted to talk to was Claudia. Agnes flipped the switch.

Her bedroom walls oozed like melted cheese out of an overcooked grilled cheese sandwich. She floated in space where the floor had been. After what seemed like five minutes, the room returned to its normal shape. She cracked open her bedroom door and peeked out. She smelled the strong aroma of freshly brewed coffee. Agnes smiled. Claudia was home.

CHAPTER
43

Sunday, October 26, 2008

The kitchen smelled like coffee, but the pot was empty. Except for the living room light, which Claudia left on for security reasons, the house was dark. Agnes did a quick search throughout the house. Claudia wasn't home.

This didn't make sense. Claudia never left the house before 7:30 a.m. Agnes walked into the kitchen trying to think of a reason why Claudia would have left earlier when she noticed smoke seeping under the kitchen door that led to the garage. A chill ran down Agnes' spine. It was Sunday, October 26, 2008, and Claudia was in the garage dead or dying from carbon monoxide poisoning just like she had every time before.

If Agnes was lucky, someday she would ask Claudia why she left the house early, but for now it didn't matter. She threw open the kitchen door. The garage was full of smoke. Fumes crawled down her throat and stung her eyes. She coughed and tried to wave it away.

"Mom! Mom! Get out of the car!"

Claudia didn't answer. The engine chugged steadily while belching out more toxic exhaust. Agnes scooted around the car to the driver's side door. The car pulsated from the radio playing at full volume. As Agnes opened the door, the soaring guitar solo from Led Zeppelin's "Stairway to Heaven" flew out like a shrieking demon.

Claudia was slumped over the seat. Agnes felt her neck for a pulse. It was there, but faint. She tried yanking Claudia out, but her unconscious body was too heavy. She barely budged. Agnes spent precious seconds searching in vain for the remote that opened the garage door.

I'm wasting time, Agnes thought. There was too much smoke. She had to get Claudia out of the garage where there was fresh air.

Muscles straining, Agnes pushed Claudia until she slid to the passenger side floorboard. Agnes got into the driver's seat, slammed the door shut, revved up the engine, and threw the car in reverse. The car jerked as it roared backwards. The rear bumper rammed the garage door, splintering it, but didn't break through. Agnes drove forward, put the car into reverse, and floored the gas pedal. The car crashed through the garage door, leaving splinters of wood and twisted metal in its wake.

Once she could see daylight, Agnes hit the brake and the car fishtailed into the yard, chewing up grass and spewing dirt before it came to an abrupt stop. She scrambled out of the car as neighbors came running to see what the commotion was about.

"Call an ambulance!" Agnes shouted before dissolving into a coughing fit. She had breathed in plenty of exhaust herself.

She went around to the passenger door, fumbled with the handle until she got it open, and pulled on Claudia's arms. A pair of hands belonging to someone much stronger than Agnes joined the effort and soon Claudia was lying on the grass.

A man who lived across the street whose name Agnes couldn't remember administered CPR to Claudia. Agnes leaned against the car. Her head spun and she felt nauseous. Everyone on the block could hear the radio blasting. "Stairway to Heaven" ended and the announcer came on the air.

"That wraps up another thirty minutes of uninterrupted music from your favorite bands. We'll be back after these messages with more of our classic rock weekend. That's more Led Zeppelin, more Aerosmith, more Lynyrd Skynyrd, more R.E.M., more of the music of your life!"

The ambulance arrived. Agnes explained what happened to the paramedic. He strapped an oxygen mask to Claudia's face. He tried to put one on Agnes, but she insisted she didn't need it. They put Claudia onto a stretcher and loaded her into the ambulance. Agnes climbed in with them. The siren wailed as the ambulance sped to the hospital. Agnes sat on the bench and wished Claudia would open her eyes. The paramedic made sure Claudia was stabilized and then checked on Agnes.

"What's that?" he asked, pointing at the straps wrapped around Agnes' head and arm.

She had forgotten she was still wearing the Time Tefillin.

"It's my time machine," Agnes said. "Please don't touch it."

He shrugged and turned his attention back to Claudia.

At the hospital, they rushed Claudia into the emergency room. A nurse pulled Agnes aside. She held a clipboard with admittance paperwork attached.

"I want to stay with my mother," Agnes said.

"You have to wait here. A doctor will come speak to you as soon as he can," the nurse said. "But first, I need to get your mother's information."

Agnes followed the nurse to the front desk. The nurse waited as Agnes filled out the form.

"That's a unique watch you have there," the nurse said, pointing at the digital clock attached to Agnes' wrist.

"It's part of my time machine," Agnes said. "Please don't touch it."

The nurse wrinkled her nose but didn't comment. Agnes handed the completed form to her.

"The waiting room is down the hall to the left," the nurse said.

"When can I see my mother?"

"We'll let you know as soon as we can."

Agnes trudged to a waiting room full of people who seemed either anxious or bored. She found an empty chair between an old man wearing a skull cap and reading a newspaper, and a young mother holding a sleeping baby.

The old man put down his paper and stared at Agnes.

"That thing on your head and your arm. Is that supposed to be tefillin?" he asked. "Only men can wear tefillin. Women aren't allowed."

"It's my time machine," Agnes said.

"Oh, a time machine?" he said in an overly sarcastic voice. "Then I better not touch it."

He resumed reading his paper.

The hours dragged by. The old man and the young mother with her baby vacated their chairs and were replaced by a crying woman and a man who pulled his ball cap over his eyes and fell asleep.

The more time passed, the more worried Agnes became. Why was it taking so long? Did that mean there was something seriously wrong with Claudia? Had they forgotten Agnes was out here waiting? What would she do if her seven hours ended, and she still didn't know Claudia's fate?

Her leg bounced and she glanced at her digital clock repeatedly. She only had five minutes left. A young doctor wearing a white coat over her blue scrubs entered the waiting room. She looked at her clipboard and then looked around the waiting room.

"I'm looking for whoever came in with Claudia Cook," she said. "That's Claudia Cook."

Agnes held up her hand as if she were eager to answer a question in class. As she approached the doctor, she couldn't read the physician's expression. Her blank stare didn't indicate whether she had good news or bad news. Agnes felt the electric tingle of the Time Tefillin. She looked at the digital clock. Her seven hours were almost over.

"Quick, tell me. How is she?" Agnes said.

The doctor opened her mouth to speak, and the room melted into yellow and green blobs. Agnes floated in the oppressing silence as shimmering shapes flowed around her. The room returned to normal just as a large man with his right hand wrapped in white gauze knocked Agnes to the floor.

"I'm so sorry," he said. "I didn't see you."

He bent down to help Agnes and saw she was crying.

"Oh man. I didn't realize I hit you so hard. You need to see a doctor? They got a bunch of them here."

"That's not why I'm crying," Agnes said.

He helped her to her feet, walked her over to a chair, and sat beside her.   Agnes looked at the large man. He had a kind face.

"It's like you came out of nowhere," he said.

"What day is it?" Agnes said.

"Day after Christmas. I made the mistake of going to an After Christmas Sale." He held up his bandaged hand. "People get crazy in those sales."

"Do you have a phone I could borrow?"

"Sure thing."

With his undamaged hand, he fished a cell phone out of his jeans' pocket and gave it to Agnes. She dialed home. The phone rang and rang and then the answering machine came on. She hung up without leaving a message. She called Wendy's, but nobody answered. They often didn't pick up when they were extremely busy. She handed the phone back to the large man.

"Thank you," Agnes said as she wiped tears away with her sleeve.

"Is everything okay?" he asked.

"I have no idea."

Judging the expression on his face, Agnes thought he was staring at the Time Tefillin. She touched the strap on her forehead.

"I won't bother explaining what I'm wearing, because you wouldn't believe me if I told you."

"You don't remember me, do you?" he asked.

Agnes studied his face.

"I'm sorry. I don't."

"It's okay. I'm glad you don't."

"Now I'm curious. Who are you?"

The man scratched his bandaged hand.

"We were only in seventh and eighth grade together. I recognized you because I read in the paper about you going to Georgia Tech."

Looking closer, peeling back the years, Agnes finally remembered.

"You're Trey Dobbs, aren't you?"

Trey smiled.

"That's me. Fart Boy."

Agnes felt a pang of guilt.

"Sorry about that."

Trey shook his head.

"Don't apologize. I got what I deserved. In fact, you helped me be a better person."

"I don't understand."

"I wasn't just a bully to you. I bullied a lot of the little kids. But then you hit with your stink bomb and kids at school called me Fart Boy for the next two years."

Agnes gasped.

"Two years? I had no idea."

"You couldn't have known. You were gone by then. You'd jumped grades. Again."

"You must have hated me."

Trey stared at the floor.

"I hated you. I wanted revenge. But then, I realized I was upset because you made me feel as helpless as I made you feel."

"I just wanted you to stop hurting me," Agnes said.

Trey rubbed the back of his neck.

"For years, I wished I could go back in time and stop myself from picking on you. Since I couldn't do that, I've tried to be a better, kinder person. I don't always succeed. But I never stop trying."

Agnes studied the straps wrapped around her finger. With her Time Tefillin, Trey could go back in time and fulfill his wish. But even if he believed her machine worked, she couldn't let him use it.

If Trey hadn't bullied her, Agnes wouldn't have made the stink bomb which led to her interest in science. If she hadn't decided to be a scientist, she wouldn't have enrolled in Professor Levin's lab to study time travel. If she hadn't been in his lab, she wouldn't have built the Time Tefillin. If she hadn't built the Time Tefillin, she wouldn't have been able to go back in time to save Claudia from the garage. Or try to save Claudia. Did she save Claudia? She wasn't sure.

"Everything is connected, and everything has a purpose," Agnes said.

"I never thought of it that way," Trey said. "But I guess you're right."

CHAPTER
44

Saturday, January 10, 2009

Agnes leaned on the railing of the Walnut Street Bridge and watched as the late afternoon sun sparkled off the river. Behind her, joggers and tourists crisscrossed the bridge. She glanced nervously over her shoulder.

"Expecting someone?" Claudia asked.

"I thought I saw somebody I knew, but I was wrong."

Agnes sat on the park bench next to Claudia. They both wore winter coats. Claudia wore sunglasses and Agnes wore her Georgia Tech baseball cap.

"I hope you don't mind I dragged you out here," Agnes said. "You must be freezing."

"I'm fine and you didn't drag me out here. This is one of our special places."

Agnes asked a question so softly Claudia had to ask her to repeat it.

"Are you still angry with me?"

"Yes," Claudia said evenly. "You disappeared for two months. I was worried sick. So was Professor Levin. Even the doctor at the hospital who came to tell you I was okay was worried. She said you literally disappeared. She kept saying literally when it was obvious that she meant figuratively. Why won't you tell me where you were?"

"I don't want to talk about it."

"Ever?"

"Maybe some time in the future. But not now."

Claudia linked arms with Agnes.

"You know who you're acting like," Claudia said. "You're acting like I did when I was your age. Is that really how you want to behave?"

Agnes rested her head on Claudia's shoulder.

"Maybe," Agnes said.

Claudia rolled her eyes.

"I can't be too mad at you. You saved my life. How did you happen to be home? You were supposed to be at school. Oh, that's right. You're still playing the mystery girl."

Agnes pulled her arm away from Claudia and turned so that they were face to face. The words rushed out like water from a busted dam.

"I'm sorry I ruined your life. If you hadn't gotten pregnant with me, then you would have gone to college. You would have shared a dorm room with Megan and both of you would have joined a sorority. You would have gone to great parties and to Florida for Spring Break. You would have gotten a college diploma and then an amazing job where you would have met a really cool guy who probably wouldn't have been as cool as Neal, but he would have helped you get over your grief for Neal. But I took all that away from you. I'm the worst thing that ever happened to you."

Agnes' hand shook as she wiped the tears from her eyes. Claudia took her wet hand and held it tightly.

"I don't know where you got that crazy idea, but you forget it right now, Agnes Cook. You are the best thing that ever happened to me. You have brought me so much joy, and I am so proud of you. So what if I got pregnant when I was sixteen? I could have gotten an abortion. But I chose to have you and I didn't do it for Neal. I wanted you."

"You had to work so hard on your own. Don't you feel cheated?"

"I have friends who went to college worse off than me. I have a nice little house, a car that runs most of the time, and the best daughter in the world."

Agnes held out her arms like a child and they embraced.

"Then why did you do it?" Agnes asked.

"Do what?"

"Try to kill yourself in the garage."

Claudia pulled away.

"Is that what you think? Oh, come on, Agnes. Really?"

"You were in the garage with the engine running. If I hadn't found you in time, you would have died."

Claudia crossed her arms.

"I was listening to the radio, and I lost track of time."

Agnes tilted her head to the side.

"Explain."

"There's nothing to explain. I was listening to all these great R.E.M. songs on the radio while I waited for the car to warm up. I last thing I remember was listening to "The One I Love." It's one of my favorite R.E.M. songs. The next thing I know I woke up in the hospital."

Agnes groaned.

"It was an accident. We should have considered that possibility, but we just assumed you did it on purpose. How foolish of us."

Claudia stroked Agnes' curly hair.

"Why do you keep referring to yourself as we? Did you become a queen during those missing two months?"

"I'm going back to school on Monday."

"Good," Claudia said, patting Agnes' knee. "I'm sure Professor Levin is thrilled to hear you're finally going to do your presentation."

"I'm not doing the presentation."

"Really? Why not?"

"The experiment didn't work."

"So, you'll do the presentation when it's ready. You've never let a failed experiment stop you before."

"Maybe. I have to think about it."

"Let's do something special tomorrow night before you go back. I know, let's go out for deep dish pizza."

"I'm sorry, Mom. I can't. I have a date."

Claudia put her hand over her heart.

"You do? When were you going to tell me? Who's the lucky guy? I want details."

"Josh Hawkins. I called him up and asked him to go to a movie with me."

"Who the hell is Josh Hawkins?"

"Fourth of July. Chester Frost Park."

"I'm still not making the connection."

"He was in my grammar school carpool. I hung out with him on the beach for like a minute."

Claudia's eyes widened.

"That was over a year ago. I can't believe you remembered him. Hey, don't get me wrong. I think it's wonderful. Beyond wonderful. What made you decide to call him?"

"I made a promise to myself I would call him if I got the chance."

Claudia put her arm around Agnes's shoulder and squeezed.

"Use protection. It doesn't always work, but it's better than nothing."

Agnes' cheeks burned with embarrassment.

"Mom! I can assure you that won't be necessary."

Orange and blue streaks stretched across the sky. The air was crisp as the day moved closer to night. Agnes had never been happier, but still she was troubled.

She could never explain to Claudia about the missing two months. When Agnes went into the past to save Claudia, she created a new timeline, one that didn't include Agnes. She only existed in the timeline where Claudia was still dead and didn't join live Claudia until later. There was no Fourth Agnes to take her place while she skipped over those two months.

If thinking about the various timelines gave Agnes a headache, how could she ever hope to explain them to her mother? She imagined how the conversation might go.

"There's something I need to tell you, Mom, but I'm afraid if I tell you, you won't love me anymore. I know what you're going to say. Nothing would make you ever stop loving me. What I have to say might change your mind. "I lied. My experiment did work. I built a time machine, an actual functioning time machine. I traveled to the future and the past. Speaking of the past, I know who the mystery girl is, the one who attacked Barry and Derrick, the one who stole Barry's car. No. It wasn't me. It was First Agnes and Second Agnes. I'm Third Agnes. It's complicated. Perhaps if I did a diagram, it would help make it clearer.

"Every Agnes went back in time to try and save you because you see, Mom, you did die in the garage on Sunday, October 26, 2008. Not once, but three times. I had you cremated and was going to scatter your ashes from this bridge.

"We didn't know your death was an accident. We blamed ourselves. We thought if we made your life better, you wouldn't kill yourself. First and Second Agnes failed, but no experiment is a failure. The purpose of experiments is to learn from our mistakes, and I learned from theirs. That's how I was able to finally get you out of the garage.

"I know you wish I could have met Neal. I did meet him. He was taking you home after you spent the night. I was behind you, chasing the car. Neal looked in the rearview mirror and for a second our eyes met. Some people might say a second doesn't count, but when it's all you have, it counts a lot.

"Time travel has taught me so much. I learned time is a river, and everyone clings to their individual boat. Some things never change. You're always my mother and I'm always your daughter. We're all connected because everything is connected."

Agnes took a deep breath.

"There's something I need to tell you, Mom."

Claudia cupped the side of Agnes' face.

"Are you going to tell me where you were for two months?"

"No. I'm afraid if I tell you what I'm going to tell you, you won't love me

     Mickey Dubrow

anymore."

"There's nothing you can tell me that would ever make me stop loving you."

Agnes made a decision.

"I hate R.E.M. I've always hated R.E.M. I can't stand their music."

Claudia scowled.

"Really? All these years I've been playing their music and you've hated every minute of it?"

"Some of their songs aren't terrible."

Claudia looked at the river. Then she laughed.

"That's okay. I love you anyway."

"Always?"

"Always."

Agnes didn't check the time. She wasn't in a hurry to be anywhere.

ACKNOWLEDGEMENTS

Endless gratitude to Michael Richter for providing an insider's view on student life at Georgia Tech, to Matthew Kennedy for suggesting a crucial plot change that transformed the novel into something better than what I had originally intended, and to Mark and Loren Falls for providing the setting that sparked this story. Special thanks to my insightful writing group Jef Blocker, Robert Gwaltney, and Marissa McNamara. I can't thank Kathy L. Murphy and Mandy Haynes enough for their tireless devotion to promoting authors and publishers with The International Pulpwood Queens and Timber Guys Book Club. And last but certainly not least, my love and gratitude to Jessica Handler. To paraphrase something she has said, we can make no journey large or small without each other.

www.ingramcontent.com/pod-product-compliance
Lightning Source LLC
Chambersburg PA
CBHW071231210726
48293CB00002B/667